A Hustler's Fantasy

An Urban Romance

Part Two

A Novel By

Shameka Jones

Text **ROYALTY** to **42828** to join our mailing list!

To submit a manuscript for our review, email us at submissions@royaltypublishinghouse.com

LEGAL NOTES
© 2016

Published by Royalty Publishing House

http://www.royaltypublishinghouse.com

CHAPTER ONE: TOOKIE

Three Months Later...

The Bahamas is nice, but I am growing home sick by the day. This is a great place to visit, but after a month, it started to get old. My family is in Dallas, and I am ready to go back to join them. I've kept in contact with Ro since I've been gone, and everything was clear. The FEDs ended up locking Inky up, and this dude name Rob that he was scoring from, about a month ago. I knew the FEDs were watching Inky's dumb ass. I'm glad that I never admitted anything to him. Even with Inky behind bars, I had a feeling that the FEDs were still watching. I can remember Brooke saying that she was going to lock me up, so I knew she wouldn't stop until she did. It didn't make a difference to me because I was going to go back home regardless.

The holidays are around the corner and I want to celebrate with my family like normal. Not only that, I am ready to get my hair cut. Since I have been here, I didn't do anything to it but edge myself up. Cutting my own hair wasn't something that I could do for real. I was looking rough, but my edge up made it to where I didn't look too bad. This caveman look isn't for me, so my first stop in Dallas will be at the barbershop.

I could hear Imani in her walker rolling around on the marble floors. Ever since we got her that walker she has been on the go. She wasn't able to walk on her own just yet, but she could stand up for a long period of time. It won't be long before she makes her way down the hallway, so I quickly got back to work. I had to move some money around, and search online for a building to rent in Dallas. Yaniyzah and Kayla have been talking on the regular, and Kayla was giving her pointers on the clothing business. Kayla had her own clothing line out, so she knows a little about the fashion world. Yaniyzah has been working on a few pieces of her own. She plans to sell her unique pieces in the store. It was a good front for us. Even if she didn't sell one thing, we could fix the books to where she will be making thousands. I had way too much cash that still needing cleaning and I need her store to do it.

"Da-da," I heard Imani call out as her walker hit the office door.

I jumped up to open the door for her. Imani was bouncing up and down in her walker, with her hands held up.

"Imani!" Yaniyzah called out.

"She's in here with me!"

"Okay."

Instead of picking Imani up, I slid her walker over towards my desk. I still had a little more work to do before I could play with her. She immediately raised her arms and began to pull papers off of the desk. I was done with them, so I let her have at it.

Just as I wrapped up work, Yaniyzah pushed the door open. She walked in with an apron around her waist, and a glass of Mimosa in her hand. Yaniyzah was the sexiest female that I have ever been with, hands down. And after putting this dick in her for the past three months, that ass is growing by the day.

"Langston, are you done with work yet?" she smiled.

"I just finished, what's up?"

"I have brunch ready. I'm going to set it out on the patio deck for us."

"Thanks, babe, I'll be right out."

I shut the computer down then reached down to get Imani out of her walker. She smiled and kicked her feet as I lifted her up.

"Hey, Mani."

She grabbed my beard like she always does and pulled on it. I don't know what it is about my beard that fascinates her so much. She is always pulling on it, or trying to put it in her mouth. Everything she sees now goes into her mouth, so we're having to watch her very closely. Almost every trinket in the house was put up high out of her reach.

Yaniyzah had a nice spread on the table when I stepped out on the patio. Omelets, waffles, fruit and Mimosas were spread out looking delicious. Yaniyzah sure knows how to treat a nigga well.

I placed Imani in her highchair then took my seat.

"Thank you, Niy, this looks nice."

"You're welcome. I felt like doing something nice for you."

"What's the occasion?"

"Nothing special, just showing my appreciation for all you've done for us."

"You know I do it out of love. I told you I got y'all no matter what."

"You say that like you don't expect us to be together or something."

"I don't mean it like that, but you know how this life shit works out sometimes." She looked at me with questioning eyes. I reached over the table and took ahold of her hand. "What do you think about going back home?"

"We are home."

"I mean Dallas. Don't you think it's time to go back?"

"I thought we were going to stay here?"

"Not forever, just until things cooled down. You like it over here or something?"

"Yeah, I do. I love it, actually."

"We can always come back, but this is not where I plan to live for the rest of my life."

"I'm scared, Langston. I don't want to go back and something happens."

"Something like what?"

"Like you going to jail or something. Why can't we just stay here?"

"Come here," I said tugging on her hand. She walked around the table then took a seat in my lap. "Because we have work to do in Dallas. You want to get your store up and running, right?"

She smiled, "Are you serious? You're getting me a store?"

"That is what you want, right?"

"Of course. But I didn't think—" She paused and took a deep breath. "Thank you, baby."

I looked at her for a second, trying to read her eyes. "You're welcome. Now let's eat."

I knew that she wasn't going to be thrilled to go back that's why I had to get her a store. The plan was never to stay here forever, I just wanted to get away from the heat for a minute to think. I know as soon as I step foot inside of the U.S., eyes will be on me. The plan is to steer clear of anything to do with drugs or cash money for a while. I'm just going to play it cool, and try to find out who is speaking my name.

As we finished up with brunch, my cell phone sounded off. There were only a few people that had my burner phone number, so I knew I had to answer. I ran inside of the house to catch it before the person on the other end hung up.

"Wassup, Q?" I answered.

"Ain't shit, big bro, how's everything out that way?"

"Everything is going good."

"Glad to hear that. I was calling because baby girls birthday is coming up, and I'm inviting you and the little ladies to Miami."

"Miami? You're throwing a one-year-old a party in Miami?"

"Yeah, since the season has started I will be in Miami at the time. It's not gonna be nothing too big, just the family. Plus, I have a game so y'all can come to that too."

"I've been thinking about coming back to the states anyway, so yeah, we'll be there."

"Cool, I'll email you the information later on tonight."

"Alright, bruh, talk to you later."

Well that makes things official. We are going to Miami for a few days then we're off to Dallas.

The thought of calling my boy Ro was on my brain, then I decided against it. I didn't want to alert anyone of my return. There were too many unanswered questions in Dallas, so I think it will be best if I just pop up. If I make people aware of my return, niggas will be on their best behavior. The last I heard, Ro and the crew were running the north side. I want to pop up and see how shit is really going.

Since Yaniyzah made us brunch, I cleared and cleaned the patio back up. When we first got here, I had a housekeeper to do all of this, but Niy wasn't feeling her being here all day every day. I didn't fire her, I just put her work on hold while we were here. Yaniyzah wanted to take care of the household so I granted her that wish. As long as the house stayed clean and I stayed fed, it didn't matter to me who did it.

I walked into the kitchen and sat on the island, watching Yaniyzah clean the dishes. Imani was back in her walker, rolling all over the place. She really thinks she be doing something when she is in there. I laughed to myself as her afro blew from the wind that she was creating.

"What's up?" Niy asked.

"I just got off of the phone with Q. He wants us to come to Miami for Princess's birthday and his game."

"When?"

"He is going to email me the information, but I'm assuming in a few days. Once we're done there, we will go on to Dallas."

"So that means I need to start packing?"

"Exactly. Just pack one bag for Miami, and I will send the rest of our things ahead."

"Okay, I'll start on that later. What are we doing today?"

"I think we can just chill around the house and get our heads ready to go back," I suggested, as I jumped down from the island. I walked over behind her and slid my arms around her waist. "Let's have some food delivered and love on each other all day."

She turned her head slightly towards me, "I love the sound of that."

"Mm," I moaned, kissing her on the nape of her neck then grabbed two hands full of ass.

"Can you let me finish the dishes first?"

"Sure, go ahead. I'm gonna take Mani outside to play."

I grabbed the back of Imani's walker to catch her as she drifted by.

CHAPTER TWO: YANIYZAH

After fighting with Imani, I finally got her down to bed. Every night there is a fight to get her to sleep, which is crazy. It used to be a time where she would lay down on her own and go to sleep. I pushed the door to the bedroom open and entered. Langston was on the phone with his Big Mama checking on her. She was his heart, and the only person that he talks to on a daily basis. While he talked to her, I went to go take a shower. We've spent most of our day outside playing with Imani. I'm worn out and more than ready for a shower then bed.

A few minutes after I stepped into the walk-in shower, Langston opened the door and joined me. My eyes were glued on his chest muscles. Langston is fine as hell, there's no denying that. I catch myself staring at him anytime he is dressing or undressing himself. I've never mentioned it to him because his head is already the size of Jupiter. He didn't need any help with building his self-esteem, that's for sure. He walked up close to me, and pressed his body against mine. It instantly made my pussy began to tingle. Sometimes I hated that he had that effect on me. I don't like for any man to have any type of control over me. I dealt with that from my father and Montrez, and I didn't want to relinquish my power to Langston just yet.

Langston leaned in and placed a kiss on my lips. His lips were so soft that it sent chills all over my body. I couldn't help but to wrap my arms around his moist skin. The soap made his skin slippery, so I slowly rubbed my hand over his back.

"Mmm," he moaned. "I like when you touch on me and show me affection."

"You don't think I show you enough affection?"

"No. You will go an entire day without touching or kissing me. When you do it's because I initiate it."

"That is not true."

"Yes, it is. Close your eyes and think about today. Think about how many times we touched then think about who initiated it."

"That was just today."

"Okay, yesterday. You got up early and went—"

"Alright, babe, I get it."

"Damn, what's up?"

"I don't know, I just…I don't want to get hurt again."

"Baby, I'm not gone hurt you. I sit here every night thinking about how I am going to build a life with you and Mani. You've shown me more loyalty than anyone ever has. Why would you be loyal to someone that you're not sure about?"

"Because that is the person that I am. I am loyal to people until they give me a reason not to be."

"Niy, I've told you over and over that I am going to be there."

"I know, and it always ends with a *but*. That but plays an important role in your sentence."

"Alright, I won't include 'but' in anymore of my statements, will that work for you?"

"Yes."

"Okay. Now kiss and rub on me again," he laughed.

The shower was already hot, but we made it steam once our bodies began to rub up against each other. Langston picked me up by my waist, and placed me up on his shoulders. I leaned back, placed my hands on the shower walls for leverage, while he began to indulge in my juice box.

"Uhh," I moaned as he sucked my clit. "Shit!"

"You like that?"

"Yes," I whined. "You already know I do."

He sucked my clit again then spoke, "I want you to ride my face."

He lifted me from around his neck and lowered me down to his waist. I wrapped my legs around him, he shut the water off, then pushed the shower door open. I placed my hand behind his head and pulled it closer for a kiss.

Langston fell back onto the bed with me right on top of him. Both of our bodies were soaking wet, but it didn't matter to us. We were hot, horny and craving for our flesh to connect as one. I crawled up his body then hovered over his face. He grabbed me by my ass and pulled my body down to his face. His tongue penetrated my hole, causing my body to shake just a little. I exhaled deeply and began to move my hips.

Once he entered my black hole, the party was on. I was so wet from him teasing me. He kept moaning in my ear, telling me about my wetness. I placed my hand on the back of his head then began to trust my hips.

"Fuuck!" he cried out.

"Is it that good?" I joked.

"Mm hmm, keep throwing that good ass pussy on me."

"Go deeper," I requested.

He pushed my legs open wider to fulfill my desire.

"Uhh, sss," I whined as he began to touch my guts. "That's it baby, that's it."

He began to speed up his strokes, which caused my orgasm to build. I wrapped my arms tighter around his muscular back. Rubbing on his muscles did something to me. It made me feel protected, even though I've never seen him fight. The more I rubbed, the closer I came to climaxing.

"You cummin'?" he asked.

"Yes baby, yees!"

He started making long, slow strokes that pulled my orgasm out.

"Shiit! Oh Jesus, Langston!" I yelled just as I exploded.

We kissed while he continued his slow stroke. This made my body shake and crave him even more.

"Ride this dick," he requested, rolling us over without pulling his dick out.

After my third orgasm, Langston finally ejaculated. We took another shower together, and now we were cuddled up in the bed naked. The television was on, but I couldn't focus on what was on it. Langston had his hands cupped around my breasts with my nipples secured between his index and middle finger. It was giving me that tingle between my legs again, but I know Langston is still in recovery mode. I lifted my arm to the top of his head, and began to twist his mane between my fingers. Instead of focusing on sex, I closed my eyes to go to sleep.

I woke up to Imani slamming her toy against my back. Rubbing my eyes, I sat up and turned to face her. She had that beautiful smile that I love on her face and slobbering everywhere. Langston was sitting on the other side of her eating a bowl of fruit. I could tell that he had been feeding it to Imani because she had strawberry seeds stuck to her chin. For a split second, she was sitting there looking just like Montrez to me. I shook my head to remove that image immediately.

"Hey, mama," I smiled at Imani. She crawled over and kissed my cheek with her mouth wide open. She left a puddle of slobber on my face that rolled down on my bottom lip.

"Good morning," Langston smiled at me.

"Morning, babe," I yawned. "What time is it?"

"Almost 10."

"Dang, I slept for a long time. I must have been tired."

"Must have been because you were snorin' and fartin' all in your sleep."

"Stop telling stories," I chuckled.

"Shiid, I ain't lyin'. And you better be glad that it didn't stink or I would have kicked yo' ass out the bed."

I looked at him with my lips pursed up. It is a possibility that I could have passed gas, but I know good and well that I don't snore. He is always talking shit about what I do in my sleep because I can't prove him wrong. He says so many things that it had me wondering if I did. It also had me wondering why he is always up while I am asleep. I didn't like the thought of him watching me or not being able to sleep.

"You want some breakfast," I asked, easing my head back down to the pillow.

He smirked, "Nah, we're good, we ate already."

"Good, 'cause I didn't feel like getting up."

Langston pulled the covers off of me and slapped me on my ass. "Lazy ass." Imani was sitting there watching then leaned over to do the same. Langston started cracking up instantly.

"Don't be showing her bad stuff."

"That's not bad. I'm showing her mama affection, something that she never shows me."

"Spoiled butt," I groaned.

I sat up and leaned over to kiss him. He moved his head to the side, avoiding my kiss.

"Nah, bro, you gotta go brush them teeth first."

"Whatever," I said rolling out of the bed to go do just that. "You won't kiss me with morning breath but you'll eat my pussy like the last supper."

"Stop runnin' yo' mouth and brush yo' tongue too."

"Shut up."

When I emerged from the bathroom, Langston was sitting at his desk. He will be there for the next hour or so, and that gave me time to begin packing. My plan was to start yesterday, but we were having a family day. I wasn't ready to go back to Dallas just yet. Even though we didn't have any family or friends here, I am willing to stay. Going back to Dallas would put Langston at risk with the FEDs. That is the last thing that I want to happen, especially since my child and I have gotten used to him. He is our sole provider, so I can't let anything happen to him. I'm not street smart, but I will do whatever I can to make sure he doesn't get locked up.

I took Imani from Langston and went into the kitchen. Langston had made pancakes and eggs for breakfast. I can tell by looking at the mess that he has left behind. Shit, I shouldn't have told him to get rid of Nicole. True I didn't want her here waiting on us hand and foot, but I could use her to take care of the dishes around here. Langston likes to eat, so I find myself cooking four times a day sometimes. We rarely ate out which was something we did all of the time in Dallas. At least with us going back I won't have to cook as much.

After cleaning the kitchen, I sat at the table eating a stack of pancakes. I'm sure Langston fed her, but Imani sat in my lap begging, so I had to share with her. My baby is getting so fat now that she is eating table food on a regular basis. Her fat ass be wearing my hip out too. I'm so glad that we got that walker. Now I don't have to tote her around as much anymore. That almost made me sad because she was growing up too fast. In two months, she will be turning one.

Imani ate, got full, and I was now rocking her to sleep. Once I get her down, I will be able to start packing. I wasn't sure when we were leaving, but Langston said to go ahead and pack. We have accumulated so much stuff over the last three months so it would take a while. I walked slowly towards the nursery to lay her down.

As I leaned over to place Imani in her crib, I felt Langston rub his muscle up against my butt. That tingling feeling instantly arrived, but I had to calm it. If he wants me to be ready when it's time to go, he needs to let me pack.

"Really?" I whispered.

"You the one walkin' around here with them lil' ass shorts on," he said grabbing a hand full.

I did a 180 degree turn, turning to face him. "When did lil' ass shorts stand for an open invitation to the nookie?"

"Since we started fuckin' and you walkin' around the house with 'em on."

"Langston, I need to start packing. I can't be messing around with you right now."

"So you gone walk around with ya ass out, teasin' me?"

I placed my hand on my forehead and laid my head back. "Ugh."

"You stressed out, huh? Having good pussy can be stressful because a nigga wanna beat up on it all of the time. I can't help it though."

"Well, I'm not your dick's personal punching bag."

"You not?" he asked in a more serious tone. "So that means I can go out and fuck with other females, right?"

"What!?" I snapped, rolling my neck.

"I'm sayin', if you ain't giving up the pussy then I get to go fuck on something else."

"That is so disrespectful."

"What you said was disrespectful also."

"We have sex every night, so don't stand here and act like I don't give you sex."

"I didn't say that, but you need to start giving it up on demand. This once a day shit ain't gone work for me. I've been takin' it easy on yo' lil' ass 'cause you be runnin' from the dick and shit, but I like to fuck three, four times a day. Every time I hit the blunt,

I want to be able to dig into them guts."

I slid from in between him and Imani's crib that he had me pinned up against. His eyes stayed on mine as I eased away. I was waiting for him to say something, but he just looked at me like I was crazy. What he didn't know is that I like to have sex more than he thinks. He is the one with the long ass refractory period. I always end up falling asleep waiting for his dick to reset. Since he is assuming, I will let him make an ass out of himself. The real reason that I was rationing it is because I'm down to my last few birth control pills. I don't want to get pregnant, so I need to ration it until I'm able to get another prescription.

CHAPTER THREE: TOOKIE

I stood at the door watching as the delivery man came to pick up the moving boxes. The thought of us going back to Dallas instantly made my heart skip a beat. I am so ready to jump into one of my rides and cruise through the city, blowing thick smoke. Being in the Bahamas without my people is depressing. I felt like I was missing out on everything, even though Ro kept me posted on what is going on. Being in the mix of things is what I like, so Monday can't get here fast enough for me.

Before I could think about me being in Dallas on Monday, I had to get through the weekend in Miami. Miami is a beautiful city, but it rained off and on too much for my taste. If it wasn't for the sporadic rain patterns, I wouldn't mind making that my third home. I'll continue to let it be a great vacation spot for us. It's only a hop, skip and a jump across the water from my second home anyway.

"Is this the last box, Mr. Williams?" the delivery guy whose nametag read Spencer, asked.

"Yeah, man, that's the last one."

"Okay, sign right here." I scribbled some bullshit on the pad, and gave it back to him. "Here is your tracking number."

"Thanks."

"Have a good day," he smiled as he bent down to pick up the last box.

"Yeah, you too."

I stuck my head out of the door, and watched until he placed the last box on the truck.

After closing the door and turning around, I saw Niyzah walking down the hallway in my direction. Imani was saddled on her hip, clapping her hands together. I stood there frozen, looking at the both of them. Yaniyzah had on her skimpy skirt, continuously teasing me with her sexiness. Last night she went to sleep before I was able to dig inside of her, so sex was all I could think about right now. There was no way that we could possibly do it with Imani being up. That caused me to redirected my thoughts elsewhere to stop my muscle from throbbing.

My cell ringing was just the thing to bring me back to reality. Reaching down in my pocket, I removed my phone and saw that Quincy was calling. I already know that he is calling to confirm us meeting them in Miami.

"Wassup, superstar?" I answered.

"Ain't shit bro, what's going on out that way?"

"Not too much, you know, doing a little packing."

"That's why I was calling. I wanted to make sure y'all were

coming."

"Yeah, we'll be there tomorrow."

"What time are y'all arriving?"

"We should be there around 9:30 or 10."

"Cool, we can meet up and get breakfast or something before I head to the arena."

"Alright, I'll call you after we check-in."

"Bet that. Neka, Talia and Quanda are flying in tomorrow afternoon."

"Word? I haven't even talked to them. It's cool that they are coming out 'cause I miss my family. I can't wait to see all of y'all."

"I know you do, and I can't wait until y'all get here. I got to go to practice, so I'll talk to you when you get here."

"A'ight, bruh."

"Who was that?" Yaniyzah asked, startling me as I hung up the phone. She sat Imani on the bed then laid across it.

"Quincy," I answered, leaning over and rubbing my hand up her leg.

She giggled then pushed my hand away. "Stop."

"What you mean stop?"

"Langston, Imani is right there."

"You better be glad that she is. You already didn't give me none last night, now you're sittin' here with this lil' ass skirt on, makin' my dick hard and shit."

"I'm sorry," she smiled. "I was tired after all of that packing I had to do."

"I had to pack up shit too."

"I said I was sorry, there's nothing I can do about last night now."

"Whatever. You know you were acting funny."

Imani crawled over and used my body to help her stand up. She held on to the front of my shirt then began smiling and dancing. I started cheering her on as she did her baby bounce while holding on to my shirt.

Since this was our last day here, I decided that we should get out of the house. Everything was cleaned up, so I didn't want Yaniyzah to have to cook today. Plus, I wanted to chill out on the beach with the family. That is something that Niyzah has been wanting to do, but I didn't too much care about doing. The beach sand wasn't really my thing. It got everywhere and it was extremely hard to get rid of.

Our swim clothes were packed and sent ahead, so I just threw on some lounge clothes. I took some cash out of the safe to pay for our outing. It was a good amount left in there from what I sent over months ago. I plan to leave the rest of it here in the safe for emergencies. I never know when I will have to leave at the drop of a dime, and won't have time to send any money ahead. It was time for me to start strategizing because I don't know what type of situation I will be returning to in Dallas.

Yaniyzah finally came walking down the hall towards me. She had changed clothes, combed her hair, and even brushed on a little makeup. I was growing impatient waiting on her to come out of the bathroom; looking at her walk towards me made it all well worth the wait. I hadn't seen her really done up in about a month or so. I can't wait to get her out of the Bahamas and show her off again. We're definitely going on more dates once we are back in my element.

"You look good, baby."

"Thanks," she smiled.

"You should have told me that you were dressing up so I wouldn't be going out lookin' all bummy and shit."

"You don't look like a bum. I actually like the way you look in your sweats. You don't have to be dressed up to look good to me."

"I look good to you in this?" I frowned.

She smiled at me with flirtatious eyes, "Very sexy."

I looked down at my clothes like I wasn't already aware of what I had on.

"This? This looks sexy to you?"

"I've already answered that question, now let's go."

She took me by the hand and pulled me towards the garage. Imani was in my arms, holding on to my nappy ass beard as usual.

I pulled into the parking lot of the Cleveland's Beach Club. I chose for us to eat here because Yaniyzah had grown a taste for Bahamian food. They had my choice of food which is lobster, so I was killing two birds with one stone. After jumping out of the car, I ran around to the passenger side to open the door for her. She stepped out, looking like a movie star, and I was standing there looking like her driver. She claimed to like the way that I am looking, so I took it and ran with it. Once I helped her out, I removed Imani from her seat.

We were led to a table outside overlooking the beach. It was the perfect view of the ocean, and it is the perfect setting to watch the sun go down. After Yaniyzah took her seat, I sat down across from her. Her skin was shining underneath the sunrays. It was like the sun had come down and kissed her skin personally. She was physically perfect to me.

"This view is amazing, Langston."

"It is even more amazing with you sitting here with me."

"Look at you being all sweet and whatnot."

"Am I not always sweet?"

"You are always nice, not always sweet. And I think it has more to do with us being way over here."

"Don't try to play me, I'm a sweet guy."

"You are a sweet guy; I'm not taking that from you. You've just been more attentive since we've been over here."

"I've gotten to know you better since we've been here too. Nothing is going to change once we get back to Dallas."

"You sure?"

"I'm positive, girl."

"What about our time together? I know you're gonna be back running the streets."

I rubbed my forehead, and exhaled deeply. "I mean, yeah, I got to make some moves, but you will still get most of my time. You shouldn't even be questioning that."

"I just want to know what to look forward to. Please make sure that you be careful."

"No doubt," I smiled. "Now gone and figure out what you and Imani gon' eat."

I took a peek at the menu when I was looking the place up, so I already knew what I was going to order. Right now, my head is focused on what I need to do when I get back. I had to put things in order, in order for me to keep my word to Yaniyzah. I'm not sure what will happen, but she and Imani will still get most of time. I just have to figure out how to do that, and keep her out of the way at the same time. I'm not trying to get her caught up in anything that I have going on.

After dinner, we took our shoes off and stepped on to the beach. The sun was getting ready to go down so our timing was perfect. We both held on to one of Imani's arms to let her sink her feet into the sand. She was trying her hardest to sit down so that she could touch it. I held her little hand tightly. That way she wasn't able to wiggle loose from me.

With Imani in one arm, I secured my other one around Yaniyzah. I pulled her in close to me, holding her tight. She wrapped her arm around my waist and we stood there looking out at the sun fading away.

"I love you, Langston."

I leaned over and placed a kiss on her forehead, "Yeah, me too."

I told Yanizah that I loved her before, but I wasn't into saying that shit all of the time. I feel like me saying it once and proving it daily is enough. Getting my head caught up in all of that love shit isn't safe. One mistake can cost me years of my life in prison. No one is worth that risk, not even Yaniyzah's sexy ass.

CHAPTER FOUR: YANIYZAH

Being in the Bahamas made me feel free. It also gave me a chance to experience another culture's way of living. But today, all of that is coming to an end. I would be lying if I said I wasn't nervous as hell about it all. The FEDs are no joke when it comes to filing cases on people. They don't stop until a case is tried, and you are convicted or found innocent. I'm not sure how deep Langston's name is in their investigation, but I want to make sure that he doesn't get locked up. Right now, I didn't have a plan A, B or C that would help him out. But I will use the tools that I learned from my father to help in any way that I can.

I walked throughout the house to make sure that I packed everything we need. All of the clothes that Imani came with are too little, so I left them hanging in the closet. I'm sure the next time that I see them I will tear up. They are so tiny, and she is growing like a weed on me. My baby isn't that much of a baby anymore. Before I know it, we will be celebrating her first birthday.

"Are you ready, slow poke?" Langston asked from behind me.

"Yeah, I'm sure I have everything that we need."

"Well, I have the boat loaded and ready to go. Let's get on out of here."

"Where is Imani?"

"In there rolling around in her walker, waiting on you."

"Whatever, I am ready."

Langston threw his arm around my shoulder then we walked out of the room. I guess this is the start of the rest of our lives. I just pray that we have a happy ending, because I've had enough losses in my life already.

Though I wasn't looking forward to going back to Dallas, Miami on the other hand, I couldn't wait to see again. The last time we were there, I was only able to see it briefly. This time, I am hoping to see a little more of it. I am also looking forward to seeing Quincy, Kayla and Princess again. They are like the cutest family ever. Kayla and I have been talking the last few months about the items that I want to put in the store. She has also been a great help with giving me contacts for everything.

The boat ride to Miami was smooth unlike last time. The ride to the Bahamas was a little rough, but Langston held me the entire time. That could have been the reason why the ride was so rough. This time I stayed in the bedroom with Imani. She was wide awake and I didn't want all of that wind blowing on her.

We checked into the same exact room at the Fontainebleau hotel as before. Imani had fallen asleep, so I laid her down in the middle of the bed. Langston was on the phone with Quincy already trying to figure out where we were meeting. He was excited about being back in the U.S., and being cooped up in this room wasn't on his agenda.

"Bet. Y'all come on over." He slid the phone into his pocket then walked over and slapped me on my butt. "What's up with that? You on yo' period or something?"

"No."

"Why you being stingy with the pussy then?"

"You are the one that said you was gone take it easy on me, 'cause I be running and shit. Remember?"

"So you tryin' to prove a point or what?"

"Something like that."

"Well, if you remember that, you better remember the shit that I said afterwards."

He walked away and went into the bathroom. I wanted to say something to him, but the knock on the door prevented that. Maybe that is a good thing because I don't want to argue with Langston. We've gotten along well for the last few months, and I don't want things to change now.

I rushed to the door to open it. Quincy, Kayla and Princess were standing on the opposite side, smiling.

"Hey, y'all," I spoke.

"What's going on, sis?" Quincy asked.

"Nothing much, come on inside."

"Hey, Niyzah," Kayla said, giving me a hug. "I'm glad that y'all are back."

"Yeah, me too, a little. Aw, look at the birthday girl, she has gotten so big."

"Yes, girl. I think she is gonna be tall like her daddy."

"Where is Imani?"

"Taking a nap, thank God."

"Where is Took?" Quincy inquired.

"In the bathroom."

"I'm right here, lil' ass nigga," Langston called out from behind us. "Hey, Kayla."

"This guy," Quincy joked. "Nigga, I'm bigger than you."

"Only in height, remember that."

"You got me fucked up, bro. They don't call me Big Daddy for nothing."

"Who is they?" Kayla rolled her neck.

"You, baby, you."

"Mm hmm."

"Y'all ready to go grab some grub? I have practice in a lil' bit," Quincy changed the subject.

"Let me get baby girl," Langston said then started towards the bed.

I grabbed Imani's diaper bag, my purse, and slid my sandals back on. Langston strolled up behind me with Imani in tow, threw his arm around my neck then we all walked out together.

By the time we made it to the restaurant, Imani was up, throwing a fit. She hates for her sleep to be interrupted. We were in a semi fancy restaurant, so it was becoming embarrassing. Langston sat and watched her clown me for five minutes before he stepped in. Once he took her from me, she laid down on his chest and closed her eyes.

"She loves her daddy," Kayla chuckled.

"He has her so spoiled."

"As she should be," Quincy smiled. "All girls deserve to be spoiled."

"Of course you will say that," Kayla smirked. "Big Daddy has Princess acting like a brat. I done had to start spanking her lil' butt."

"Don't be spankin' on her. Her daddy is a millionaire, she is supposed to act like that," Langston joked.

"I don't care if her daddy is a billionaire, she is gonna get her butt whooped if she acts up. I'm not gon' let no little person run me."

"Leave our babies alone," Quincy laughed. "Don't be acting all jealous."

Kayla smiled and shook her head. "Whatever, Big Daddy."

Quincy leaned over and placed a kiss on her cheek. "Whatever, Big Mama."

Quincy and Kayla's relationship was so cute to me. They said that they loved us together, but we didn't have any real time behind us yet. When we get to at least the two-year mark, I'll look at our relationship as cute.

While Kayla and I started our conversation about the store and clothes, Langston and Quincy had a side conversation going. I was straining my ear trying to listen to them and Kayla at the same time. I'm sure it is something that they don't want us to hear because their voice became lower as they conversed. I wasn't always nosey, but I know Langston had some plans for when we get back to Dallas. I just want to know what we will be stepping back into and how to prepare for it. Their voice lowered again, so I removed my nose from their business. Whatever is going on, I'll have to find out about it later.

After we finished up with breakfast, we decided to head back to the hotel. Quincy had to go to practice, and their siblings' plane was getting ready to land. The number of siblings he had was overwhelming. I felt the same way I did the day that I was getting ready to meet Big Mama and Quanda. I was a little intimidated about meeting them all. Never had I ever been around so many people that I didn't know. The good thing is that Quanda and Neka will be here, and I've met them both before.

"Oh look, they are already here," Kayla beamed as the cab driver pulled up to the hotel.

"Let the turn up began," Langston smiled.

"Are you ready to meet everyone, Yaniyzah?" Kayla asked.

I smiled nervously, "Yeah."

Langston paid the cab driver then we jumped out. He had Imani and Princess in each of his arms as we walked towards the group.

"Hey, y'all," Kayla greeted them all with excitement. "Glad to see you all made it here safe."

"Yes, girl, I am so ready to unwind," the female that resembled Kelly Rowland spoke. "Hey, Tookie, long time no see, bro."

"It has been a long while. What's going on, Shay?"

"Nothing much, living and enjoying life. This right here is my husband, Anson. Babe, this is Bootie and Neka's big brother, Tookie."

"Nice to meet you, man," Anson said, dapping him up.

"You too. This is my girl, Yaniyzah, and my baby girl, Imani."

"It's good to finally meet you, Yaniyzah," Shay smiled. "Kayla and my sister Neka have mentioned you before."

"Yes, I met Neka and her sister Jasmine a few months ago in Dallas."

"Oh, okay. Jas is our baby sister."

"Do y'all need any help?" Langston asked.

"Nah, we got it," Anson replied.

Kayla went on introducing us to her other friends, Taylor and Tay, her sisters, Kendyl and Jordan, and their men. Everyone was coupled up, with children following behind them. Langston, Imani and I fit right in with the crowd. This weekend should be an eventful one.

Once we made it back to the room, Imani was wide awake. Langston sat in front of his laptop to do some work I guess. I lay across the sofa watching Imani crawl around. She started to crawl towards Langston then her sippy cup on the table caught her attention. After pulling herself up, she grabbed the cup and turned it up. It wasn't but a swallow in there so she threw it when she realized it was empty. Langston looked at her, and she began to reach for him.

"Come on," he coached with his hands out.

Imani held on to the table as she made her way towards him. It was some space between the table and Langston's hands, so I watched closely to see what she was going to do. Without hesitation, she let go of the table and took a step. I jumped up from sofa as she took her second step. She must have heard me because she tried to turn to look and fell to the floor.

"Oh my God," I smiled with my hands covering my mouth.

"You see that," Langston laughed.

"Yes, I can't believe she took steps."

"Mani, you did it," Langston clapped his hands. "Yay, mama."

Imani smiled and clapped her hands also. Tears started to fill my eyes as Langston picked her up from the floor. I can't believe that my baby is trying to walk on her own. He stood her up on her feet again then let her hands go. She was just standing there smiling her butt off. When she tried to clap, she fell back down to the floor. I walked up behind her and stood her up again. She took two more steps then grabbed ahold to Langston's thigh.

"You did it, mama," I praised.

"Why you cryin'?" Langston questioned.

"Because my baby is growing up too fast."

"Don't cry about it. We want her to be able to walk."

"I know, but it seems like it was yesterday that I had her."

"Come here, crybaby," he said, grabbing my waist.

I took a seat in his lap then pulled Imani up to join us. Just as Langston wrapped his arms around us, there was a knock at the door. I got up from his lap to let him go answer.

Quanda and Neka dropped in to visit with us. Langston was more than excited to see his sister Quanda. They were very close, and you could tell by the way they embraced each other. He hugged Neka, but not the way he did Quanda. I guess they shared a closer bond since they had the same exact blood pumping through their veins. He forgot all about whatever he was doing on the laptop and started showing his sisters that Imani could take steps. I sat there smiling as I watched them all interact with my baby. They have accepted her as their niece and they treat her as such. It makes me feel good to know that me and my baby are accepted into their family.

CHAPTER FIVE: TOOKIE

Now that my sisters are gone, it is time to get fresh for Quincy's game. My hair still looks like shit, but my goatee and my outfit will be on point. I wasn't worrying about my hair too much because I wasn't trying to impress anyone here. Yaniyzah will take a day and a half to get ready, so I let her in the bathroom first. Imani and I played with her toys while Niy did her thing.

Once Yaniyzah had her face painted on, I jumped in the shower. Niy took so much time doing her hair and makeup that it only left me time to take a hoe bath. I wasn't tripping hard on it because I didn't stink. When I emerged from the bathroom, Imani's clothes were on, and Yaniyzah was slipping her dress on. I stood there for a minute watching her while I dried off. She was looking so good that it took everything in me not to grab her up. I have two days of semen built up that is ready to be released. She's been playing with me, but tonight she gone have to give that ass up.

"Get dressed and stop looking at me," Yaniyzah joked.

"I can't seem to take my eyes off of you. You look hella good."

"Thank you, I've been waiting to dress up for something."

"Shit, I can't wait to take you out more."

She laughed, "Get dressed, Tookie."

"Ahhh, you called me Tookie."

She laughed harder, and Imani joined in with her. Imani mimics everything that we do, so now I'm trying to be conscious about the things I do around her. That still didn't stop me from walking over to her and copping a feel.

"Baby, get dressed," she whined.

I kissed her cheek, "Okay."

We all stood in the lobby of the hotel waiting on the party bus to pull up. All of the kids were running around playing and screaming. Imani looked like she wanted to get down to join them, but she wasn't stable enough to walk yet. In no time, she will be running around helping fuck up shit too.

On the way to the arena, the bus was loud. The kids were still playing while the adults had different conversations going on. I kept my hands around Yaniyzah and my face buried in the side of her neck. She was looking so delicious that I couldn't help myself.

"Dang, Niy Niy, what did you do to my brother while y'all were on vacation?" Quanda asked.

"Nothing," Yaniyzah giggled.

I removed my head from her neck to look at Quanda. "Mind yours."

"Well, whatever you're doing, girl, keep doing it," Quanda

smiled. "Maybe you can tame that wild animal."

"Tame these—"

Yaniyzah slapped me on my arm, "Watch your mouth."

"Tell her to leave me alone then."

"I've never seen you like this before," Quanda cooed.

"And with all that extra stuff you doing right now, you never will again."

"Don't be like that, Took," Neka added. "I think it's cute."

"Babies are cute."

They all began to laugh and I snuggled my face back into Yaniyzah's neck. She smelled just like strawberries and I wanted a bite so bad.

Once we were all in the stadium, it became hectic. Everyone was trying to keep track of their kids as they ran around begging for popcorn, cotton candy and souvenirs. We had no choice but to stand in the long ass lines to hush them up. Imani was crying for Talia's cotton candy, so I knew I had to get her one of her own. Yaniyzah begged me not to but I ignored her. My baby wants some cotton candy and she is going to get it. Plus, I didn't want to hear her whining about it.

"Niy, get whatever it is you want and stop pouting. I done

already bought the shit, so stop complaining about it."

"She don't need all of that sugar."

"Baby, I'm not gone let her eat the whole damn bag."

"That's what you say until she starts whining again."

"Well, if you already know it then why complain about it?"

"'Cause she will be getting on our nerves later on."

"It's alright. Order me one of those lil' bitty ass $20 pizzas."

Yaniyzah started laughing because she was saying how high everything is at the arena before we left. I wasn't tripping about the inflation of this bullshit, but she didn't like to spend money on unnecessary things. That is one of the main reason that I fuck with her. She wasn't around to spend a nigga's money on dumb shit. I hadn't had a chance to spoil her just yet, but it is definitely coming. She deserves more than the world, and I am the nigga that's going to give it to her.

We finally made it to our seats which were damn near courtside. The players were already on the court shooting around. When Quincy saw all of us, a huge smile appeared on his face. I know that he is happy to have his entire family here to support him. Seeing my brother out on that court made me feel proud. Out of all of us, I'm happy that someone made something of themselves.

Imani wouldn't be still for nothing, so I guess Yaniyzah was right about that cotton candy shit. I tried to play it off like she wasn't moving too much, but Yaniyzah noticed it. She laughed at me and wouldn't take Imani. She didn't want candy on her dress, and she wanted me to deal with her since I gave her the sugar. It wouldn't be bothering me as much if the game wasn't so good. Quincy was out there balling and I didn't want to miss anything.

"Lord Jesus, Imani," I exhaled as she jumped up and down in my lap.

"Why don't you give her some more cotton candy, maybe she'll calm down," Yaniyzah smirked.

"What you want me to say, Niy, that you were right?"

"You don't have to because I already know. I just hope you learn to listen to me sometimes."

"I do."

"Mm hmm."

She reached down into Imani's bag and grabbed her sippy cup. She filled it with water then gave it to her. Imani took a few sips until she realized it was water inside. She snatched the cup from her mouth and raised it. I already knew that she was going to throw it, so I took it from her.

"No, no, Mani."

"You did that," Niyzah chuckled.

"Whatever."

Halfway through the game, I spotted Sonja. Sonja is Quincy and Neka's mother, and she still looks hella good. I'm not sure how old Sonja is, but her body was the shit. I could see that fat ass all the way from here. She is dating Quincy's basketball coach, so she had a courtside seat. Now she was up out of her seat yelling on the court. She was doing more yelling at the players than the coach. I couldn't help but to laugh at the look Quincy had on his face. I know he wanted to tell her to chill out. She was into what she was doing, so there was nothing he could do about it but play.

After the game, we all stood in the tunnel as the team walked through. We were waiting on Quincy, who was probably on the court doing an interview. He had a triple double tonight, so I know they would want to talk to him. He finally came strolling through the tunnel and everyone started cheering loudly for him. Kayla made sure to grab him first for a congratulatory kiss. He made his way towards us and dapped me up.

"The bruhs going out to celebrate tonight, can you get out?"

I looked at Yaniyzah and she shrugged her shoulders. "Yeah, I think I can make it."

"Cool. We're meeting up in about two hours, so make sure you're ready."

"Even when I'm not ready I'm ready."

"I already know 'cause that's how you roll," he laughed.

"Alright, bruh, see you later."

He went on to hug Sonja then ran to the locker room. We all began to migrate towards our waiting bus. Quincy didn't say where we were going tonight, but I guess I need to jump fresh. I'm hating the fact that my hair isn't cut. Now I have to walk into the spot looking like I just got out of the pen. Oh well, fuck it.

Since the guys were going out, the girls linked up in Kayla's suite with the kids. I could tell that Yaniyzah was hesitant about joining them, but I told her that she needs to get to know them. They were apart of Quincy's family, which makes them part of my family. I want her to get comfortable because I plan to have her around for a long time. Quincy and his people are always taking family trips, and I plan for us to start joining them on some. I want for all three of us to see life outside of Dallas, Texas.

I was dressed in Louis Vuitton from head to toe, my Rolex was on my wrist, and of course my frames were covering my eyes. I threw a few chains around my neck then topped it off with my diamond studs. After picking my hair out, I was rocking a nice baby 'fro. I looked myself over in the mirror one more time before heading down to the lobby. When I stepped out of the room, Anson was coming down the hall towards me. He had on an all-white

Gucci outfit with the shoes to match. I eyed his fit because I hadn't seen that shit in any stores in Dallas.

"You ready to have a good time tonight?" he asked.

"Yeah, but where we going?"

"Where else would we go in Miami? King of Diamonds, nigga."

"Word? Hold up then, let me go get some more cash out the room."

"A'ight, I'mma get the elevator."

I ran back into the room to grab five stacks. I had a little cash in my pocket but not for the strip club. And there was no way that I was going to pull any cash from the ATM.

By the time we made it down to the lobby, all of the other guys were there. We headed right on out of the lobby and onto the party bus we rode on before. This time it was liquor waiting on us. Everyone grabbed a glass and started pouring up.

"Y'all know we don't get to do this shit often," Quincy said, raising his glass. "So tonight we are going to live it up."

"I'm down with that shit," Slim cheered. Slim is a rap artist that is married to Kayla's fine ass sister Kendyl.

"You better," Anson laughed. "'Cause you know Kendyl ain't

letting yo' ass out the house when she find out where we went."

"She ain't gon' find out as long as y'all nigga's keep yo' mouths closed."

"I ain't scared of my ole lady so that's on you," Anson joked.

"Nigga, you know Shay don't play that shit either," Quincy laughed.

"Y'all need to be worrying about Jackson's ass over there being quiet. He is the one that tells his woman everything." Anson mentioned. Jackson was one of Quincy good friends, and he played professional football.

We all turned to look at Jackson.

"Man, fuck y'all," he frowned. "Kori is a detective and she will find shit out if I don't tell her. And y'all niggas acting like y'all gone be invisible or some shit. Everybody knows who we are so it'll fuck around and be on Mediatakeout or The Shade Room in the morning anyway."

"Well, whatever," Slim said, taking a shot. "I'm gon' enjoy my last night out then."

We all laughed then joined him in taking shots.

The strip clubs in Dallas didn't have shit on this club. I mean, our establishments were better looking, but these females had prettier faces. From the time that we walked through the door, they have been on our dicks. Strippers were trained to spot money and to go get it. The owner hooked us up with the entire VIP section. The girls were already hanging on and we hadn't even gotten our cash yet. I'm not gone lie, I missed shit like this. I've been cooped up in the house for so long that I felt like a kid in a candy store. There were so many beautiful women walking around that I didn't know who to get a dance from first.

"Come here for a minute, bro," Quincy said to me.

I got up from my seat to follow him. We walked further down the VIP section into a private section. I didn't know what the fuck was going on but I continued to follow him. We strolled down to the last booth where Anson was seated. I looked Quincy upside his head like he was crazy, but he kept a smile on his face.

"What's going on?" I asked as we approached the table.

"Remember when you were telling me about what you got going on in Dallas?"

"Yeah."

"Well, Anson can help you."

"What the fuck, bro!? You told him about my shit?"

"Chill," Anson interjected. "Your brother is just trying to look out for you."

"Yeah, Anson knows how them muthafuckas work, so I asked

him to give you a few pointers."

"Fuck all that explaining shit. Sit down, man, let's rap a bit."

I mean mugged Quincy as he walked away. He knows damn well that I don't like people that I don't know in my business. I don't give a fuck what he can help me with, I still didn't want this nigga in my business.

"How can you help me?" I asked, getting right to the point.

"The first thing that I can tell you is whatever they have on you is not enough or you would have at least been questioned by now. Quincy said that you keep shit under wraps, so you know it has to be someone that knows you that spoke your name. Before you step back in Dallas, you need to make a mental note of everyone who knows about your operation. Everyone. One by one, see who has gotten into any trouble with anything that they needed help getting out of. Nine times out of ten, that's gonna be yo' snitch. Friend or foe, you got to get rid of that muthafucka. If you want to keep ya hands clean, I have people that can take care of that for you."

"What the fuck do you do?"

"Now why would you ask me that question? Ain't you the same nigga that just marched yo' ass over here mad and cryin' because Quincy told me what you do?"

"Well, now that you know what I do, I need to know what you

do. You know, for security reasons."

"I'm a retired assassin and I run an assassination business."

"Real talk? How the fuck you get to do something like that?"

"Terrorist don't always kill themselves. Sometimes they need assistance with getting to hell quicker."

"I hear you. That's some playa ass shit though. To be able to kill people legally."

"Yeah, it's pretty cool."

"So listen, they put this FED bitch on me but I found out about her. Do you think they will send someone else?"

"They might, or they may just wire something up. Say the bare minimum until you find out who the culprit is."

"I got you."

"Do yo' girl know what's up?"

"She didn't at first, but her father is a damn FED too."

"You sure she isn't snitching?"

"Yeah, she kind of put me on to them watching a nigga."

"You might can use that to your advantage. Hang around pops and see what he has to say."

"She don't fuck with him like that."

"Maybe she needs to start. That's her father, so no matter what, he doesn't want to see her in any real trouble. If something is coming her way, he will warn her and that will help you."

"You might be on to something, but I want to keep her out of the shit."

"If she is your girl, they will fuck with her regardless to get you. You got to take two leaps and jump in front of this shit. I'll have my people look to see if any informants are in the system. If so, I will send them to Dallas to let you know."

"Good looking out. I know you charge for your services, so what's my total?"

"The advice is on the house. If you want further services, I will bill you."

"Cool, get my info from my brother."

"Alright. Now let's go watch some ass."

I laughed, "Right on."

After going through two bottles of Ace of Spades, two bottles of Hennessey, and a bottle of Crown, we finally stumbled back to the bus. Everyone was loud and drunk as fuck now. I had so many asses in my face that I was in a rush to get back to the hotel. At one point, I forgot that the dancer wasn't Yaniyzah and I bit her on her ass. I knew then that it was time for me to go.

When I walked into the room, it was quiet. I didn't turn on the light, so I bumped into everything as I made my way to the bedroom. Imani was lying in her crib sound asleep. I looked over at Yaniyzah who was bundled up under the covers. Normally, I don't wake her up for sex, but I'm not having that shit tonight. I told her ass to stay up, so now she got to get up.

I kicked my shoes off then dropped my pants. As I walked towards the bed, I pulled my shirt up over my head. I snatched the covers off of her, and she was lying there butt naked. Well, at least she knew what time it was. I leaned down to bite her butt then I kissed it. She moved a little, but she didn't wake up. I took my hand and separated her butt cheeks. I slid my tongue across her clit then she took a deep breath.

"Wake yo' ass up."

"What time is it?"

I climbed in the bed then separated her legs, "That don't matter." I grabbed her ankles, pinned them against the headboard, and dove in head first.

"Shit, Langston!"

I dug my head deeper into her pussy. I missed tasting her, so I wanted my whole damn face in it. It tastes like she was the one eating the cotton candy and not Imani.

Once I had her pussy soaked, I release her legs and pulled her closer to me. She was lying there with a smile on her face. I leaned in to kiss her while I eased my dick inside of her hot pocket.

"Mm," she hummed.

"You like the way this dick feels inside of you?"

"Sss, yes."

"Why you holding out then?"

"I'm not."

I threw her legs up on my shoulder and dug deeper inside of her. Her pussy was so tight and wet that I had to divert my mind for a minute to keep from nutting.

"Shit, girl, you got some bomb ass pussy."

"Fuck, baby. Fuck!"

"Give me that pussy! Open that shit up!"

"Ahh! You gon' wake Imani up. Fuck!"

"Naw, you gone wake Imani up."

I picked Yaniyzah up and walked us into the living room. The last thing I want to do is wake Imani's ass up. She can sense when a nigga wants some pussy, so she will try to stay up. I fucked

Yaniyzah against every wall, table, cabinet and chair in the hotel. Being that I hadn't had none in a few days, I held on to that nut for dear life. Now that that's out of the way, a nigga can sleep like a baby.

CHAPTER SIX: YANIYZAH

The sex last night was so amazing that I had to wake Langston up early with head in bed. He deserved it since I had deprived him. Imani was still sleeping, so the timing was perfect. I made sure to suck his dick longer than I ever had. Instead of the loud fucking that we normally do, we opted to make sweet love. I rather make love then fuck anyway because Langston gets so aggressive. Sometimes it's cool to have a screaming orgasm, but I like a slow, long nut.

"Damn, baby," he said, breathing heavily. "When you learn to ride dick like that?"

"This morning."

"Who taught you how to do that?"

"You did."

He slapped me on my ass, "Damn right. What time is it?"

"Time to get up."

I slid to the edge of the bed then stood up. My legs felt like noodles from cummin' so many times. Slowly, I walked towards the bathroom.

"Wake up in the mornin' to the best head. Niyzah's ass gettin' fat 'cause I keep her dick fed. Pussy so good got a nigga breakin' bread. Dick so good got her walkin' bowleg," he sung as I walked

away.

I laughed then closed the door on him. It was too early for him to be joking around already.

After a long, hot shower, I finally came out of the bathroom. Imani was up crawling around on the bed while Langston talked on his phone. I tied my robe up around my waist then there was a knock on the door. Langston looked up at me; I waved for him to stay seated, and I walked out to answer it. When I opened the door, a female was standing there dressed like Cinderella.

"Good morning," she smiled. "You are cordially invited to the first birthday of Princess Inergee Williams." Langston walked up behind me with Imani in his arms. "Here is a gift to help you get ready for the big day."

"Thank you," I said, accepting the gift box.

"You're more than welcome. Have fun."

Langston closed the door. "Open it up, let's see what's inside."

We walked to the sofa and took a seat. With the assistance of Imani, I pulled off the wrapping paper then opened the box. Inside was a Disney Princess dress, some hair bows with some matching slippers.

"Aw, how cute," I smiled, admiring the outfit.

"Look, Mani, you're gonna be a princess today."

Imani reached over into the box and pulled the dress out. We watched as she swung it back and forth then put it right in her mouth. I already knew that's where the dress would end up. Langston sat Imani on the sofa to go shower and get himself together.

Princess's party was in the hotel, so once we were dressed, we headed down. Imani was looking so pretty with her outfit and hair done up with bows. I guess Imani was excited about her dress because I didn't even have to fight with her while I combed her hair. Langston was looking sexy dressed in all red. I matched him with my red spaghetti strapped dress that stopped right under my knees. I wished that I could have taken a picture of us, but I didn't have a phone. Langston made me get rid of it on the way to the Bahamas. I hadn't thought too much about a phone, but once we make it back to Dallas, he will have to get me one.

Once Langston opened the door to the party, it was like we were stepping inside of a fairytale. Disney Princesses was the theme. Every princess that was ever made had a section in the room. Different Disney Princesses walked around playing with the children. It was over the top, but I expected that much. Kayla was so creative and she put most of it together by herself. I had never seen anything like this, and it made me begin to think about what I want for Imani's first birthday.

"Hey, y'all," Quanda spoke as she took Imani from Langston.

"Hey," we spoke in unison.

"This is beautiful, isn't it?"

"Yeah," Langston said as he looked around. "This is some playa ass shit right here."

"I already see the wheels turning in your head, Tookie," Quanda laughed.

"I know, right. My baby got to have a bad ass party too."

"Oh Lord," I giggled.

A lady that was dressed up like Princess Tiana walked over to play with Imani. Imani was smiling but kept pushing the lady's hand away from her. She wasn't feeling her at all, so the lady smiled and walked away. Maybe a character party might not be a good idea for her.

As we walked further into the party, I began to see a great amount of tall, fine brothers. I know that they were basketball players because they were abnormally tall. I'd be lying if I said the sight of them all didn't make me moist between my legs. Langston was the shit to me, but all of these rich ass niggas made me look twice. Most of them were with their wives and children. They were all rocking fat ass rings and wedding bands. I hadn't thought that far into the future for Langston and I, but I hope that he sees that I am fit for a fat ass rock too.

My heart dropped when I saw Inergee enter the room. Inergee is the top female rapper in the game right now, and I am one of her biggest fans. Kayla had mentioned before that she was Princess's godmother, but never did she mention that she would be at the party. I contained my excitement as she walked through. A big guy, who I am assuming is her security, walked behind her with a giant gift bag. She captured everyone's attention and all eyes were on her. I spied Langston with his mouth opened and tongue hanging out. I didn't hesitate to move through the crowd towards him to push it back in his mouth.

After watching Inergee talk to Quincy, Kayla and Princess, Quincy brought her over to introduce us. Both Langston and I had the biggest smiles on our faces as she spoke to us. I knew that she was pretty, but she was even more gorgeous in person. She has the smoothest caramel skin tone with not one blemish in sight. All I could do was look at her in amazement. I had never been this close to anyone famous before. I wasn't in to basketball, so Quincy and the other basketball guys weren't considered celebrities in my eyes. They are athletes and that is a big difference in my book.

"She is so pretty," Inergee smiled, referring to Imani.

"Thank you," both Langston and I spoke.

"She looks just like the both of you." Everyone always says that, but Imani looked nothing like Langston. She looked like Montrez and his mother. I guess the saying is true; if you feed and take care of someone long enough they will begin to look like you. "Too bad I didn't get to get in the family and have one of these pretty brown-skinned girls of my own," she cut her eyes at Quincy.

I couldn't help but raise an eyebrow at her statement. I thought that she was friends with Quincy and Kayla, I didn't think that she was checking for Quincy. The way that her eyes lit up while she talked to him made me realize that she is.

"Stop that," Quincy shook his head. "We're about to sing happy birthday, so let's make our way on over."

I grabbed ahold to Langston and let him lead the way. My mind was still on Inergee's statement, so it made me think about Kayla. Did she know that her child's godmother is crushing on her husband? It also made me wonder if Inergee and Quincy ever had a thing. I know that he was in her video a few years back, but I thought that they were just industry friends back then. From the looks of it, they had more than just an industry connection.

While the guys took the children to pet the animals, I huddled up with the girls and listened to them talk. Shay was talking to her sister Ty about controlling her mouth. She had an attitude about something to do with her husband. Ty was married to Keebee who also plays basketball. As they talked, I peeped out all of their outfits. It made me anxious about opening my store in Dallas.

"You need to learn how to keep your mouth closed sometimes,

Ty. You can't tell that grown ass man what to do."

"If he just listens to me then we won't have to go through this."

"What makes you think you are an expert at everything? You're not his fuckin' equal so quit trying to be that. Your job as his wife is to assist him, not help him, do you know the difference?"

"No, but I'm sure yo' ass gone tell me," Ty rolled her eyes

"Damn right. Let's say you see him struggling to move something heavy. If he doesn't ask you to grab the other end, don't take it upon yourself to jump in. Don't make him feel less of a man because you wanted to help when he didn't ask you to."

Listening to her advise her sister made me think about our situation. My plan was to help Langston out with this FED shit, but I didn't want to overstep my boundaries. He hasn't asked me for help and I don't want to intrude. I'm sure he had a plan of his own and I don't want to fuck it up.

The party was finally beginning to wind down. I sat at the table feeding Imani the last bit of cake she had on her plate. She was smiling and slobbering all over the place, but I could see the sleep in her eyes. She had been up longer than usual today, so I know she will sleep hard tonight. That will be great for our last night in Miami. I want to get freaky and have sex on the balcony tonight. With Imani sleeping hard, we should be able to get buck wild.

Langston walked up as I was cleaning Imani up. He kissed me on my cheek then sat down next to me.

"Did you have fun today?" he asked.

"Yes, I enjoyed myself."

"Me too. I think Imani had fun also. She was so excited to see the pony; I think I might have to get her one."

"And put it where?"

"I don't know," he laughed.

"Stop trying to give her the world. Let her grow to enjoy things a little at a time."

"I'll try, but I love spoiling her."

I leaned over and kissed him on the lips. "I know you do," I said, wiping my lipstick off his lips.

"Here is Imani's goody bag," Kayla said as she walked up.

I took it from her. "Oh, thank you."

"Did you guys enjoy the party?"

"We did. You did a great job," I praised.

"It turned out just the way I wanted it. But girl, I am so glad it is over."

"I'll be saying the same thing in a few months. You've given me a lot of ideas for Mani's party."

"If you need any assistance, let me know."

"Okay."

"Well, let me finish passing out these bags. I'll talk to y'all later on."

"You ready to get out of here?" Langston asked.

"Yeah, Imani is tired too."

He grabbed Imani, while I grabbed our things. As soon as Langston patted her on the back, Imani yawned then laid her head on his shoulder. My baby is tired and we're leaving just in time. Once I get her changed and down for a nap, I can show my big baby some attention.

CHAPTER SEVEN: TOOKIE

It has been a while since I have been this tired. Something must have come over Yaniyzah because she wore me out last night. Normally I have to ask for some pussy, but she has thrown it at me consistently over the last 36 hours. Don't get me wrong, I'm not complaining one bit. Maybe she is taking my advice to fuck me more than once a day. Whatever it is, believe that I am a happy recipient.

I rolled over and pressed my naked body onto Yaniyzah's. Usually she plays sleep, but this time she turned to face me. I reached behind her to grab a hand full of ass while I leaned in to kiss her.

"You ready again?"

"I can be," I smiled. "It don't take a nigga long to get ready."

She reached down and began to fumble around with my muscle. Morning breath and all, we began to tongue kiss. My temperature started to rise and my blood got to flowing.

"Ma-ma," Imani's soft voice called out.

We untangled our tongues and looked over at her. She was bouncing up and down in the crib, smiling at us. Yaniyzah pulled away from me then got out of the bed. I watched as she walked her naked ass to the bathroom to get her robe. I wanted so badly to be up in them guts right now. We missed our window for sex, but that is due to Imani going to sleep early last night.

While Yaniyzah took Imani to feed her some breakfast, I jumped in the shower. This is our last day here in Miami, so everyone was planning to spend this day shopping and sightseeing. It has been a minute since I've shopped, and I am ready to spend some money. I want to get some shit that niggas are not rocking in Dallas yet. I'm sure I will be able to find more than a handful of unique pieces here.

"Baby," Yaniyzah said, gazing up at me. "I want a phone."

"What you want a phone for?"

"For the same reason you have one, to talk to people. I haven't talked to any of my friends in months."

"Okay, we'll get you a phone. Just don't go running yo' mouth about where we've been or what's going on."

"I know that, Langston. You don't have to tell me."

"Well, I'm just putting it in the front of your brain. What kind of phone you want?"

"The newest one that is out."

I laughed, "Okay, we'll get it when we get home."

"Thanks, baby."

I slid my briefs and wife beater on while I ironed my clothes for the day. It was a hot day in Miami, so I had on a pair of cargo pants and a Ralph Lauren cotton shirt to throw on. I'm not going to do too much today because I'm trying to stay cool.

After waiting two hours, we were finally heading out the door. My sisters were already out, so we were going to meet up with them later. First, we had to find us something to eat. Imani had eaten oatmeal, but I'm sure she can eat some more. Yaniyzah and I hadn't eaten at all, so we both were starving.

We decided to stop at Pepper's to grab something to eat. Yaniyzah was ready to shop, so she didn't want to go sit inside of a restaurant. Whatever she wanted to do, I am down with. Low key, I wanted to grab something quick and get to shopping myself. I didn't want to be out here all day because I wanted to get rested up before we make it to Dallas. I already know once I make it there I will be going nonstop.

After we suppressed our hunger, we met up with my sisters to shop. They both already had several bags swinging from their arms. Seems to me that they had done enough shopping for the day. I already know that Quanda is hanging around to talk me into buying her something. She knows that I will buy her whatever, so I know she is waiting to ask me to buy something expensive that she does not want to spend her own coins on.

"So, do you have a plan for when you get back home?" Quanda

questioned.

"Not really a plan, but I have a few ideas of what I need to do."

"I got a few people that will give me information. They haven't gotten anything useful so far, but they promised to get me anything that they find pertinent."

"Do you trust these people?"

"Of course I do, or I wouldn't be talking to them about getting me info."

"Alright, well keep me posted on whatever."

"You know I will."

"I love you, sis," I said giving her a hug.

"I love yo' big head ass too," she laughed. "Now buy me this bag."

"I should have known that you were buttering me up for something."

I didn't get a wink of sleep last night. After fucking around with Niyzah, I stayed up thinking. I took the advice that I got from Anson and decided to make a list of who knows about my drug distribution. Everyone that is on this list is close to me, so it will hurt me to find out that someone I know is the snitch. Before tucking the note away, I stared at all of the names. Jefe, Nacho,

Punchie, Onion, Lil' Toot and Joy. I didn't bother to write Yaniyzah and Ro's name down because they found out about me after the fact. I doubt if Jefe or Nacho has anything to do with it, but I can't eliminate them just yet.

After packing up my things, I went to wake up Yaniyzah. We had two hours left before we had to leave for the airport. Hopefully two hours was enough time for her to get dressed and packed.

"Wake up, baby, it's time to get up."

"Mm," she groaned.

"Come on, you already know it takes you a day and a half to get dressed."

"You trying to be funny?"

"Not really. Come on, baby, chop chop," I clapped my hands together.

"I'm getting up."

While she went to go take a shower, I put my bags by the door. My cell started to ring so I ran back to catch it. The number wasn't familiar but I answered anyway. This phone only rings when someone I know is calling. I picked up the phone but I didn't say anything.

"L," my Big Mama's sweet voice spoke through the phone.

"Hey, Big Mama, what's going on?"

"I'm calling to check on you. Are y'all still flying in today?"

"Yes, ma'am."

"Well, there has been a car sitting down the street from my house for two days."

"Two days? Big Mama, why am I just now hearing about this?"

"Because I didn't think too much of it at first. Your brother, Quentin Junior. came by looking for you and pointed them out to me. He said that it is an undercover car."

"Okay. What did Junior want?"

"I don't know. He wanted to talk to you about something. He left his phone number."

"Alright, I'll get it when I get there."

"I don't think that you should come by here right now, L."

"Big Mama, I ain't gon' let no police or, anyone else for that matter, keep me from seeing you."

"You are so hardheaded boy."

"Always have been."

"How is Yaniyzah and Imani?"

"They're fine. Niyzah's in the shower and Imani is sleeping."

"Well, while you're being hardheaded, keep them in mind."

"I am."

"I don't want to keep you, I just wanted to inform you of what was going on."

"Alright, Big Mama, I'll see you when I get back."

"Okay, love you, son."

"I love you too."

As I hung up the phone, Yaniyzah emerged from the bathroom. I sat at the head of the bed watching her dry herself off. If we didn't have to get out of here, I would have gotten me one more nut.

After meeting Quanda and Neka in the lobby, we jumped into a cab and rode to the airport. While the girls chatted, I sat thinking about my next few moves. I closed my eyes and envisioned a chessboard. I thought about all of the pawns on my board, and which one is scared of doing their bid. No one had made any mention of going to jail, so I have to check for myself. Once we are back in Dallas, I will have Quanda look into it for me. That is my first move, then I'll look at the board later.

It took forever for us to get through the security check. By the time we made it to the gate, they were beginning to board. It was perfect because I didn't feel like waiting around anyway. Yaniyzah, Imani and I had first-class seats, so we jumped right in line. I looked around to make sure no cops were hanging around before I headed through the tunnel. The coast looked clear, so I turned to make my way.

Before we even took off, I fell asleep. Yaniyzah woke me up to tell me to lift my seat. I looked out of the window and saw us flying over downtown Dallas. The sight of the skyline made me jittery. I wasn't nervous at all; I was just excited to be back home.

My plan was to go by Big Mama's house, but she convinced me not to. Her word is bond to me, and I am going to listen this time. She had never been wrong about anything before, so this time isn't any different. Instead of me trying to prove that no one can stop me from doing anything, I rather approach everything with caution now. If I just had me to worry about I would say fuck the police, but now I am responsible for Yaniyzah and Imani. I promised her that I would always be here for them and I want to keep my word.

"Get at me ASAP about that," I said as I hugged Quanda.

"I will, just give me a few days."

"Okay, I'm gonna get a new phone, so I'll call you tomorrow with the number."

"Alright, y'all be careful. Bye Niy Niy, bye Mani."

"Bye," Yaniyzah smiled then hugged Quanda. "Bye, Neka and Talia."

"Bye, girl," Neka waved. "Don't forget to call me."

"I won't."

I am so glad that my sisters finally liked a girl that I like. They have been so hard on the others that it was mind blowing to see them being cool. The fact that they love Yaniyzah and Imani like I do lets me know that I found the right one. I've never been one that wanted to get married, but if she acts right long enough, I just might make her Mrs. Williams. Don't smile, I said I might.

Stepping back into my loft was like taking my first breath. It felt so refreshing to actually be back home. Since the season had changed to autumn, it wasn't hot inside. Before I could relax, I looked around to make sure that everything was still like we left it. Yaniyzah took Imani to the bedroom to lay her down.

Everything checked out, so I took a seat on the sofa. After I turned on the television, Yaniyzah came and took a seat in my lap. I wrapped my arm around her waist then laid my head on her chest.

"Are you happy to be home?" she asked.

"Hell yeah."

"Me too. What are we gonna do today?"

"I just wanna relax and enjoy being home."

"I thought we were going to go get me a phone?"

"We will. Who you trying to talk to so bad? I'm right here."

"My friends. I haven't talked to them in months."

"You'll have plenty of time for that. Just sit here with me and watch TV."

She secured her arms around me and laid her head on top of mine.

CHAPTER EIGHT: YANIYZAH

Langston rambling through the closet woke me from my slumber. I rubbed my eyes as I sat up in the bed. He came rushing out of the closet, then paused once he saw me.

"I didn't mean to wake you."

"What are you looking for?"

"I got it, go back to sleep."

"Are you about to leave?"

"Yeah, I got a few runs to make, but I'll be back."

"Why can't we go with you?"

"You already know that I can't have y'all in the car while I am handling business."

"What about my phone?"

"Girl, you gon' get that damn phone. Just stay here until I get back, can you do that?"

"How long are you gonna be gone?"

"Until I get back." This is the exact reason why I didn't want to come back here. I knew once we got back to Dallas he was going to begin to leave me in the house alone again. "Stop pouting, alright? I won't be gone all day, but in the meantime, you can use the house phone."

"You have a house phone?"

"Yeah, all you have to do is plug it up."

It made me feel better that I am able to call my best friends while Langston is gone. But, I am still disappointed that he is leaving. He didn't even mention that I could drive his car this time.

"Can I take one of the cars out?"

"Not today. Stay put because no one knows that we are back yet. After I get back this evening, you can start using it again."

"Okay," I smiled then threw the covers off of me. "Do you have to leave right now, or do you have time for round one?"

He licked his lips and smiled at me. "Look at you tryin' to make a nigga late and shit."

"If you don't have time then…" I said pulling the covers back over me. "I'll go back to sleep."

He pulled the covers off of my feet, and pulled me to the bottom of the bed. I giggled uncontrollably as he snatched the covers off of me. I didn't have any undergarments on, so he pushed my legs open and dove right in. I arched my back and gently placed my hands on the back of his head.

"Shhhit," I whined. "Damn you be eating my pussy good."

"Yo' pussy taste good."

While he licked me up, down and all around, I moaned to myself. I wanted to make sure that I didn't wake Imani before I get this good dick.

Langston stood up straight and slid his pants down. I watched as he slid his briefs halfway down.

"Uh uh, what you doing?"

"What?"

"You better get naked. You not gone fuck me like I'm a side chick."

He laughed then began to untie his shoes. I continued to watch as he took each piece of clothing off and carefully laid them down. I grabbed him by his waist to pulled him closer to me.

"Give me this chocolate."

I spit on his dick then wrapped my mouth around it. Langston let out a deep breath as he fingered my hair to pull it out of my face. While I massaged his muscle with my mouth, I looked up at him. He was biting his bottom lip, looking right at me.

"Damn, you look sexy as fuck doing that shit. Keep that shit up." I moved my head faster then began to massage his balls. "Fuck."

"You like that?" I asked, licking the tip.

He sucked his teeth. "Ss. You already know you got a nigga sprung off that shit. Can a nigga get some of that good ass pussy though?" he said leaning down to kiss me.

I leaned back and gapped my legs open wide. "We ready."

He rubbed his dick around my pussy before slowly beginning to push inside of me.

"Shit, you are ready."

"Mm, I told you," he laid on top of me and snuggled his face into my neck. "Langston."

"Hmm?"

"I think we need to start using condoms."

He stopped his thrusts, "Why?"

"Because I'm out of pills."

"Well go get some more of them shits."

"I have to make an appointment, but I will still have to wait before I start taking them again."

"When did you take your last pill?"

"Yesterday."

"Well, I'll pull out."

"That doesn't always work. Imani is the product of that."

"I'll get some later," he kissed me then began to move his hips again. "Right now, give me this gushy stuff."

"You are so nasty."

"Get nasty with me."

After Langton ejaculated his babies on my butt, he jumped into the shower. I walked around the room gathering my clothes to put on for the day. Langston said that he will only be gone for a few hours, and I want to be ready when he gets back. I've bugged him enough about my phone, so I didn't want to have to make him wait on me.

"Da-da," I heard Imani calling out. "Ma-ma!" she screamed.

I laughed to myself. "Here I come, baby."

When I stepped into her nursey, she began to bounce up and down. She was looking too cute with her hair all over her head.

"Mama, mama," she sung.

"Good morning, Mani."

She smiled and wrapped her arms around my neck. I walked into her adjoining bathroom to wash her face. She hates for me to wash her face, so I know I have a fight on my hands.

Once I got Imani presentable, I sat at the dining room table, feeding her. Langston came out of the room, brushing his hair. He smiled as he walked towards us, then leaned over to kiss Imani on the cheek.

"Here," he said setting a cordless phone on the table. "Make sure you call them people to get some more of them pills. We don't need no extra youngins runnin' around here no time soon."

"I will."

"Alright, I'll be back in a lil' bit."

"We will be ready when you get back."

"Please?"

I laughed, "I'm not that bad."

"Shiid."

He kissed me on the cheek then walked away. Imani began to grunt so I knew it was time to stuff some more oatmeal in her mouth. She is too greedy.

After sorting through my things, I finally found a paper with my doctors' information on it. They couldn't get me in until next week, but I went ahead and made the appointment. Since Imani and I were both dressed, I kicked back on the sofa. I was bored out of my mind, so I picked up the phone to call my bestie, Shannon. I haven't spoken with her in months, and I know she is going to curse me out. She had no idea why, or that I was leaving.

The phone rang three times before Shannon finally picked up.

"Who this?"

"Oh, you don't know a nigga no more?" I said in a deep tone.

"Don't play on my phone if you don't wanna get yo' feelings hurt. Who the fuck is this?"

"It's Niy, girl," I laughed.

"What!? Bitch, where the fuck you been?"

"Living life."

"Where are you now?"

"I'm—," I paused before I accidentally told her I was back. "I'm en route to Dallas."

"When will you be here?"

"Tomorrow."

"Girl, I can't wait. Where is my niece?"

"Right here. She has gotten so big, Shannon."

"I know she has. I miss you guys."

"We miss you too. Where's Courtney?"

"That tramp is probably somewhere tramping as usual."

Courtney and Shannon were sisters, but if you didn't know you wouldn't be able to tell. They talked to each other like bitches off to the street. Don't get it twisted because they've always had each other's back when it came to fighting.

"Don't even start."

"I'm not. Where is yo' fine ass man at, girl?"

"Bitch, don't be askin' 'bout my man like that."

She started laughing, "He is, shit."

"Whatever. He is out right now."

"When y'all get back, you need to hook me up with one of his fine ass homeboys. Hell, I'll take one of the fat ones. You know I likes me a chubby nigga."

"You are always tripping me out," I laughed.

"Speaking of trippin', yo' baby daddy been looking for you. He called me crying about wanting his family back."

"He is so full of shit."

"I already know."

I went on talking and catching up with Shannon for the next three hours. We had so much catching up to do.

Five hours later and Langston hadn't shown his face yet. As I watched the seconds tick away on the clock, I grew restless. I knew when we made it to Dallas he would start this disappearing act. He is out of his mind if he thinks that I am going to be cooped up in this apartment all winter. If he is going to be out in these streets, so am I.

After feeding Imani again, I laid her down for a nap. Langston still hadn't brought his ass back, and now I am mad. The wireless stores are getting ready to close, so that means that I am not getting my phone today. We've barely been back 24 hours and he is already breaking promises to me. I'm not putting up with any bullshit this time. And as soon as he gets here I will make him aware of that.

When I heard the front door open, I wanted to jump for joy. I am happy that Langston is back, but I didn't want to show it. I'm still frustrated about him leaving me here all day. He walked into the room smiling like he hadn't done anything wrong. The first thing that I noticed was that he had his hair cut. That made me even more mad, but I can't deny that he is looking handsome as fuck right now.

"Hey, baby."

"Hey baby?" I asked with an attitude. "Langston, where in the fuck have you been all day?"

"First of all, don't start questioning me as soon as I walk through the fuckin' door. I was out handling business, and that is all that you need to know."

"But you lied to me twice today. You said you weren't gonna be gone long, and you said that we were going to get my phone."

He had a bag in his hand that he threw towards me. I kept my eyes on him as I reached out and grabbed the bag. With my eyes still planted on him, I removed its contents. When I saw it was a phone, I smiled then jumped to my feet in the middle of the bed.

"Thank you, baby," I cheered, as I jumped towards him then wrapped my arms around his neck.

"Oh, now you wanna be on the tip of a nigga's dick and shit? Get on with that fake shit, Niy."

"It's not fake, you know all I really wanted was a phone."

"Now that you have it, I don't wanna hear no more bitchin'."

"Okay," I kissed his lips. "I missed you today."

"You did?" he asked, picking me up from the bed.

"Yeah, I'm not used to being away from you that long. For the last three months, I've been around you like every second of the day."

"Well just say that off top, don't come fussing at me as soon as

I walk through the door. If you miss a nigga, tell me then give me some head or something. Don't try to start an argument with me to get my attention."

"You want some head?"

"You ain't never got to ask me no shit like that. Where's Imani?"

"Sleep."

"Fuck that head then, I want some of that pussy."

"Did you remember to get some condoms?"

"I did," he smiled.

I immediately started kissing him to get the party started. Imani has been sleep for a while, so it won't be long until she is up again.

CHAPER NINE: TOOKIE

My plan was to alert the guys that I was back today, but I was still checking out their operation. Ro said that they had the north side on lock, so I was checking it out for myself. I saw a lot of product being moved which was a good thing. The bad thing is that I could see it. This operation was sloppy as fuck, and I didn't too much care for this set up. It was too out in the open for my taste.

I stepped out of my ride, and walked towards one of the youngins that was slanging. He saw me coming, so he kept his eyes on me.

"What you need?" he asked as I approached him.

"What you got?"

"That raw white girl."

"Oh yeah?"

"The best shit in Dallas."

"Who product is this?"

"This Whop shit."

First impression is everything to me, and I didn't like this shit one bit. The fact that he gave up Whop's name so easily doesn't sit well with me.

"A'ight bro."

"You want the white girl or nah?"

"Nah, nigga, I ain't on that shit."

He stood there looking at me crazy. I turned to walk back to my car and head to another spot that was theirs.

The next two spots that I stopped by was up to my standards. Them niggas wanted to know who I was, and why I wanted to know who package they were pushing. I damn near had to bust my gun on the second dude for jumping fly. Even though I almost had to put my foot in his ass, I liked the way that he operates. He is one of the few niggas that will stand tall when the people come asking questions. That first nigga definitely has to go. He is too weak to work these streets.

I picked up my phone to call Ro. I've seen enough of his corners, now it's time for me to talk to him. Things have to be tightened up around here to steer clear of the police.

"What it do, boy?" Ro answered.

"Tryin' to see what's up with you."

"Where you at?"

"I'm in the city, nigga. You know better to be askin' me where I'm at."

"My bad, bro, I didn't know. Swing by the house."

"Alright, I'll be through there in a minute."

I hung up with Ro then pulled into a gas station. I wanted to get some burner phones for us to talk on. If we need to talk, I want us all to have a separate phone to talk on. I don't know what's going on out here yet, and I don't want to get myself caught up on a wiretap.

I drove around the block twice before I pulled into Ro's driveway. Like I said, I don't know what's going on in the streets, but I had to make sure that he wasn't being watched. Yaniyzah said that her father had a picture of me talking to some people that she has seen me with before. I don't know if Ro is one of those people and is being watched. Every move I make now has to be done cautiously.

"My nigga!" Ro smiled when he opened the door. "Man, it's good to see yo' ass, get in here."

I dapped him up as I walked through the door.

"Shit, don't I know it. It feels good to be back."

"Besides, I have all this money stacked up for you and I'm running out of places to put it."

"That shit sounds like music to my ears. Where's Shanie?"

"Here I am," she called from the kitchen. I looked over at her and she was big and pregnant.

I walked over and hugged her. "Hey girl, how you doing?"

"I'm alright."

"How is my godson?" I said rubbing her belly.

"He's fine. Keeping me hungry, that's for sure."

"Feed that baby."

Ro was seated in the living room; I opened the fridge to get a water, then went to join him.

"So you back, huh?"

"Yeah, man, I was getting home sick."

"Well, at least you're coming home to some cash."

"That's always a good thing. You haven't had any problems with the laws have you?"

"So far so good."

"What about the lil' niggas?"

"They're straight."

"I checked out a few of y'all corners today. One nigga gave up Whop's name quicker than a hoe will give up the drawls. I don't like that shit one bit."

"Me either. Which nigga is this?"

"He's on that Parklane block."

"I'll make sure to handle that shit."

"How is everyone? Have you to talked to Toot, Punch or Onion?"

"I've talked to all of them?"

"Do they know about the business?"

"Toot and Punch know a little because I've had to supply them, but they don't know where I'm getting it from."

"What Onion doing?"

"I don't really know.

"Is he getting money?"

"If he is, it's not with me."

I shook my head and took note. When I get home, I have to make sure to put a check by his name. That is, after I find out what he has going on.

"Well, since I am back, I will get back on the money shit with the Cartel. You can stay on the drug shit. I got to get this business together so that I can clean this money."

"What business?"

"I'm gon' open up a store for Yaniyzah. Once I get that going, our legal cash flow will begin. After that, we will be able to ball how we want to."

"I'm glad because I am ready to move out of this piece of shit ass house. I want to bring my son home to some nice shit."

"I don't know if we'll be able to do it that quick, but in due time my nigga."

"I've waited this long, another year won't hurt."

Ro helped me take the bags of money to my car, then I dipped out. I didn't count the money there because I didn't want to be gone all day. Yaniyzah hates for me to be gone all day, and I didn't feel like her mouth today. Now that Ro knows that I am back in town she will be able to get out of the house. Hopefully her friends and the store will keep her occupied while I take care of business.

Yaniyzah's laughed echoed off of the walls when I entered the loft. Since she's gotten that phone, she hasn't taken it from her ear. Imani was sitting on the floor playing with her toys. I walked up behind Yaniyzah and kissed her on her neck. She smelled so sweet that I began to suck on her skin.

"Girl, let me call you back, my man is home. Alright, I'll see you tomorrow."

"Who you seeing tomorrow?"

"Shannon, and stop putting passion marks on me."

"Oh yeah, how is she doing?"

"She's alright."

"I found you a store."

"Is that what you've been doing today?"

"No, that's what I was doing yesterday. You were too busy trippin' on a nigga for me to tell you," I said taking a seat.

"I apologized." She crawled over into my lap. "What more do you want from me?"

"Nothing," I smiled. "You want to go out for dinner?"

"Of course I do."

"Gon' and get dolled up, I'll make us a reservation."

While she rushed off to start getting ready, I got down on the floor to play with Imani. Once I sat down, she forgot all about her toys. She began to crawl all over me like I was a jungle gym. I wrestled with her and roughed her up a little bit. She is so strong to be so little.

Yaniyzah must have been ready to get out of the house because she was ready in record time. For the first time, she was waiting on me to finish. I brushed my fade once more, dabbed on some cologne, then stepped out of the bathroom. Imani was sitting in the middle of the bed, taking off the shoes that I am sure Yaniyzah just

SHAMEKA JONES

put on.

"What you doing, lil' girl?"

She jumped then looked back at me smiling. Yaniyzah was leaning forward, buckling her heels. She looked back at Imani and shook her head.

"She is always doing something."

I took the shoe out of her mouth and slipped it back on her feet. "Leave these shoes on."

Imani smiled at me then grabbed her foot again. I reached over and pulled her from the bed before she could take it off.

Yaniyzah stood up, "I'm ready."

"Alright, let's go. We're gonna stop by Big Mama's first."

"Okay."

She snatched up her phone and purse from the bed, then followed me out of the door.

When I turned on Big Mama's street, I saw the undercover car parked. My first mind was to keep going, but I said fuck it. I am not going to hide from these muthafuckas. If they want me then they can come and get me. I'd rather for them to pick me up and question me anyway. At least that way I will know what they had. Anson said they wouldn't approach me until they had something,

100

so I know they are still fishing for information. As long as everyone else stands tall, one snitch won't hurt nothing.

Before we could even make it on the porch, Big Mama was opening up the front door. She held her stomach as she began her old lady chuckle.

"Hey, Big Mama."

"L," she hugged then began to pat me. "It is so good to see you."

"It's good to see you, too."

"Yaniyzah," she smiled and hugged her. "You and Imani are looking well."

"We are."

"She has gotten so big. Y'all come on inside this house."

Big Mama's face was lit up like a Christmas tree the entire time we talked. She is happy that I am back, and it showed all in her face. She may be just a little more excited than I am.

"L, did you see that car up the road?"

"Yeah, I saw it. I'm not worried, Big Mama, so I don't want you worried either."

"That's easy for you to say. I worry about all of y'all all of the time. I can't help not to."

"Well, I'm fine, mama."

"Where are you guys headed to all dressed up?"

"Out to eat, Niy is tired of being in the house."

"I know that's right, girl. Do you want me to keep the baby?"

"Nah, we gon' take her with us."

"Well, you need to get going so y'all won't be out too late with her."

"We are, I just wanted to stop by. I'll be back in a few days."

"Okay. And Yaniyzah, bring this baby by here to visit with me. You don't need L with you to bring her."

"I will, as soon as I'm able to get some car keys," she cut her eyes at me.

Big Mama started laughing and I waved them off. I'll take her off of restriction tomorrow.

"Yeah, yeah, let's get on out of here before it gets too late."

"I'm glad y'all stopped by to rap a tad," Big Mama smiled. "Be careful out there. Yaniyzah, take care of my babies."

"I will, Big Mama."

"Oh, give me Junior's number," I said, remembering one of the reasons why I came by.

"Wait right here."

The entire drive to the restaurant, I kept my eyes in my mirrors. I didn't see the undercover car following me, but that didn't mean that they weren't back there somewhere. I made sure to weave in and out of traffic just to be sure. If someone was following me, they will have a hell of a time keeping up. I noticed Yaniyzah looking out of the side mirror so she was looking out too. She is always watching my back, and that is the reason why I love her so much.

CHAPTER TEN: YANIYZAH

As soon as Langston hit the door, I got Imani and myself dressed. He gave me the keys to the Escalade, but told me not to go too far. I didn't care where I went, I was just excited to be able to roam freely again. Once we were all the way dressed, I called Shannon.

"Hey, girl, you back yet?"

"Yes, we are. Where are you?"

"I'm at home."

"Okay, me and Imani will come by in a little bit."

"Alright, see y'all when you get here."

I double checked Imani's diaper bag to make sure I had everything that she needs. She has already taken it upon herself to take her shoes off. I threw them in the bag, then grabbed it and her.

When I pulled into Shannon's apartments, all eyes were on my whip. It's Langston's ride, but we will just call it mine for now. The tint was extra dark, so they weren't able to tell who was driving. I drove around in front of Shannon's building and parked. It was a group of people standing out front, so I double checked myself in the mirror. I've never given two shits about my appearance, but Langston says that I represent him and I have to stay fresh.

"Best friend!" Shannon hollered as soon as she saw that it was me. She ran up to me and gave me a big hug before I was even able to open Imani's door. She pushed me completely out of the way. "Give me my niece, I miss her."

"And here I am thinking that it was me that you missed."

"You're my bitch, you know I do."

I pulled the diaper bag from the back seat, then followed Shannon towards the crowd. I put a smile on my face as I began to see familiar faces. A few of these bitches I used to kick it with before I got pregnant. Once I wasn't able to kick it no more, they kicked me to the curb. It was all good though, because now they were standing around with jealousy in their eyes. I was never one to stunt on people, but I am glad that I pulled up in a fly whip with my expensive threads on.

"I see you, Niy," Bresha spoke first. Bresha didn't hate on the fact that I got pregnant, but she stopped hanging around me like the rest did.

"Yeah, my man takes good care of me," I bragged.

"I see, you done caught you a big fish."

"Something like that. Wassup, Aspen?"

"Nothing much, what's going on, Yaniyzah?"

"You know me, spending my time being a mommy."

"Motherhood looks good on you girl."

Her twin sister, Denver, stood there eyeing me, not saying a word. She is one of the bitches that used to have so much to say, now that ass is on mute. I wanted her to say something to me so bad, but she knew better. Aspen and I were cool, but I can't stand Denver's bitch ass. The only reason that we never threw hands is because of Aspen. I've never known for identical twins to be so different like they are.

Shannon's mama house smelled just like I remembered when we entered. She always uses those Hawaiian Breeze Glade plug-ins that I love. Courtney emerged from one of the back rooms as soon as I sat on the sofa.

"Hey, girl," she sung. "Where the hell you been?"

"Relaxing on beaches and shit."

"You lookin' hella good, and you look like you've gained a pound or three."

"Thank you."

"Look at Imani," Courtney cooed. "Still beautiful as ever. You know yo' punk ass baby daddy been lookin' for you."

"So I've heard."

"I told you that hoe ass nigga wasn't 'bout shit when you met him. Now that you got a new nigga, he wanna act all caring and shit. He comes askin' me where you was at, I told his ass you went to the moon to get away from his ass. The son of a bitch said he was gon' slap me, but his punk ass ain't did it yet."

"He ain't gon' slap shit," Shannon frowned. "He need to slap a perm on his mama's nappy ass head. That bitch's shit is tougher than Jesus, and we all know he had hair like wool. Thank God Mani didn't take after them."

"You sure that's his baby?" Courtney laughed. "'Cause she too damn pretty to be his."

"Uh, excuse me, I am her mama."

"But you ain't that cute to overshadow his ugliness."

"Bitch, whateva."

"I'm just playin', girl. Shit, you need to have you a baby by that nigga Tookie. I know he's papered up and will take care of it."

"Don't wish that on me. I don't want any more babies right now and neither does he. We are just fine with Imani; he claims her as his anyway. That fool hit his own best friend upside the head with a bottle because he said she wasn't his."

"You still need that insurance baby, because he isn't obligated to take care of Imani. What if y'all break up, what then?"

"We done already talk about that so that's the least of my worries. He said that he will have my back forever and I believe him."

"Don't be no fool, girl. You better be stackin' yo' paper."

"Get out her business, Courtney. She just came from a long ass vacation with her man, she knows him better than we do," Shannon added.

"Whatever. I'm 'bout to dip, I'll see y'all later."

"Bye, girl."

"Make sure you got yo' key," Shannon called out.

My cell started ringing, so I dug it out of my purse. It was Langston calling.

"Hello."

"Hey, I need you to meet me at Uptown in Cedar Hill."

"Okay, I'll be there in a little bit."

"Bet. I'll text you the building number."

I hung up the phone and looked over at Shannon. She was playing with Imani, but looking at me smiling.

"You got to go?" Shannon asked.

"Yeah, I got to meet La—Tookie in Cedar Hill." I had to remember to refrain from using his real name around people. "You wanna ride with us?"

"Hell yeah, I've been trying to get out of this house all day."

While Shannon and I cruised the streets of Dallas, she caught me up on almost everything. She made me aware of who was no longer together, who is pregnant by who, and who didn't go to college as planned. We were only gone for three months, but it sounds like I've missed a lot. Well, not really because I was where I wanted to be. I hate that I missed it all, but it was well worth missing.

Although it was a Wednesday afternoon, the shopping strip was packed. It looks like Langston is on to something with getting a store here. The traffic flow is heavy for a weekday, so I know it will be outrageous on the weekends. Langston's main reason for getting this place is to clean money, but I think we will make some good money in this area.

"What y'all 'bout to do? Shop?" Shannon inquired.

"Nah, we're gonna look at a store. Tookie is gonna get me a boutique."

"What!? Say swear."

"Swear."

"Damn, bitch, you hit the jackpot with this one. This nigga already breaking that kind of bread for you? Must be nice."

"You know I've never been the one to like a dude that throws his money around. But, to be honest, I don't have any complaints."

"You better not, especially after dealing with Montrez's punk ass. Hold on to this nigga for dear life, and don't let go for shit."

"I don't plan to."

I spotted Langston's Corvette so I pulled in next to it. We were in the back of the buildings, and I had no idea which door to go through. Just as I had that thought, Langston walked out of the door in front of me. He walked over to the truck and opened my door as I killed the engine.

"Hey, baby. Oh, I didn't know you brought company."

"You remember Shannon."

"Yeah, 'sup girl?"

"Hey Tookie Man."

He helped me down from the truck, then pulled the back door opened to get Imani out. She had fallen asleep on the long ride over here.

When I walked into the store, all I could do was smile. It was much bigger than I expected but I love it. There were so many ideas going through my head that I could barely contain myself.

"So what you think about it?" Langston asked.

"I love it, of course."

"Yeah, this spot is the shit," Shannon said, admiring the store.

Langston wrapped his arm around my waist and pulled me close to him. "Is it big enough for you?"

"It is actually bigger than I expected."

"That means you need to get to work on your clothing line."

"Are you getting the store?"

"It's already yours," he smiled, then pulled the keys from his pocket.

"Really?" I beamed. "I don't even know what to say besides thank you, and that doesn't seem sufficient enough."

"I have a few things in mind," he leaned over and licked my ear. "Too bad you brought your friend with you, we could have broken the store in."

I giggled playfully, then shook my head at him. Everything with him resulted in sex. If that is all he wants, I can definitely take care of that. But I still feel like I need to do something special for him. I have to show him my appreciation in a way other than sex. Sex is not a gift, even though that is all he ever asks me for.

"That's all you ever want to do."

"I can't help that the shit is good. You should be taking it as a compliment."

A HUSTLER'S FANTASY 2

"I do, but there is more to me than pussy."

"Of course, your head is amazing too."

I punched him in his side, "Shut up."

He chuckled, "Oh, you don't want yo' girl to know that you got a good head on your shoulders?"

"No, sir."

"Okay, I'll keep it a secret. So as you can see, we have a lil' work to do, but it shouldn't take long to get the store opened."

"How long do you think it will take?"

"Maybe a month."

"I need to call Kayla because she is supposed to send some clothes. Oh, and I need to go get some fabric for my designs."

"Well, go do what you need to do. Just make sure you meet me at the loft at 7:30 to go eat dinner. I'll take Imani with me."

"Where you going?"

"Home, why?"

"I just want to know where you will be at with m—our daughter."

"You better had straightened that shit up quick. You know I wouldn't take her if I was going anywhere that she couldn't."

113

"I know that much."

"Come on, let's get out of here."

By the time we got all of Imani's things transferred into Langston's car, she woke up. I thought that she would want to come with me, but it seems like she was happy to be going with him. She loves her daddy and I can't even hate on it. He is always playing with her, so she knows that it will be fun with him. He is like a little kid when it comes to playing with her. I, on the other hand, will play for a little while then I'm done.

Shannon smacked her lips. "Bitch, don't ever let him go. You're pushin' this fly ass whip, the nigga just bought you a store, and he took Imani without you having to ask. Like I said, hoe, you hit the muthafcukin' jackpot."

"I know," I said humbly. "I need to get him something."

"Girl, niggas like that only want loyalty. Look, Niy, I don't know what Tookie Man does, but I know he gettin' that paper, so you just stay 10 toes down for that nigga. It's not every day that a nigga comes rescuing bitches with a baby. Niggas don't even wanna buy a bitch a burger no more because he thinks that's trickin'. Stand tall for that nigga, and make sure to keep these skanky ass, dehydrated tramps away."

"I am," I said throwing the gear into reverse. "I plan on doing all of that."

"So when you gon' hook me up? A bitch pussy is as dry as Dutchess lips right about now."

I burst out laughing, "Bitch, shut up. I'm gonna hook you up. I haven't met all of his friends, and I don't know who all is single. But don't worry, I will think of something."

CHAPTER ELEVEN: TOOKIE

It is three o'clock in the morning, and I am still up thinking about my next move. Now that everyone knows that I am back in town, I know the bullshit will begin. As long as I stay three steps ahead of everything, I will be fine. The only people that I know for sure isn't snitching is Ro, Niy, and Quanda. When I hit the streets in the morning, I will be on the search for that person or persons.

I heard Imani coughing so I got up to go check on her. Yesterday, I noticed that she wasn't as active when I tried to play with her. She may be coming down with something, or it could be something dealing with the climate change. As I walked into her nursery, she started coughing again. I tiptoed over to her crib to look at her. Her eyes were still closed but she was rubbing her eyes. She scrunched up her face as if she was going to cry, so I reached down to pick her up.

I walked into Imani's bathroom to search for some medicine. She felt a little warm so it was evident that she was sick. I found some Motrin for babies and read the back label. I had no idea how much Imani weighed so I picked up the scale from the floor. She was still wiping her eyes as I sat her on it. Twenty-two pounds. I poured the medicine to the fill line then gave it to her. She licked and smacked her lips like it was the best thing on Earth.

After I fixed Imani a cup of cold milk, we sat in front of the TV watching *Super Why*. Well, I was watching because Imani's eyes were closed as she sipped. Before she was even done, she dropped the cup and slobber leaked from her mouth. I held her until the show went off, then went to lay her back down. I switched on her night light and the stars began to orbit around the room.

Yaniyzah was still sleeping peacefully when I walked into the bedroom. I took all of my clothes off, then slid in next to her. My eyes were wide open, and sleep seemed so far away for me. Yaniyzah didn't like to be awakened, but I needed some pussy to put me to sleep. I've smoked two blunts and all it did was make me high, not sleepy. I ran my hand down her thigh, hoping that it would wake her. She was in a deep sleep because she didn't even move. I dipped under the covers, and lifted her leg up. She didn't have on any underwear, so I softly licked her clit. At first she whined like a kid that didn't want to be awakened, but it quickly changed to moans of pleasure.

Once I had her pussy wet, I slid back up behind her. I lifted her leg back up over my forearm, then slowly entered her from the back.

"Uh," she gasped.

"Mm," I moaned, then licked her earlobe. "Is this my pussy?"

"Yeah."

"Damn I'm happy, my shit good as fuck too."

"Is it?"

"Hell yeah," I said lifting her leg up higher. I sucked her neck and I slowly dug deeper into her.

"Shhit baby," she whined.

"You like this dick?"

"I love my dick."

I flipped her over on her back, then laid in between her legs. She wrapped her arms around my neck and we began to kiss. We grinded our hips against each other, making passionate love. Her pussy began to open up, so I knew her orgasm was near. I sped up my thrust to get her on across the finish line.

"Fuck, Langston."

"You cummin'?"

"Uh, sss, uhh."

She clinched up and held me tight. That gave me my answer. I didn't want to fuck on her all night, so I started concentrating on getting my nut. This time I didn't bother to put on a condom; I had to pull out which was something I hated. I much rather burst my nut inside of her like I'm used to doing it.

"Ahh, shit."

"You cummin' baby?"

"Yeah."

"Do you have on a condom?"

"No, I got it." I pulled my dick out, and she sat up and started sucking it. "Ooh, shhhit. Uh." My nut started to fill her mouth, but she kept on sucking. "Fuck, baby, fuck. Okay. Gimme me my damn dick," I laughed as I snatched it out of her mouth.

She laughed and semen flew from her mouth and nose. "Oh my God," she laughed harder.

"That's yo' spot," I laughed as I drug myself out of the bed. "That's what you get for being nasty."

"You the one that like that nasty shit."

"Sure do." I pulled her chin towards me then tongue kissed her. She played with my balls while we did so. I didn't want to keep her up all night, but it seemed to me that she wanted a round two. "Come join me for a shower."

The smell of bacon filled my nostrils, and woke me from my slumber. I felt worn out, so I rolled over to look at the clock. It had only been three hours since I had closed my eyes. I wanted to get up but my body wouldn't let me. I rolled back over to go to back to sleep. In another hour or so I should be good to go.

Not even an hour later, Yaniyzah came waking me up with breakfast in bed. I still didn't want to get up, but I got up to eat. I sat up against the headboard, then dug in.

"I think we should have some type of get together," Yaniyzah spoke.

"Why do you think that?"

"To celebrate us being back. We can just have something small with our close friends, you know."

"That might not be a bad idea. When do you want to have this party?"

"I don't know, next weekend maybe."

"That's cool. Invite a few of your friends, and make sure they're cool."

She rolled her eyes at me. "You're always telling me things that I already know. I know what to do and what not to do, Tookie Man. I know who to trust in my circle."

"Alright then. Did you talk to Kayla or whatever about the clothes?"

"I did. As a matter of fact, she said that she was coming to Dallas next weekend. Quincy has a game in L.A., but she is coming here to drop some things off."

"Oh, cool. I wonder why bro didn't call me."

"I don't know."

"Oh. Have you talked to your father?"

"No, I haven't even thought about contacting him. Why?"

"I think you should, you know. Stay close to him and be my extra ears. And since I mentioned that, during the get together, I need you to let me know who I was in those pictures with."

"Okay."

"I see Imani is feeling better."

"What was wrong?"

"She had a lil' fever last night. I gave her some medicine though."

She looked over at Imani who was chowing down on a piece of pancake. She seemed to be back to her normal self.

After I finished my breakfast, I pulled out my cell to call Junior. I've been meaning to call him, but it kept slipping my mind.

"Hello?"

"Junior?"

"Yeah, who is this?"

"Took."

"Oh, what's up, bro? I'm so glad you finally called."

"Big Mama said that you wanted to talk?"

"Yeah, I wanted to ask you about working."

"Send me your address, and I'll swing through later to rap with you."

"Alright."

I'll check up on him later on today. Right now, I need to go meet up with the guys. I hadn't talked to Whop, Fish or Cocka yet, and it is time that I do. They were in charge of the drug business, and I needed to voice my concerns to them. I left Ro to educate them, but he didn't do a good job. I like things to run clean, and the way that they have it right now is not it.

I pulled up to Yaniyzah's old apartment and got out. Ro's car was already here, so I'm hoping the other guys were as well. I jumped out and ran up the stairs. Fish opened the door for me with a big smile on his face.

"My nigga," he sung. "It's good to see you back."

"It's good to be back. I see life has been treating you well," I said, admiring his new gear. He was fresh to death and so were the other guys. I also noticed that they had put new furniture in the apartment and a big screen television was mounted up on the wall.

"Life is great."

"Wassup, Tookie," Whop dapped me up.

"From what I hear, you."

"What's that mean?"

"We'll talk about it. Wassup, Cocka?"

"Chillin', bro, making this paper."

"Already."

I slapped him five, then took a seat on the leather sofa. This place looks nothing like it did when Yaniyzah stayed here.

Time is valuable to me, so I didn't waste any time telling them what was up. I let Whop know that he has to get rid of that soldier on the corner. They had to get rid of those corners period. They had to think big, and to do that, they need to stop pushing small amounts. Another thing they had to do was get a trap for their workers to serve in. That out in the open shit is a guaranteed way to get busted by an undercover. You can't get familiar with regular clientele selling to anyone that walks up.

"So, I got these burner phones, right. They are only for us to communicate on. Nobody, I mean nobody else should have this number, not even yo' broad. When we talk, there is no name calling. Say what's up in code or whatever, or set up a meeting spot to talk. If anyone slips up and say a name, everybody needs to get rid of their phones. We have to take every precaution because the FEDs could be watching me. If they associate me with y'all, you could become a target. Make sure your soldiers will stand tall for you, or get rid of them now. We can't have any weak links on the team. One weak link on a chain will fuck up everything."

"Yeah, and I ain't trying to fuck up my money," Ro expressed. "I know y'all like getting money too, so let makes sure we stay on point and alert."

They were all in agreement with what we were telling them. I passed them the bag to let them all take a phone.

"I see that y'all have fixed up the place, but this lease is up at the end of the month. Y'all need to find somewhere else to stay, and I'll lease it for you if need be. I'm sure all three of y'all are tired of sharing this lil' ass apartment anyway."

"I sleep at my mama's house," Fish mentioned.

"Well, if you two want to stay somewhere else, find that shit."

"I got you," Whop shook his head. "I need somewhere to bring girls to anyway."

"What girls? You don't have no girls," Fish joked.

"Well I'm having a lil' get together next weekend, so swing through. Niy might have a home girl or two there to choose from."

"They ain't gon' want our young ass," Cocka complained.

"You have to look at yourself as a man. You are making grown moves, so you need to act the part. All you need is some money and some good dick to keep them happy."

"We'll see."

After a smoke session with the guys, I had to head on out. I had to go speak with Junior about whatever he is trying to do. All he said was that he wanted to talk to me about working. That could be a number of things, especially when it comes to me. Although he is my brother, I still have to check him out. I didn't kick it with dude, so I have no idea of what he has going on.

"Langston?" I heard my name called from behind me. It caused me to paused because my real name was called. I turned around to see Ms. Vickie standing in her doorway.

"Yes ma'am, it's me."

"How are you?"

"I'm great, how have you been?"

"I've been well. Where are my girls?"

"Probably out in the streets somewhere."

"Well, you tell Niyzah to bring Imani to visit with me."

"I will make sure to tell her."

"Okay, it was good seeing you again."

"You too, Ms. Vickie."

As I made my way to the car, I pulled out my phone to text Yaniyzah. I'm sure I will forget to tell her to call Ms. Vickie, so I had to tell her while it is fresh on my brain.

When I pulled up in front of Junior's house he was standing outside, along with our sister Queenie and a few unfamiliar faces. I threw the gear into park as Junior made his way towards me. I pressed the button to let the window down to expose my face.

"'Sup, Took," Junior said, reaching his hand out.

I slapped him five, "Get in."

He didn't hesitate to run around to the passenger side of the car. As he pulled the door handle, Queenie walked up to my window.

"Where y'all 'bout to go? I wanna go."

"Damn, can you at least speak first?" I asked.

"My bad, hey brother."

"Hey, big head ass girl."

"Where y'all 'bout to go?"

"None of your business," Junior interjected. "Get yo' ass in the house."

"Your name is Quentin Junior. not Sr., so you are not the father."

"Burn off on her, bro," Junior groaned.

"We're outta here, Queenie," I smiled, then pushed the button to let the window up.

"Y'all make me sick!" she yelled right before the window closed completely.

"Damn she gets on my nerves."

I laughed, "That's what sisters do, bro. What's up with you though?"

"Man, my mama done lost her job, and they won't give her any type of unemployment. Shit is getting scarce around here, so it's time for me to make some moves."

"What kind of moves?"

"I don't even know. I'm down to do whatever is necessary to make sure nothing gets cut off, and we don't go hungry."

"What is it that you think I do?"

"I don't know, don't nobody know that shit. But I know you're getting to the money. I want in on whatever, bro."

I took a deep breath before I started talking. I needed to think about what I was going to say. The last thing I want to do is bring my little brother into my business while shit is lukewarm. At the same time, I understand exactly where he is coming from. Once Big Mama was placed on social security, I had to get out and get it on my own too.

"Alright bro, you can be my right had man."

"Doing what?"

"Starting tomorrow, you will be my driver, assistant, and whatever else."

"Okay."

"I'm gonna come get you in the morning. Get the envelope out of the glove compartment."

I already knew that he was in need of some money when he mentioned working. I took seven thousand out of the safe to give him. He opened the envelope and flipped through the money.

"Thanks, bro," he smiled.

"Take care of business with that."

"No doubt."

"Listen Junior, you are my brother but I have rules. Don't tell anyone that you do anything other than drive for me, and that's only to family. Don't tell anyone else that you work for me, keep your mouth closed."

"I already know the code. Plus, you're my brother, so I wouldn't do no fuck shit."

"And don't tell yo' punk ass daddy neither."

"Fuck him, man. I called him last month for some money, and that nigga is still on his way."

I shook my head as I turned back on the block that Junior stayed on. He finally sees what us older children seen years ago. Our father stayed making empty promises. The fucked up thing about it is his brothers are nothing like that. Uncle Ralph and Uncle Tex took care of their kids. Then, too, they didn't have as many as my father did.

CHAPTER TWELVE: YANIYZAH

Langston and I sat in the room of the clinic, along with Imani, waiting for the doctor to enter. Finally, I will be able to get my prescription and not have to worry about getting pregnant. We were using condoms the first few days, then Langston had a change of heart. He didn't like the way that sex felt with it, and I can't deny that I feel the same way. We both have gotten used to the feeling of sex without the rubber in between us.

Doctor Gordon walked in the room with her eyes on the chart. As soon as she lifted her head and saw Imani, a smile came across her face.

"Oh goodness, she has gotten so big."

"Hasn't she?" I beamed.

"Yes, and as cute as can be." She looked up at Langston then shook his hand. "Hello, I'm Dr. Gordon."

"Nice to meet you, Dr. Gordon, I'm Langston."

I had to keep myself from gasping. I've never known for him to introduce himself to anyone using his real name. The way he rolled the L off of his tongue brought me back to the evening I met him. He tried to play me by give me his nickname. I've never went for that nickname shit, so he wasn't going to be an exception.

"Nice to meet you as well, Langston." She turned her attention back to me. "So, Ms. Owens, how has everything been since having the baby?"

"Everything has been great; I haven't had any problems."

"That's good to hear. So you are here to get your prescription refilled?"

"Yes."

"Okay.

She went on asking me a million questions. I answered everything honestly, even when she asked if I we had been using protection. Langston's face was in his phone, but his eyes darted up at me after I answered each question. At least he was listening; I hope he heard her when she said that we needed to be extremely careful. She stressed how easily it is to get pregnant after having a baby and stopping the birth control.

After leaving the doctor's office, Langston and I stopped to pick up some lunch. He was spending the first half of his day with Imani and I. I am grateful because he has been spending most of his days handling business. I missed him so much during the daytime, so I'm soaking up every moment right now. Shannon and I were meeting up later to plan the get together for this weekend.

When we passed the exit for our loft, I turned my head to observe Langston. He had his eyes on the road trying his best not to look over at me. I didn't open my mouth to ask him any questions, but I kept looking over at him after each exit we passed up. It was obvious that he wasn't going to tell me where we were going, so I put my elbow on the door panel and gazed out of the window. He finally acknowledged my curiosity by placing his hand on my thigh. Of course he didn't say shit, but at least he knows that my mind is wandering.

"Where are we going?" I had to ask.

"You've rode this long without asking, you may as well wait 10 more minutes."

"I hope it is to somewhere that we can sit down and eat because the food is getting cold."

"It is," he smiled.

I couldn't help but smile back at his cute ass. He always irritates me by not telling me anything, but at the same time, he is good at surprising me. I just hope whatever it is it's worth the wait.

Langston pulled up into the driveway of a house in the southern suburb of Dallas. I had never been this far south of Dallas, so I had no idea of where we were. He hit a button, then the garage door began to raise. Then it hit me, this had to be his house that he told me about.

"Is this your house?"

"This is *our* house," he said as he shut off the engine.

"What?" I sang. "You finally trust me enough to show me the house."

"Like I said, this is our house."

He jumped out of the driver seat, then came around to open my door. After helping me out, he grabbed Imani from the back seat. I held onto the food bags as we made our way to the door.

Walking inside of the house was like walking into a whole new world. This house was decorated way better than the loft and it was nice. He had famous paintings that were hanging along the walls. It didn't look like something he did on his own, but I wasn't too sure. His house in the Bahamas was decorated nicely as well. The house in the Bahamas is bigger, but this one was definitely more expensive. Now I see why he had us staying in the loft; he didn't want us to fuck up his expensive things.

"So, what do you think?" he finally asked.

"I think it is beautiful. Who decorated for you?"

"You tryin' to play me? I did."

"Really?"

"Boy, you have no faith in your man, do you?"

"You know I do."

I wrapped my hands around his waist to pull him closer to me. He leaned down and placed a kiss on my forehead that I wanted on my lips. I grabbed the back of his head to pull him down to my lips.

"Shit, act like you like a nigga then."

"You tryin' to play me?" I asked, mocking him from before.

He grasped a hand full of my ass. "I'm trying with play with you."

"Your daughter is awake."

"I know, that's that only reason that I haven't snatched yo' ass up, and pulled them damn clothes off."

"There will be plenty of time for that later. I'll make sure to put Imani to bed early tonight."

"I might not be out that late. I have a few runs to make, then I have to stop and check on the store."

"Which reminds me, the racks will come in tomorrow. Will you be able to be there, or do I need to go?"

"I don't know, but I'll let you know tonight. For now, let's eat."

As soon as we finished up our meal, Langston's phone began to ring. I already knew what time was, but I was starting to get in my feelings. Is it selfish that I wanted him all to myself? I had gotten so used to him being around, and I don't like the fact that he is gone 9 or 10 hours a day sometimes. Even with me having things to do, I still missed him like crazy.

"Why you lookin' all funny?" he inquired as he disconnected the call.

"No reason."

"Don't start that again, what's wrong with you?"

"It might sound selfish, but I just want you to be with us all of the time."

"I am with y'all all of the time."

"You are when you're not working," I bashfully stated.

"So what do you expect me to do, not work?"

"I do want you to work," I giggled. "I just want you with me too."

"It's just one of me, baby, and I can only do so much with only 24 hours in a day. Unless you know how to clone a nigga."

"Don't make me ask Google."

"Girl, don't do that shit. You gon' have the government lookin' at yo' ass," he laughed. "But for real, I'll be home earlier this evening. I just have a few runs to make, then the store shit. You just make sure that you are naked when I come home."

"Okay. Are you talking about here or the loft?"

"Whichever one you want to call home tonight."

"I'll be at the loft, it's too expensive in here."

He chuckled, "That's cool." His text message alert went off, interrupting him. "I'm 'bout to roll. Here are the keys to the car, and make sure to lock up when you leave."

"I will. Be careful, and I love you."

"Yeah, me too."

He stood up to give Imani and I a kiss before walking out of the door. It bothered me when I told Langston that I loved him and he didn't say it back. He had only told me once, and we weren't even face to face. It had me wondering if he just said it because he was going through something. I quickly shook that thought out of my head. I know that he loves me; it will just be music to my ears to hear him say it again.

Right after Langston left, I took a look around the house. It was a nice sized three-bedroom house with two bathrooms. The master bedroom was huge, it damned near took up one side of the house by itself. I was in love with the bathroom. Inside was a garden tub and a walk-in shower. It also had two sinks and two toilets. That was something that I had never seen before. And I forgot to mention that everything was gold. This house is nice, but it didn't have that homely feel to it. For now, I much rather stay in the loft.

I left the house heading straight to Shannon's house. If I wanted to beat the rush hour traffic, I had to step on it. After texting her that I was on my way, I put the pedal to the metal. I had spent too much time walking around inspecting Langston's house. It had no signs that a female had been there like the loft did. That almost made me reconsider moving there. If it wasn't so far south I wouldn't mind. Living out that way would definitely mean that I would be running into traffic. Staying downtown was better because it was 10 to 15 minutes away from everything.

When I arrived to Shannon's apartment complex, I pulled right in front of her building. I didn't bother parking because we didn't have time to waste. It was people hanging out in front of the building as usual, but I didn't pay them any attention. I shot Shannon another text to let her know that I was here. There was a knock on the window that caused me to jump. I looked up and Montrez was standing there with his forehead pressed against the window. I didn't want to let the window down, but I knew that he could see me.

As the window went down, a smile appeared on his face. I couldn't see my face, but I know I had a frown on it. He was the last person that I wanted to see right now.

"Where my baby, Z?"

"She is in the back seat sleeping."

"Open the door, I want to see her."

I sucked my teeth, then pulled the door handle to open my door. There was no way that I was going to let him inside of this car. I wasn't going to risk Langston killing me behind it, because I would probably kill him if I found out he had a woman in his car.

"Damn, baby, you look good," Montrez admitted.

I didn't even acknowledge his statement as I pulled the back door open. Imani was sleep so I knew that she would have an attitude about being woken up. I'm sure that will scare him away quickly, then hopefully he will leave us alone. As I handed Imani over to Montrez, Shannon came walking down the stairs. She paused and placed her hands on her hips to look at us. Imani was still sleep even though Montrez was trying to wake her.

"Where you been at with my baby, man?"

"I've been on vacation with my baby."

"Why you change yo' number?"

"Because I lost my phone in the ocean, and I didn't want that number anymore."

Shannon walked up and stood there. She was eyeing Montrez like he was her long lost baby daddy. I maneuvered my head to tell her to get in the car.

"Well, I need your number. I'm Imani's father and I need to be able to reach you."

"For what?"

"What you mean for what? So that I can see her."

"Oh, now you want to be a father to her? Damn near a year later?"

"Better late than never."

"Yeah, okay. How about you give me your number instead."

"Come on, Z, you already know that you are not gonna call." I stood there looking at him. "Can you at least bring her to see my mama? She has been asking me about her."

"I'll see."

"Please. I know I haven't always been there for you, but I want to do that now."

"I don't need you to be here for me."

"I guess you think since you got a new nigga and shit you don't need me no more?"

"When I did need you Montrez, you weren't there, and I definitely don't need you now. You're right, I do have a new nigga and he takes very good care of me and my child."

"Our child."

"Whatever."

"I just want to spend time with my baby, that's it. All I'm asking is for you to bring her around."

"I told you that I would see."

"That's not a good enough answer for me."

"Well, you better make it good enough," I said, pulling Imani from his arms.

I put her back into her seat, and fastened her up. Montrez was still standing there, waiting for what I don't know. I closed her door, then turned to open my door. Montrez grabbed my hand and spun me around to face him.

"Don't be trying to keep my baby from me because you wanna play family with this nigga."

"I'm not keeping her from you. This is only your third time seeing her since you and yo' mama put me out. So let's get that straight, you kept yourself from her not me. And as you can see, she is not that much of a baby anymore."

"Stop being so fuckin' smart before I slap the shit outta you. I know that shit. I'm trying to be a father to my child and you're acting like a bitch. You always have."

"You don't know shit about me being a bitch. You don't know me period. We only dated for two months before I got pregnant, so of course I was a bitch the entire time. If you knew anything about hormones and a female being pregnant, then you would have known why I acted the way I did. Not to mention the shit I had already went through with my dad. You are lucky that I even try to be cordial with you after that. Trust, you don't want to see me act like a bitch."

"Just bring her by my mama's, a'ight?"

I rolled my eyes at him, then pulled my door open. This conversation was over before it started, and now it was definitely over. I already told his dumb ass that I would see. He wanted to get a confirmation from me today that I would, but I couldn't give him that. I still felt some type of way about his mama, and I didn't want to see her fat ass. Even though he is her father, I think I may need to talk to Langston about it. I'm pretty sure that I already know what he is going to say. *Hell nah*. After hopping inside, and buckling my seat belt, I burnt off in Montrez's face.

CHAPTER THIRTEEN: TOOKIE

My face was in my phone as I rode to Nacho's place. I had my brother Junior driving me around in the new Tahoe that I'd just purchased. I traded in the Benz since I hardly drove it anyway. That way my little brother could have something to ride in. It is my truck, but after my work is done for the day, I let him take it home. Yaniyzah and I can't drive all of these cars at once, plus he needed a nice ride to be my apprentice.

"Pull in the driveway and wait for the garage to come up," I instructed Junior.

"Alright. Whose house is this again?"

"Nacho."

I was telling Junior things little by little. I didn't want to give him information about everything just yet. Right now, his job is to keep the police from fucking with me, while I conducted my investigation on everyone. The garage door began to open, and Junior slowly crept inside.

Nacho was smiling ear-to-ear when I stepped out of the back seat. He looked extremely happy to see me.

"My brother," Nacho greeted me with a hug.

"What's up, man? Long time no see."

"I know, man. Are you back for good?"

"Yeah. Nacho, this right here is my brother Junior. He is going to be assisting me from now on."

"I'm glad to have you back. I hope he is more consistent than Ro."

"What happened?"

"He is too slow. He has been late to several pick-ups and drop offs."

"Well, I'm back so things will return back to normal. What else have I missed?"

"Nothing else. The drugs have been moving quickly, so I have no complaints in that area."

"Cool."

"Let's go inside and handle this money business."

Junior and I followed behind Nacho into the house. As we walked towards the basement, I noticed him looking around the house in amazement. I can tell that he is not used to seeing nice things. I haven't taken him to any of my homes yet, so he hadn't seen what having real money looks like.

Once inside of the basement, Junior and Nacho sat at the table with me while I counted the money. It had been so long since I have had to count money, but I felt like I hadn't missed one day. Junior's eyes were big as light bulbs as he watched me count it all up. He is anxious to learn everything that I know, but I will continue to take my time with him. In due time, I will have his ass running things, and I will be able to spend more time with Yaniyzah and Imani like she wants me to.

"Nacho, have the police or anyone been scoping your place?"

"No, I've kept an eye out on my camera's, and I haven't saw any suspicious activity around here. Are they still looking at you?"

"I don't know for a fact, but I am sure they are around somewhere."

"Jefe told me about what was going on so I made sure to pay close attention to everything. Whomever is talking to the cops about you aren't talking about the money laundering."

"That's because no one knows about that. It had something to do with the drugs."

"Which is weird because you hardly even touched the yayo."

"That's why none of this shit is making sense to me. It has to be someone that either wants to see me locked up, or know that I don't mess with it for real and figured that the FED's wouldn't find anything linking me to it."

"I don't know brother."

"Me either, but I will find out very soon."

After the count was finished, we left Nacho's place heading for Onion's house. I had been calling him since I made it back in town, but he hadn't hit me back. He is the first person on the list that I want to speak with since he hadn't been around much. Ro had no idea of what he has been doing but I plan on finding out. Once I talk to him Lil' Toot is next on the list.

When we pulled up in front of Onion's house, I saw that Lil' Toot's car was parked out front. This was perfect because I could kill two birds with one stone. Junior killed the engine, then we both jumped out. I warned Junior before we went inside to keep his mouth closed and his ears open. He had to be my extra set of eyes and ears around everyone.

I rang the doorbell and waited for an answer. Ten seconds later, I heard the door unlocking. Onion opened the door with a smile on his face like he was happy to see me. That couldn't be possible when the nigga wasn't answering or returning my calls.

"Took," he dapped me up. "When the fuck you get back in town?"

"A few days ago, I've been trying to call you."

"Man, this stupid ass bitch done got mad at me and broke my damn phone. I've been using a bullshit burner. Come on in here, bruh."

"This my bro, Junior."

"I remember Junior. What's up, bruh?"

"Chillin', man."

They dapped each other up, then we trailed behind him.

Lil' Toot was seated inside of the game room when we entered. When he saw me walk into the room, he jumped up out of his seat.

"My nigga! Where the fuck yo' yesterday mornin' breath smellin' ass been at?"

"I just walked in the door and you are already with this shit. I wasn't even gonna say nothing about yo' volleyball built ass." I dapped him up. "What's good my nigga."

"Shit, trying to make it, you hear me."

"Yeah, I hear you. What's been going on around here?"

"Not too much," Onion answered. "Everything has been chill."

"What you been doing?"

"Fucking hoes and getting' this money."

"Where Punchie?"

"I talked to him yesterday," Toot spoke. "Does he know that you are back?"

"Nah, I haven't been by there yet."

"I'm 'bout to call that nigga now and tell him to swing by."

While Toot called Punchie, they continue playing the Xbox game. Junior and I grabbed a bean bag and took a seat next to them. I began to twist up a blunt to smoke while we waited for Punchie to come through.

"How you gettin' money, O? Ro said you not coppin' from him?" I continued my questioning.

"'Cause he got that white, I'm on that green. Since Ink got popped, folks been needing that weed."

"Who yo' connect?"

"Right now I'm coppin' from this nigga name KeKe in the Cliff."

Onion was giving up a lot of information, so I doubt if he is snitching. I'm not 100% sure, but I don't think he would be talking this much if he was snitching.

It took him an hour, but Punchie finally pulled up on us. The first thing that I noticed was the scar across the side of his head. I almost feel bad about putting it there. He was excited to see me like the other guys were. They all wanted to know where I had been, so I told them traveling the world. I didn't want them to know that I was running from anything, and I damn sure didn't want them to know where I really was. The Bahamas is a place for only my closest confidants to know about. They were my boys, but I wasn't even going to let them know about it. That is a safe haven for me and my family only.

"So, what happened with Inky?" I asked, starting the conversation. My intentions were to find out everything that I could in as little time as possible.

"That nigga got caught during a buy or something like that," Punchie admitted.

"I told you them people were looking at him, and you wanted me to hit him off with a package."

"Shit, I didn't know. But it wasn't a huge bust, so he'll probably do five years or something like that."

"I'm glad that you didn't fuck with him," Onion added. "But I wish you would have let us in on the connect like you did Ro."

"Ro doesn't have the connect, he knows the person that knows the connect."

"Why you didn't put me on to that shit?" Punch inquired.

"At the time, I didn't know if the FEDs were watching you too, or what. Ro asked me right before I left, so I introduced him. You getting work, right?"

"Yeah, but I rather have the connection."

"I'll try to hook that up for you. Before I forget, I'm throwing a lil' something at the loft Saturday, y'all come through."

"You already know that we are there," Toot smiled. "You inviting some hoes?"

"Nigga, you are always on hoe watch. Niy is inviting some of her girls, but I don't know how many."

"Tell her to invite every bitch that she knows," Punchie said, laughing. "I need me one of them young humble broads."

"I don't know any of them like that, but good luck on whatever."

We all laughed, then Toot passed the blunt around that he had just rolled. It felt like normal to be with my boys, and I didn't get any bad vibes from either one of them. Maybe it wasn't one of my boys that was talking to the cops. I couldn't eliminate them just yet, so I was going to keep a close watch on everybody.

Since I had a chance to talk to my boys together, I saved myself a lot of time and gas today. I had one last stop to make, and that was to Big Mama's. It has been a few days since I stopped by, so I had no choice but to go today. Even though is wasn't Tuesday, I stopped and picked her up a bouquet of flowers. If she was mad about not seeing me, they would surely cheer her up.

Big Mama was sitting on her porch as usual when we drove up.

She sat there eyeing the truck until we stepped out. I saw her smile as soon as she saw that it was me. Or, it could have been the flowers that I had in my hand.

"Well now," she joked. "The brothers are hanging out. How are you, Junior?"

"I'm fine, Big Mama, how have you been?"

"I've been doing good, baby. L, where have you been hiding?"

"I haven't been hiding."

"Mm hmm. I guess since you are a family man now you don't have any time for the old lady."

"Lies. You know if I don't have time for no one I have time for you."

She chuckled then hugged me. I made sure to hold her tighter and longer during this hug. I need for her to know that I missed her too. I've been away from her too long, and I've only seen her once since I have been back. She wasn't used to this new routine, but neither was I.

"Come on inside," she waved.

Junior and I sat at the kitchen table eating Big Mama's dinner. Neither one of us had eaten anything since we had been together. I don't know if Junior had the munchies, but I damn sure did. Not only that, I missed the shit out of her cooking. Yaniyzah can cook but it's nothing like eating Big Mama's food. It was just something different about her cooking.

"L, I hear that your mama is about to get out."

"Oh yeah? What's that mean? Is she planning to get herself right this time?"

"I don't know, son. I guess you will have to ask her those questions."

"I don't want to ask her anything. I want her to stay as far away from me as she can."

"Don't be like that, L, give her a chance."

"Big Mama, how many chances do you think I'm supposed to give her?"

"As many as it takes. Don't turn your back on your family."

"Sometimes family don't mean as much to some as it means to the rest. I love her 'cause she gave me life, but I do not like her."

"I already know that I can't make you do anything. You are grown and you make your own decisions."

I was just waiting for her to say *but*, but she never did. Big Mama knows that she can't change my mind on what I want to do. But, it has never stopped her from trying to change it before. I'm sure once my mama gets out she will change her tune about my decision.

It was getting late, so it was time to head on home. I know that Yaniyzah is at home looking at the clock, waiting on a nigga. I'm trying my best to use my time wisely to keep her from having an attitude.

"What you think about the meeting with the bruhs?" I asked Junior.

"It was cool. None of them seemed like a snitch to me, but who knows."

"Right. I didn't get a bad vibe, but we're gonna keep our ears open at this lil' kickback. You can invite a few people of your own if you want to. More females than males, I don't want a bunch of niggas walking around my shit."

"I got you. I think it would be better if you had it at your house instead of the loft."

"I was actually thinking that earlier. I'll talk to Niy about it and see what she has to say."

Junior pulled into the front of the loft, then turned back to face me. "Alright, big bro, see you tomorrow."

"Come get me at 10. We have some shipments coming to the store that I need to be there for."

"Alright."

I opened the door, "Be careful, man."

"Bet."

We slapped each other five, then I stepped out. I stood on the sidewalk and watched as he drove away. Once I was no longer able to see the taillights on the truck, I turned to go inside.

CHAPTER FOURTEEN: YANIYZAH

Since the store was coming along great, I spent yesterday ordering things online. I haven't had time to work on my own designs yet. Shannon and I purchased a lot of fabric, and we even came up with some new designs, but hadn't began working on them. Once I get some time to actually work on them, they will stand out and make my store unique. I can't wait to see how it all will turn out after everything is done.

Langston was out for the day, so I was trying to find something to occupy my time. Kayla and Princess were coming to town today, but that is later on this evening. I've thought about calling my father several times, but my fingers wouldn't let me dial the number. I didn't even know the first thing to say to him. Looking at Imani rolling around in her walker gave me the confidence I needed to make the call. Even though he was upset about me being pregnant, he fell in love with Imani when he saw her.

"This is Don Owens," he answered.

My heart was pounding, but I managed to squeeze some words out. "Hello, Daddy."

"Yaniyzah!?"

"Yes."

"Where in the world have you been, girl? I've been looking for you for months."

"I've been traveling the world."

"Really? Where are you now?"

"I'm back in Dallas."

"Are you able to grab some lunch with me around noon?"

"Um, yes, I can do that."

"Okay. Let's have lunch at your favorite spot, and bring my grandbaby."

"I will, see you in a little bit."

"Alright, baby."

He didn't seem to be upset about me being away so I felt better. It seems like he was happier to hear that I am back than anything. I had a little over an hour to get dressed, so I grabbed Imani's walker, and pulled her to the bedroom. I need to be able to see her while I get dressed, plus I need to change her shirt.

After Imani and I were dressed, we jumped into the 745, and headed to Uncle Julio's. Imani and I were dressed alike in our pink and purple sweat suits, with some fresh Air Max to match. I'm running a little late, but my dad should expect that from me. I am hardly ever on time for anything unless Langston is pushing me to be. Knowing my workaholic father, he will probably be late

A HUSTLER'S FANTASY 2

himself.

As I pulled into the restaurant's parking lot, I saw my father entering. I knew I wouldn't be considered too late fooling around with him. Langston didn't like for me to park his cars around other cars, so I drove around to the back of the parking lot. I grabbed my purse, then got Imani out of her seat. She was smiling like she knew where she was about to go.

When I pulled the restaurant door open, my father was standing at the hostess stand. He turned in our direction, and a smile spread like a wildfire across his face.

"Hey, Niy," he hugged me. "You look nice baby girl."

"So do you, Daddy."

"How is our little princess?" he said as he stroked Imani's chin. She sat there staring at him with no emotions.

"She is fine."

He reached his hands out for Imani, but she turned her back to him.

"It's okay, you don't know Pop Pop but you will."

"Mr. Owens, your table is ready," the hostess called out.

He stepped to the side to let me walk in front of him. Imani was holding on to me tight, but looking back at my daddy. She has only seen him once, so I'm sure she doesn't remember him. I just hope she doesn't act a fool while we are in this restaurant. Langston is the only person that can calm her down and he isn't here to do that.

After we placed our orders, my father began asking me questions. I knew that he would have some, but I didn't expect so many at one time.

"So you've been traveling, huh? I guess this new guy is better than the last one."

"Yes, he is."

"How so?"

"He's kind, he is honest, he takes good care of Imani and I."

"How is he with her?"

"He loves her, and she loves him the same. I think she loves him more than I do."

"You love him? Already? You've only known him for about what, 5 or 6 months?"

"Yeah."

"Yaniyzah, you have to be careful, baby. You thought you loved her father just a year ago."

"I am careful, and I've never told you that I loved her father."

"You didn't have to tell me; it was all in your actions."

"I didn't feel the same way about him as I do Tookie. It's very different."

"What's different about it?"

"I already told you."

"You need to elaborate. You haven't told me anything about this guy."

"Well, for one we haven't been talking for me to tell you anything. All I can say is that he treats me well. He loves and treats Imani like she is his own."

He sat there looking at me like he was waiting for more. I wasn't going to tell him anything about Langston because he wasn't his business. If he wants a relationship with me and my daughter that is fine, but if it's only to get closer to Langston he can forget it.

"You're not gonna tell me about him, are you?"

"No."

"Since you're not gonna tell me about him, I will tell you what I know about him. I know that he is 24, which I think is a little old for you. He obviously has money because he took you to see the world. What I don't know is how he can afford to do that. I mean, he has a little money in the bank, but not for a life time sweetheart."

"Daddy—" I cut my sentence short when our waiter arrived with the food. The conversation was beginning to get deep, so I am glad he finally showed up. Imani was bouncing in her seat and getting her lips ready.

As the waiter walked away, my father slid a card towards me. "Look, Niy, I don't know what this guy does that you have gotten yourself involved with, but there are speculations that he sells drugs."

"He doesn't sell drugs, Daddy."

"I'm tellin' you the word, girl. Be naïve if you want to, but you know who I am."

"I'm not naïve, Daddy. I know what he does and it's not selling drugs."

"Okay, well keep this card for emergencies. This is the best lawyer in Dallas. If you or this guy find yourself in any trouble, call her. I heard what you said about him, but I've heard differently."

"What have you heard? As a matter of fact, what do you have proof of that he is doing?"

"I know he makes money through a night club."

"Okay."

"That's all I know. His name came up during an interview a while back. It was told that he sells drugs, but there is no proof of that. Niy, if he does, tell him to steer clear of it for a few weeks. No charges will be brought against him if he keeps his hands clean."

I just looked at him without any expression. I know he is trying to read my face like he always does. I'm not changing my story about Langston no matter what he said he knew. Even though my daddy seems like he is trying to help, I'm still not saying one word to him.

"When can I meet this guy?" he continued.

"I'll ask him about it later."

"I need to meet the guy that is taking good care of my daughter and granddaughter."

While he continued to talk, I started to feed Imani and myself. She was tired of waiting, and I was done talking. I didn't want to say too much to my daddy because I knew Langston would inquire about our conversation. I want to be able to tell him that I didn't say shit and it be the truth.

After lunch with my daddy, I drove back home. Imani had gotten full and fallen asleep, which was perfect. Her napping will give me a chance to get some work done around the loft. I have to get Imani's room ready for Kayla and Princess. They are staying a few nights with us, so I need to change all of the bedding.

It took me no time getting the bedroom ready for our guests. Imani was still sleeping so I was now bored. I went into the kitchen to see what I could cook for dinner. After looking in the fridge, it was evident that I needed to go to the grocery store. I hated going to the store, especially when I had Imani with me. By the time I made it to the register, she had taken it upon herself to open half of the things in the basket. I grabbed my cell to call Langston. I'll just have him grab a few things on his way in.

"'Sup, baby," Langston answered with the music blaring through the phone.

"You busy?"

"A little, what's on yo' mind?"

"We need groceries."

"Go get it then."

"I didn't get any money from you."

"A'ight, text me what I need to pick up and I'll get it on my way in."

"Okay, and I need to talk to you about something when you get here."

"As long as my pussy is wet when I get there, we can talk

about whatever you want to."

I rolled my eyes and shook my head. Everything always ends in sex with him.

"Just don't forget the groceries."

"I'll bring home the bacon, babe," I could hear him smiling through the phone.

"See you later."

"Bet."

I stood at baggage claim with Imani on my hip, waiting on Kayla and Princess. We were just alerted that their flight had landed, so they should be walking this way shortly. Imani began to wiggle herself out of my arms. I stood her up next to me and held her hand. She started screaming, then tried to pull away from me. I looked and saw Kayla and Princess walking in our direction. Princess started screaming and clapping, so Kayla put her down. As she made her way towards us, I let Imani's hand go. She began to walk towards Princess like she was a professional. Not once did she stagger, but she was walking like a mummy. They hugged each other, then the both of them fell to the ground. Kayla and I both burst out laughing at them, along with some onlookers.

"How cute," Kayla cooed.

"I know, right. Welcome to Dallas."

She hugged me, "Thanks for having us."

"Girl, please. You are here to help me, I should be thanking you."

"I can't wait to see the store."

"I can't wait to see these clothes."

We gathered our babies to go get the bags.

We had to rent a luggage cart to carry all the baggage that Kayla brought along. She had several boxes that I took for being clothes for the store. Some random guy walked up to us to help. He even rolled the cart to the Escalade, and loaded it all up for us. It was nice of him to do it for us, but even better that he didn't try to flirt. Most men only do things for a woman that he wants something from. When we tried to tip him, he quickly declined, and told us to have a nice day.

As soon as we walked through the door, Kayla and I took the boxes to Langston's office to open. We had the girls sitting in the playpen that was against the wall.

"Girl, this is cute," I said as I pulled one of the dresses from the box.

"It's a few of those in there, but it's not the cutest one to me. Keep looking."

"You make me not even want to put my shit out."

"Everybody likes different things, so don't second guess yourself. I've seen so many pieces that I believed put my clothes to shame, but people love a variety of unique designs."

"You're right."

"Where is Tookie?"

I looked down at my watch. "He should be here in another hour or so. I gave him a grocery list, so ain't no telling what he is at the store picking up."

"If he is anything like his brother, he will come in here with everything except what you told him to get. Big Daddy be like, *they didn't have what you was looking for so I got this*," she said, mimicking his voice. We both laughed. "For real, I'm like, how the hell does the store just happen not have shit when you go. He gets on my nerves with that shit."

"Nah, Took is more than likely to pick up double of everything so that he don't have to go back."

"See, that's smart. Big Daddy is so spoiled he just doesn't want me to ask him to go. That's why I ask his ass every chance I get."

We laughed then I heard the loft door open and close.

"Niy!" Langston called out. "Where yo' fine ass at?"

Kayla and I giggled to each other, then I walked over to the doorway.

"Here I am."

"My pussy wet?"

"Watch your mouth, we have company, and your daughter is still up."

"Company?" he asked, strolling towards me.

"Yeah, did you forget that Kayla and Princess were coming to visit?"

"Shit, it is Friday," he hugged me then started towards Kayla. "Hey, Kayla, excuse my language."

"No apologies needed. You and your brother definitely share the same DNA," she and Langston laughed as they shared a hug. "How have you been?"

"Better than ever. How is lil' bro?"

"He's good."

Langston slid past her to go play with the girls. While he and Kayla talked, I continued going through the boxes and separating the clothes. I can't wait to see what it looks like when they are hanging in the store. There is still work to be done, but looking at these clothes made me excited.

CHAPTER FIFTEEN: TOOKIE

Our usual wakeup time around here is between 8 and 8:30. It was 7:30, and I could hear Niy and Kayla up talking. I didn't know if they had been up all night or woke up extra early. Either way, I need them to be the fuck quiet so I can get another hour of sleep. I rolled over, pulled the covers over my head, and closed my eyes.

My sleep was interrupted again when I felt Yaniyzah climbing into the bed. She slid over close to me, then climbed on top of me. When she laid on me, I secured my arms around her.

"Morning, baby," she spoke.

"What are you doing up so early?"

"I'm gonna go show Kayla the store, then we have to go pick up the rest of the stuff for the get together. What you got to do today?"

"I need to go get my hair cut."

"Is that all?" she asked, rubbing my muscle.

"Yeah, what's up?"

"Can you watch the girls for a few hours?"

"Is that why you're in here playing with my dick and shit? I should have known that you wanted something."

"I'm willing to give a little to get a little."

"Your little better be great."

"Come join me in the shower, and I'll let you be the judge of that."

She tried to lift up, but I held on to her tight. I didn't care too much for sex in the shower, I would much rather have it right here. I rolled us over then pushed her shirt up.

"Why you get in the bed with me with all of these clothes on?"

"Because the plan was to get out of the bed and into the shower. If you quit being lazy we can get it in before Mani wakes up."

Yaniyzah turned on the shower, then slowly she began to undress. I stood there watching her put on a little show for me. After she was naked, she pulled my pants and briefs down. While she did that, I lifted my shirt over my head. She ran her hands down the center of my chest, then squatted down in front of me. I leaned back to rest my body against the bathroom counter.

"Shit, girl, y'all must be planning to be gone all day?"

She pulled my dick out of her mouth, smiled, spit on it, then deep throated my shit. I got weak and lost my grip on the sink. My hands slid back, knocking the toothbrush holder over.

"Fuck," I moaned, then sucked my teeth. I swear every time she sucks my dick she gets better at it. Slowly, I moved my hips to match her speed. One of her hands gently stroked my balls while she massaged my dick with the other. I enjoyed the view of her giving me that sloppy toppy. The way her lips pulled my pole let me know that I had to stop her. I didn't want to cum before I had a chance to get in them guts. "Is my pussy wet?"

"Yes," she smiled.

"Let me see."

She stood up straight, then I picked her up to sit her on the cabinet. I pushed her legs up to the mirror and inspected her pussy with my tongue. She was ready for me, but I had to return the oral favor. I licked around her clit before gently taking it in my mouth.

"Shit, babe," she moaned as she rubbed her hand across the top of my head.

I pulled her legs apart so that I could see her facial expression. She was biting her bottom lip as I suspected. I removed my mouth from her clit to flick it with my tongue. Her eyes opened and she looked high as hell. I chuckled at the expression that she had on her face.

"I ain't gon' let you cum in my mouth," I said, pulling her closer to me by her thighs.

Her forearm knocked over the toothpaste holder. "Why, I let you cum in mine?"

"That's 'cause you nasty," I joked. "I wanna see you cum on this dick though."

"Just for that, I'm not doing it again."

"Yeah you will," I smiled, rubbing my dick around her clit.

"No I'm not."

I slapped her on her ass, "Stop talkin' back." Then I slid my dick inside of her.

"Mm," she moaned.

"Mm hmm, you ain't got shit to say now."

"Stop talkin' shit and fuck me; not too hard because we have company."

I had forgotten all about Kayla and the kids that fast. Lord knows I was getting ready to fuck the shit out of her for talking shit to me. After a few strokes, I noticed some blood.

"You on yo' period or something?"

"I wasn't, why, do you see blood?"

"Yeah a little."

"Good."

By the time we got out of the shower and dressed, Kayla had cooked breakfast. Imani and Princess were both sitting at the table eating pancakes.

"I figured y'all would be hungry after that workout, so I made breakfast for everyone," Kayla smiled.

Niyzah stood there looking all embarrassed. I walked over to the cabinet and removed two plates. Shit, I was hungry, so I wasn't going to hesitate.

"Thank you, sis. Niy, you gon' eat?"

She shook her head yes, and started towards me. I winked at her to make her smile. She gave me her bashful smile as she moved me out of the way. I held onto her waist while she fixed our plates. No matter how much we have sex, I just can't keep my hands off of her. If we are in the same room, I have to be touching her somewhere.

While we ate breakfast, Yaniyzah told me about her seeing her father yesterday. She said that he wants to meet me, which was expected. I had no plans of ever meeting this man, but only because he was a FED. This is something that I have to think long and hard about. Did I really want to show this guy my face? Did I even have a choice? I'm dating this man's daughter, so I know at some point that I will have to see him face to face. I didn't too much care for how he did Yaniyzah when she told him that she was pregnant. He already has two strikes against him, I'm just waiting for the third.

When Niyzah and Kayla left, I moved the coffee table back, and sat the girls on the floor. They had a gang of toys surrounding them. I sat down on the outside of the toys, going through my phone. I had several text messages asking me about the kickback. After responding to each one of them, I started playing with the girls. Hopefully, I'll play them out and they will take a nap.

Two hours had gone by and the girls were still going strong. There was no sign of sleep in their eyes, so I gave up on that thought. I kept thinking about my haircut, but I knew that was out of the question. Instantly, I got the idea to call Neka.

"Hello," she answered, trying to sound cute.

"Ain't nobody checkin' for yo' unattractive voice ass."

"Who is this, Tookie?"

"Yeah, big head, what you doing?"

"Combing Talia's hair."

"You coming to the kickback?"

"Yeah, Quanda told me about it. I'm coming through."

"Okay, cool. Your nieces are sitting here with me asking about you."

"Who, Mani?"

"And Princess."

"Oh, they're here?"

"She and Kayla are."

"They must have left you there with the girls?"

"Yup, and they want their aunt Neka to come get them."

"Don't be trying to bait me in. What you trying to do?"

"Go to the barbershop."

"Alright, I'll swing through in a lil' bit."

That was music to my ears because the girls were beginning to get into shit. Princess was walking around, and Imani was right behind her, walking and falling. They had already pulled the DVDs off the shelf, now they were pulling the magazines out of the bin. Honestly, they were destroying the place, but I didn't feel like running after them. As long as they aren't crying I am good.

By the time Neka sashayed her ass into the loft, I had given up on the haircut. Even if I did go, I would probably have to wait. Scoota's chair stays full on Saturdays, and I didn't want to have to wait at all. If I had gone earlier, I wouldn't have had to.

"I changed my mind now."

"You should have told me that before I drove over here."

"You can still take 'em though."

"Where are their car seats?"

"Ah shit, they are in the truck that Niy is driving."

"So I couldn't have taken them anyway. Good, that means you can keep Talia too while I run a few errands."

"Y'all not finna stick me with all these kids. I am not the babysitter."

"I know, you are the father and the uncle. Talia, don't you want to stay with Uncle Tookie?"

"Yes, I want to play with the babies," she cheered.

I chuckled at her calling them babies when she was barely older than them herself.

"See brother, she wants to stay with her cousins. She will be more of a help than a burden."

"If I keep her, then you have to keep Mani for us when I want to take Niy out."

"Damn, just for a few hours? You drive a hard bargain."

"I'm a hustler, baby," I smiled.

"A con artist is more like it, but I got you."

"Alright, and hurry yo' ass back. The fuck y'all think this is?"

Three hours later, Niy, Kayla and Neka came walking

174

through the door laughing. The girls had fallen asleep an hour ago, and I had just got finished cleaning everything back up. They had toys everywhere that I had to put back. I had messed the kitchen up making them lunch, and everything else that they had begged for. I was so happy to see their asses finally wind down.

"Shh, don't wake them up."

"Where they a hand full?" Kayla asked.

"Three hands full, and don't y'all ever ask me to keep all of them again. They never stopped moving until an hour ago."

"You did good, bro," Neka complimented. "They are still alive and so are you."

"You just don't forget our deal."

"I said I got you."

"The good thing is that the house is ready," Yaniyzah hugged me. "Everything is done, so all we have to do is get dressed and go over there." She held a Louis Vuitton shopping bag up. "I got you something to wear."

"Word? So you was thinkin' 'bout yo' man while you were out?"

"You know I was."

I kissed her on her cheek as I took the bag. Hopefully she

picked me up something that I will rock. She was pretty good at putting threads together, so I trust that whatever is in this bag is the shit.

I stood in front of the mirror admiring my outfit. Yaniyzah had purchased me a pair of stone washed denim pants, with a marble printed cashmere sweater. It was also a pair of Louis Vuitton sneaker boots at the bottom of the bag. The shoes set the entire outfit off; I couldn't help but smile. My girl knew how to dress me right. My whole joint was on point, just how I like to be.

Once we were all dressed, we loaded up the kids and headed over to the house. Yaniyzah agreed to have the party at the house, because she didn't want any strange people walking around where we sleep. Even though I didn't want them in my house either, I agree with them not being in the loft. Plus, it was more space at the house to maneuver, and we wouldn't have to go outside to smoke.

Stepping into my house was always like taking a breath of fresh air. The atmosphere in here is so peaceful to me. After all the people leave, I will have to burn some sage in this bitch. There is no telling who will bring any kind of negative energy into my space.

"This house is nice, Tookie," Neka smiled. "Why don't y'all stay here?"

"Ask Niy."

"I just like the loft better for Imani."

"I like this better, it's way more room."

"That's what I told her," Kayla spoke. "This is a very nice house."

"I bet it don't have shit on y'all house," I stated in more of an inquiry.

"Our house is nice," she said, smiling hard.

"I already know."

I walked further in the house to look around. They had the dining room and kitchen area packed with tables, chairs and store bags. Countless bottles of liquor lined the countertops. It looks like we are going to have a good time tonight. The doorbell rang, then I heard Shannon and another female's voice. I already know that this is about to turn into a pussy fest for the time being, so I fixed me a drink, then started towards my bedroom.

After turning on the television, I sat on the side of the bed to roll up. It was going to be a long evening, so I rolled up 10 blunts. These, along with what I know my boys will bring, should be enough. Yaniyzah pushed the bedroom door open, then walked over to sit in my lap.

"How is everything going?"

"It's coming along, we just have to get the food finished."

"Did Kayla like the store?"

"She said she loved it. It looks way different from when we first went there."

"I pay them niggas enough, it better."

"What's left to do?"

"We have two more inspections and the license to wait on, then we will be free to open at any time. You need to get some flyers together so we can pass them out. We got to promote that shit."

"Kayla and I already designed some flyers, I just need you to get them printed."

"Look at you, staying ahead of the game."

"You said I have to stay two steps ahead."

I smiled, then leaned in for a kiss. That one statement made me feel proud. At least she has been listening to what I have been telling her.

When Ro, Toot and Junior showed up, I emerged from the bedroom. The women still outnumbered us, but at least I wasn't the only male in the house now. After making us a stiff drink, we went out to the patio. I lit up the first blunt for us to smoke, while the girls finished preparing the food. Junior and I listened attentively to Toot and Ro talk. Toot was inquiring about stepping his re-up game up. He said that he has some new territory that he has been testing out, and the results were amazing. Ro looked to me a few times for some input, but I kept my mouth closed. I wasn't saying shit around anyone until I find out what I need to know.

Punchie walked out onto the patio along with Onion and Big Sorry. Excitement filled my soul because I hadn't kicked it with all of my boys in a while.

"Big Sorry," I boasted. "What's good my nigga?"

"Yo' lil thin ass," he dapped me up.

"Thin? Shit, you the one that look like you've lost a few pounds."

"Yeah, I've been doing a lil' working out. My doctor said I need to get healthy and shit."

"Already, it looks good on you."

"Fuck all that, who is them females in there?"

"I know right, I was wondering the same shit," Onion asked.

"I don't know who y'all are peepin', but two of them are spoken for. Niy and Quincy's wife Kayla are off limits, everyone else is free game."

"Well, I'm 'bout to go up in there and see what's up," Punchie mention.

Everyone laughed then began to make their way inside. Since most of the people are here, we went ahead and joined the women. I was trying to give them a little space while they finished up with the food. Once inside, I noticed that Quanda, Sloan and a few more faces were present. I wasn't familiar with the two females, but I am assuming that Yaniyzah knows them. As soon as I see her I will be sure to ask. I don't want anyone that we didn't know to be in my house.

Yaniyzah walked out of the kitchen and scanned the room. I had my eyes planted on her until she finally locked eyes with me. She smiled then nodded for me to come.

"You hungry?" she asked as I approached her.

"Just a little."

"The food is ready if you want to eat."

"What you got in there?"

"Chicken tetrazzini, some wings, Rotel nachos and meatballs."

"All that, huh? What you trying to do, make these muthafuckas stay all night?"

"I just wanted to make sure to accommodate everyone."

"Who is them two chicks right there?"

She moved her head to the side to look. "Oh, that's Akera and

Maxine, they are Shannon's cousins."

"Okay, cool, as long as you know them."

"I do. Now, do you want something to eat?"

"Yeah, bring a nigga some of that tetrazzini, and a few of them meatballs."

"You want some balls?" she giggled.

"See, now you don' ruined meatballs for me, scratch them shits."

She continued giggling, "They're good though."

I smiled and shook my head, "I can't even fade that shit right now. Bring the tetrazzini and don't say shit to ruin that for me."

"I'm bringing balls anyway," she laughed harder, then walked away.

She plays too damn much. I'm still not eating them shits. I won't be able to bring myself to even put that shit in my mouth right now.

I sat at the table eating with Toot, Punchie and Junior. Junior has been doing a great job with sticking around to listen in on conversations. As I took a bite of my food, I noticed Courtney watching me. I looked at her for a second, then turned to look at Junior.

"Lil' bro," Junior looked up at me. "Look over to your left and tell me if that bitch in the red shirt is still looking at me."

He took a sip of his drink as he casually looked over. I placed my eyes on Punchie and took another bite. Junior sat his can down, so I looked back at him.

"Yup, who is that?"

"One of Niy girls, or so she is supposed to be."

"She got that flirtatious look on her face."

"I don't like that shit. I might have to talk to Niy about her."

"She still looking fool," Punchie spoke. "I'm gonna go talk to her and see what's up."

Punchie rose from the table to make his way over. I kept my attention on my plate because I didn't want to look over and see her eyes on me again. Yaniyzah walked up behind me, then placed an alcoholic beverage in front of me. I grabbed and pulled her down to my lap.

"Sit yo' sexy ass down right here."

"What's going on, babe?"

"Nothing much. Where you been?"

"In the room with the kids. Kayla is in there supposed to be watching a movie, but she fell asleep on them."

"You don' wore her out, better her than me."

"You'll be later."

"Aw shit," I sung. "Now you're speaking my language."

"I know."

"Ay', let me ask you something." I leaned in closer to her ear to whisper. "Remember when you told me that you saw pictures of me at your father's house? Is it anyone here that was on them?"

She leaned over to my ear, "One of them is at the table." I knew that she had to be talking about Onion because she has seen Junior before today. "The other one is over there in that green Gucci sweater." I looked up and noticed that she was pointing out Toot.

"Anybody else?"

"Those are the only two that I see here, but it was one more."

"We'll talk about that later. What my baby in there doing?"

"Destroying your room," she laughed. "I'll fix it."

"Don't worry about it. Where them dominoes, I'm 'bout to whoop these nigga's ass right quick?"

"I'll go get 'em."

"Take this plate with you."

I slapped her on her ass and watched as she walked away. As soon as I looked away I saw Courtney looking at me again. Big Sorry was all up in her grill but she was eyeing me. I didn't like that shit one bit, and I will definitely be telling Yaniyzah that I don't want her around. She can't be a loyal friend to her if she is eyeing me. Those are the types of people that I do not want in my circle.

Before we started the game of dominoes, I went into the room to check on the kids. Kayla was still stretched out across the bed. Princess and Imani was jumping and crawling all over her, but she didn't budge. Once Imani noticed me in the room, she wanted me to pick her up. I sat down on the floor to play with her, Princess, and Talia. They wanted to come out of the room, so I had to chill with them for a while.

Kayla finally woke up from her nap. By then, the kids were beginning to settle down. I walked out of the bedroom to join everyone else. The music was going, so now it was looking more like a party. Whop, Cocka and Fish were now here. Yaniyzah and her girls were dancing in the middle of the living room, and a few of the guys were out there with them. She was smiling hard having herself a good ole time. I stood there watching to make sure that none of them niggas danced up on her.

The domino table was full, so I made another drink, then made my way towards my sisters. Quanda and Neka were huddled up in a corner talking and I wanted to be nosey.

"What's going on over here?"

"Nothing much," Neka spoke first. "Is Talia still up?"

"She'll be out in a minute, all of them are sleepy."

"Good."

"What's been up with you though?" Quanda inquired.

"I've been chillin'."

"I got some information for you."

"What you holding on to it for?"

"You know I wasn't gon' call you with the shit; plus, I knew that I was going to see you today."

"Well, what's good?"

"According to my source, Onion and Toot have been arrested in the last year. Both were for traffic violations, but they could have been questioned about other stuff."

"Is it anyway that you can find out if they were?"

"I'm still working on it. I'll keep you updated."

"Mm hmm. You just make sure you tell me as soon as you find out something, and not a minute later, ya dig."

"I got you."

"Yo' girl got some ratchet ass friends," Neka laughed. "Look at their thot asses, especially that one in that red shirt. That hoe don' been in every nigga's face in here."

"Oh yeah?"

"Yeah, and you need to keep Niy away from her before she become a lil' thot."

"Now you know I ain't letting that shit happen."

Yaniyzah looked back as she danced and her eyes landed right on me. I nodded my head for her to come over. She smiled then sashayed her way to me. I pulled a blunt from behind my ear and slid it between my lips. As she wrapped her arms around me, I lit it up and took a drag.

"Where have you been?" she asked.

"In there with the kids. Kayla was sleep on them and Imani is too small for Talia to keep up with."

"Thank you for being a great daddy."

I took another drag, "No doubt. Why yo' girls so wild?"

She chuckled, "They're just having fun. It has been a while since we have kicked it together."

"I don't want you acting like them, all wild and shit. Keep it classy, ma."

"Always."

Sloan walked over towards us, so Yaniyzah gave us some space. We had to discuss the club business. Now that I am back in town, I need to continue cleaning money through the club. He has been missing the extra cash that I had been throwing him, so he was all the way down with it. Business between us will start back next weekend. That means that I will be back on the scene, and the spotlight will be back on me.

"Bro, you know I would stay, but I have to get to the club," Sloan spoke.

"I know, G. Go make sure that your shit is straight. I'll walk you out."

I passed the blunt I had to him as we headed towards the door.

"Okay, are we doing the same amount?"

"Yeah, I want to keep everything the same as it has been. I don't want to set off no alarms and shit."

"I understand that. Other than that, is everything else straight? I mean, you dropped off the scene for a minute, you good?"

"Yeah, I took my girl on a vacation and we didn't want to come back."

"A'ight, I can dig it. Well, I'm gone."

I took the blunt from him, then dapped him up. I stood there smoking as I watched him get into his car and pull off. That nigga finally upgraded his car I see. He drove that old ass box Chevy forever, now he was whipping an Impala. Sloan had money in his pocket to get something better, but that nigga is cheaper than Julius from *Everybody Hates Chris*.

Just as I was about to turn to go back inside, I spotted a car creeping up the street. I stepped back off the curb when it slowed down in front of me.

"Why didn't I get an invitation?" a female voice asked.

I ducked my head down to see into the car. It was Brooke, or should I say Marlana Brooks.

"You already know that you gets no invites into my house. Fuck you want?"

"To let you know that I still have my eyes on you."

"I'd rather you have yo' mouth around my dick, know what I mean? You do know how to suck dick a lil' bit."

"You're still a disrespectful bastard."

"And you're still an annoying bitch," I shot back. "If you leave me the fuck alone, you won't have to worry about disrespect."

"I'm not worried."

"What's wrong, ma, you need some more of the dick? You liked it, didn't you?"

She laughed then burnt off. Damn, now this bitch knows where my house is. Man am I glad that Yaniyzah didn't want to move in here. If she had, we would be moving right back out. Now that this bitch is back sniffing up my ass, I have to make sure to move extra careful. The only good thing about this situation is the fact that I know she is watching me now.

CHAPTER SIXTEEN: YANIYZAH

Now that the weekend is over, it is time to get back to the business. It is time for me to concentrate on making new clothes and promotional items for the store. Kayla is leaving this evening, so we have to conduct business for the remainder of the day. Hopefully she has enough energy today to get some work done. After sleeping Sunday away, I hope that today she is a ball of energy.

Just as I finished up with breakfast, Langston strolled into the kitchen with Imani in his arms. Both of them had bed heads looking rough, but they were so adorable. Even Langston's tough ass was looking delightful this morning.

"Morning, babe," I spoke.

He kissed me on my cheek, "Morning. What you got going up in here?"

"The usual. It's done if you want to eat."

"My stomach is feeling a lil' queasy right now so I'mma wait."

"What you eat?"

"Yo' pussy was the last thing I ate," he smirked as he rubbed his belly.

"Well, it is deadly," I shot back.

"You're right, that shit gon' be the death of me. What you got up for today?"

"Fabric cutting for the most part. I have to take Kayla and Princess to the airport at 3. What you got up?"

"I got a lil' rippin' and runnin' to do."

"Be careful," I paused, then looked down at the stove. "My father said that they are just about to wrap up the case. They have nothing on you, so as long as you stay away from drug activity you'll be good."

"When did he tell you that?"

"The other day when I met up with him."

"Why are you just now saying something about it?"

"When I told you about him wanting to meet you the conversation went elsewhere. Plus, Kayla was at the table. I've been meaning to tell you, but we have been a little busy lately."

"We're never too busy to talk, especially about shit that is important."

"I'll remember that."

I began to fix my plate with enough for Imani to eat. I already know that she will be digging all in my shit. After fixing my plate, I set it on the table, then took Imani from Langston. He walked into the office area to get on the computer to work. I put Imani in her seat, then took my seat. While I closed my eyes to say my prayers, Imani took it upon herself to dig in my plate. I heard the spoon move just as I was wrapping up.

By the time Kayla and Princess woke up, Langston was on his way out the door. After feeding herself and Princess, Kayla came into the office to help me cut patterns. Every few seconds, I would look over at her. I wanted to ask her if she was pregnant, but I didn't want to pry. If she was, and wanted people to know, she would say something, right? But curiosity killed the cat.

"Are you okay, Kayla?"

She darted her eyes over at me, "Yeah, why?"

"Just making sure. You've been sleeping a lot."

"If you are trying to ask me if I am pregnant, the answer is...yes," she sighed.

"You sound disappointed."

"I am...a little. I'm not ready to have another baby just yet. Big Daddy is on the road most of the year, and Princess is already a handful."

"What did he say when you told him?"

"I haven't. I don't know how he is gonna feel, and I don't want to do anything that will mess up his game right now."

"I understand that much."

"And if you tell Tookie, Niy, please tell him not to say anything to Big Daddy about it."

"Okay. Kayla, can I ask you for some advice?" I asked in a more serious tone.

"Sure."

"You know that Tookie is not Imani's biological father, right? Well, now her biological father wants to be in her life, and I don't know what to do."

"What do you mean that you don't what to do? He is her father, so you can't just keep her away from him."

"And I don't want to; well, not necessarily. Him and Tookie have had words, and I don't know how to handle it with Took playing the father role."

"You need to let Tookie know what's up. If she was biologically his, he would want to be around her too."

"I hear you, but I also know Tookie. If I let him know, he wouldn't want me or Imani around him. He has done more for me and Mani than her father has. I still have to respect his wishes as well."

"I agree, but right is right. If you think that he will flip out about it, then keep it to yourself. But if you are taking that little girl around her father, you need to be honest with Took. Or be ready to deal with the backlash."

Rather I'm straight up with Langston or not, there will be backlash. At least if I do it without notifying him, I can act dumb. If I tell him about it, then do the opposite, he will be even madder. I didn't want to be selfish towards Montrez, but I didn't want to piss Langston off either. No matter what I decide, someone was going to be mad.

I stood on the outside of security check as Kayla and Princess walked through. Once they were cleared, I waved goodbye, then made my way back to my ride. When I got Imani and I back in the car, I noticed I had a missed call from Shannon. I didn't have shit to do, so I hurried up and dialed her back.

"Wassup, cow?" she answered.

"Nothing much, leaving the airport. What's up with you?"

"Yo' crazy ass baby daddy. He done came over here twice looking for you. He wants to see Imani."

"I'll call him."

"Please do so that muthafucka can quit coming over here. What you 'bout to do?"

"I don't know, probably go home and finish up on these dresses. You know the ones that you are supposed to be helping me with."

"Oh yeah, I was supposed to be helping you, right? I'll help you tomorrow, I have a date tonight," she giggled.

"Who are you going out with tramp?"

"Punchie."

"Punchie?"

"Yeah, I'm going on a date with chunky trunks."

"And you haven't said anything? You a hoe for that."

"I was gonna tell you after the date."

"Whatever, broad. Call me later and tell me everything."

"A'ight."

I hung up with her, then scrolled through my contacts for Montrez's number. Even though I was having second thoughts about calling him, I reluctantly pressed call. After three rings, he picked up.

"Yo', who dis?"

"This is Yaniyzah."

"Oh, wassup, Z? Where my baby?"

"She is in the back seat."

"You're out, can you bring her by my mama's house?"

I thought about it for a second, then muttered the word, "Okay."

"Cool, we are here now, so come on through."

"I'll be there in a little bit."

I hung up with him as I exited the airport. This feeling of being sneaky didn't sit right with me, but I have to do what I have to do right now. Hopefully Langston will be understanding whenever I reveal it to him.

When I pulled in front of Montrez's mother apartment building, all eyes were on my ride. Everyone was standing around waiting to see who stepped out. I applied some lip gloss to my lips, then grabbed my purse before stepping out. As I made my way towards the back passenger door, Montrez walk up on me.

"Get off of me," I pushed him, then pulled the door open.

"Don't act like that. You know you still love me."

"Uh, no I don't. I haven't loved you for a long time. As a matter of fact, I'm not sure if that was even love that I had for you."

"Yo' mouth can say what it wants to, but our love child is proof that you loved me. Otherwise, why you have my baby and shit?"

"Because I wanted to have her," I said as I pulled Imani out of her seat. "It's my body and I can do whatever I want with it."

"Looks like you've been taking good care of it, I'll tell you that."

"My man takes good care of it."

"Fuck that wannabe thug ass nigga. I'mma drop his hoe ass the next time I see him too."

"Grow up. You need to be worried about her, not him, because that is what he worries about, not yo' ass."

"I don't give a fuck, I'm beefin' fa' that nigga now."

"Whatever, Montrez. Do you want to spend time with your daughter or not? I got shit that I need to be doing, and it doesn't consist of standing here listening to you talk shit."

"Give her here then."

I extended my arm out for him to grab her. She turned away just like she did my dad, but he took her anyway. She kept her eyes on me as I followed behind them to the apartment.

As soon as Montrez opened the door, I heard the radio playing as usual. Janet Jackson's "Let's Wait a While" was coming through the speakers and Montrez's mother was singing along. My mind instantly went back to when I first heard her singing. I can't deny that she had a great singing voice, but I would never tell her that. She was always such a bitch to me, so I never tried to be nice to her. Maybe if she wasn't a bitch she could have had a music career. You can't be mean to people and expect to get a blessing like that.

Nothing much had changed, and she was still jamming old school music. If it wasn't for Ms. Piggy, I wouldn't know any of the songs from back in the day. Even if her television was on, her radio would always be turned on, just at a low volume. The house was spotless as usual, which was the one thing that I did like about staying here. They stayed in an old ass apartment, but she made sure to keep it extra tidy.

"Mama!" Montrez called out over the music.

We both took a seat on the couch, and Imani was still eyeing me. She kept trying to reach for me, but Montrez would tickle or talk to her to grasp her attention. Ms. Piggy emerged from the back room. She paused where she was when she saw me and Imani. She smiled then walked over to turn the radio down.

"Well, look what the fuck the wind blew in."

"How you doing, Ms. Piggy?" I spoke and forced a smile.

"Fine, I guess. You ran off with my damn granddaughter, so I don't know how I feel right about now."

"I didn't run off with her. We went on a vacation."

"Yeah, judging by the clothes y'all have on you must've found a balla."

"I wouldn't say all that, but he does okay for himself."

"Girl, don't sit up here and lie to me like I'm the damn police. Shiid, Trez told me what kind of car you was drivin'. Only a nigga with money would let a chick he just met drive around in some shit like that."

This is exactly why I didn't want to come over here. I knew she would be asking me questions and assuming shit the entire time. Montrez's punk ass had been running his mouth to his mama like a lil' bitch as always. She always knows about everything that's going on between us. Montrez is grown, and it is time that she takes her nipple out of his mouth.

"He treats me nice, and he treats Imani nice as well."

"Well, as long as he treats my granddaughter right, he is okay with me."

I looked at her closely to see if she was bullshitting me. I couldn't tell, so I looked away.

"Ma, how you gon' say some shit like that?" Montrez asked.

"What? What you want me to say? Her broke ass needed someone to rescue her ass, 'cause you damn sure couldn't do it."

"I didn't need rescuing. I had a job and an apartment before I met him."

"I heard. I also heard that you let your boyfriend control shit. Don't forget that we were there when no one else was."

"Momentarily."

"Chile, please. If it wasn't for me, you would have been in the streets."

"If it wasn't for your son, I could have still been home with my father."

"Yo' fast ass is the one that opened your legs for him." I sat there silent, not saying another word. I've went back and forth with her long enough. "Boy, bring my grandbaby over here so I can see her."

Now I am regretting the decision I made to come over here. If I wanted to be ridiculed I would have called my father. At least his talking is beneficial to me.

"And just because you and Trez are not talking don't mean I don't want to see my grandchild," she continued. "No matter what's going on with y'all, keep the baby out of it. Ain't that right, Cocoa?" she said as she rubbed Imani's face.

I didn't stay at Ms. Piggy's too much longer. She was wearing out my last nerve, so I had to dip. Once she saw us getting into the Escalade, she really thought she knew what she was talking about.

She started telling me the prices of trucks like these, but I tuned her ass out. My ear wasn't a toilet to catch all that shit she was spitting. I didn't have time for her or Montrez, and if they keep playing with me, they might not see Imani again.

CHAPTER SEVENTEEN: TOOKIE

Junior and I stood watching as Jose welded some stash spots into the truck. Now that I am back to collecting the money, I need to be able to secure it well. In case I am pulled over, I don't want the police to be able to find it. The thought of money is on my brain, so I may as well call Joy. Ro told me that he never picked up that money from her, and I need to pick that up. I thought about letting her have it, but I have had a change of heart. With Yaniyzah and this store in my pockets, I want all of my lil' ends.

"Hello?" Joy asked in a questioning tone.

"Hey, baby," I smiled.

"Who is this?"

"Oh, you don't know a nigga no more? That's fucked up. I thought you loved me, girl."

"Took, what you want?"

"You already know not to ask me no questions like that. What's up, girl?"

"Nothing much."

"I'mma swing through and get that from you. You still got it, right?"

"Yeah. I moved though, so I will have to send you my new

address."

"Text it to me, and I'll text you when I'm on my way."

"Okay, see you later."

Though I am happy in my relationship with Yaniyzah, I'd be lying if I said I wasn't excited about seeing Joy. She was the first girl that I ever loved or trusted. If it wasn't for her being a scary cat, we would still be together. My feelings for her never completely left, but Yaniyzah has done a good job with overshadowing them. I love Yaniyzah, but today that love will be put to the test. I used to have a weakness for Joy, so I'll see if she is still able to make my heart melt.

"I'm finished bro," Jose spoke, stepping from the back of the truck.

"Let me take a look."

Sauntering towards him, I scrolled through my phone for Sloan's number. My plan is to stop by the club on my way to Joy's.

"See," Jose started. "You have two compartments back here. The truck has to be in neutral with the bright lights, and hazards on to open up."

"That's sweet right there."

"Yeah, I've learned how to do a few combinations."

"This will work. We'll be back in a few days to drop off another stash."

"Cool, man."

We dapped each other up, then Junior and I were out.

The stop by Sloan's club didn't last long. He was on his way out but he waited on me. That was perfect because I had other shit to do anyway. After I finish up with Joy, I have to stop by and check on the youngins. They went ahead and moved into a new spot, so I wanted to take a look at it. I don't know if they scoped the place out for police before they decided to move in. Even though they are technically working for Ro, they were still my investment.

Joy had moved further north to Richardson, so our drive was a long one. On the way, we blew a fat ass blunt. I was high as hell and glad that I wasn't the one driving. Junior drove into the apartment complex, then stopped right in front of her building.

"Chill out here for a lil' bit, lil' bro."

"Who lives here?"

"One of my old broads. She is holding some money for me that I need to get."

"Do you need me to scope this place out?"

"You don't have to, but make sure to keep your eyes open. If you see some strange shit, hit me up. I shouldn't be in here too long though."

"A'ight, bro."

"And while you are out here, hit Whop up to let him know we are swinging by there."

"Bet."

I jumped out of the back seat, and ran up the stairs that led to her apartment. Before I knocked, I did a breath test to make sure that I was straight. I just smoked but it was okay, considering.

When Joy opened her door, all I could see was her long ass legs. I don't know what possessed me to look down at them first. They had me mesmerized, so I began to scan her body upwards. As soon as my eyes landed on her breasts, it took me back to old times. Even with all this attraction that I had to her, I still didn't feel any sparks flying as expected. I thought that I would have been drooling by now but I wasn't. That confirmed to me that the feelings that I once had for her were fading away.

"Are you gonna speak or stand there fantasizing?" she asked, breaking my thoughts.

"How you doing, Ms. Lady?"

"I'm fine," she smiled then pulled me in for a hug.

"A nigga can see that."

"There you go already."

"What? I can't give you a compliment?"

"You can, but you know how you do. Don't you have a girl or something?"

"Yeah, but that don't have anything to do with complimenting you. It ain't like I'm tryin' to fuck or nothing."

She looked insulted, or maybe she was disappointed.

"Good. You can have a seat while I get the money."

While she disappeared to the back, I walked around slowly, admiring her apartment. It was nice, and it had me wondering where she got her money from. As far as I knew, she was still in school. She didn't work when we were together, so it made me wonder if she had taken any money from me. Well, not taken because I used to throw cash at her, but it looks like she saved it or something. I figured if she had stolen from me, she would have kept this money I came to get.

"Here you go."

"Is it all still here, or did you spend some?"

"It is all there; I don't want any of your drug money."

"Drug money?" I laughed. "Girl, you talking crazy."

"Don't lie to me like I'm yo' new broad. I already know what the deal is."

"Nah, this is legit money right here. I didn't want to keep all of the money I'm making at the club in the bank."

"Langston I was with you when you picked the money up."

"You don't know what you're talking about Joy."

"Well, whatever it is, I didn't touch it."

"What's up with you though? You've been snappy since you opened the door?"

"I'm not snappy."

I smiled while I looked her dead in her face. She can say what she wants, but I know when she has a lil' attitude. That is some shit that I wasn't going to deal with today, especially not from her.

"Alright then, Ms. Lady, I'm outta here."

She sighed and stood up. "Well, it was good to see you again. Even if it was a short time."

"I don't want to be just chilling over here. Plus, you act like you don't want a nigga here."

"No I'm not. So, where you been?"

"On vacation."

"Where?"

"All over the world."

"You took yo' girl with you?"

"Of course. You already know how I do, or have you forgot."

"No, I remember a few trips, but I don't remember seeing the world."

"You missed out on that one."

"I see. Do you love her, Tookie?"

"Don't do that. And I'm not 'bout to sit up here with you and talk about her. That is my lady, and that's that."

"Okay. As long as she makes you happy, that's all I care about."

"Now you care about my happiness?"

"Yes, I do. I couldn't be that girl that you wanted me to be, I just hope that she is."

"She straight. Since you in my business, what you got going on?"

"Just focusing on finishing school. I have one semester left."

"That's good, I'm proud of you."

"Thanks," she smiled.

Now the softness was coming out of her. She had her wall up when I mentioned not fucking her, so I am happy to see it was crumbling. Maybe she had hopes of having sex with me when I came over. If she did I hate it for her.

Joy and I talked so long that I forgot that Junior was in the car. When I did remember, I got up out of there. On my way out of the door, she planted a kiss on my lips. That was the first time since I had seen her that I felt a little spark. I began thinking about the old days, then I had to snap out of it. I'm not a cheating ass nigga and I wasn't going to start today. The last thing I want to do is hurt Niy now that I had her wide open. She would probably leave with no problem now that she is back speaking to her father. I still hadn't made time to meet him, but I need to do so real soon. I wanted to get a look at this man, even though I didn't want him looking at me.

When we made it to Whop and Cocka's spot, Ro's car was already there. They stay in a townhome that had a connecting garage. That was the first thing that I noticed and that was perfect. They didn't need for anyone to see them bringing bags in and out of their apartment. Junior pulled into the driveway alongside Ro's car, then we both hopped out.

"Whose spot it this?" Junior asked.

"This is the youngins' new place. We don't have to go to the north side no more."

"Cool, 'cause them laws be hot out there anyway."

I rung the door bell and waited for an answer. Cocka came to the door with a big grin on his face.

"Welcome to mi casa," he greeted us.

"Nigga, get yo' corny ass out the way and let us in. This ain't even yo' shit by yo'self."

"Well, we casa, then; us casa, nigga."

Junior and I both had to chuckle at his statement. This nigga Cocka don't have a bit of sense. We follow him into the living room where everyone was sitting. They were sitting around counting money that was scattered about on the table.

"What's good, niggas?" I spoke.

"Took," Ro started. "'Bout time yo' ass fell through."

"You know a nigga been trying to get shit back in order. Twenty-four hours ain't enough time in a day for me."

"I feel you on that one," Whop added. "Especially when you're hustling."

I took a seat at the table with the guys, but I didn't touch anything. They had money piled up all over the table, which meant that they were really out getting that paper. It took everything in me to not jump in and start counting. I am so used to being a part of the hustle that I felt left out. I'm still trying to get used to being on the outside of things. Even though I still had places to collect money from for Jefe, I wanted to count the cash in front of me. To occupy my time, I pulled out a bag of weed, and began to roll up.

We blew four blunts while they finished up the count. Whop also spoke to me about letting a few of their crew members go. After telling him the importance of being low key, he didn't have a choice. If niggas were calling their name on the streets they wouldn't hesitate to sing like a mockingbird to the police. Those are the type of people that you do not want in your crew.

"So, Took," Ro started. "Did you ever find out who was speaking on yo' name?"

"Nah, I'm still working on it. I got a lil' info, but it ain't shit to jump on just yet."

"You still think Punch said something?"

I shook my head side to side, "Man, I'm not even sure."

"On some real shit, I need to know, too. I've been serving them niggas and I ain't tryin' to get caught up."

"All I can tell you right now is to move carefully, watch everything and everybody."

"Right on."

"Anyway, I went by Sloan's today, so I'm back on cleaning

money. And we gone party this weekend."

"Fa sho' my nigga," he slapped me five. "Damn, I'm glad my nigga is back. Shit just wasn't the same without you, bro."

"I know, 'cause y'all niggas whack."

He laughed, "Whatever, bro. You just make sure that you jump fresh."

"You already know that you don't have to tell me that. But I've chilled enough, so it's time for me to move around."

"Alright then, bro."

"Check y'all lil' niggas later."

"Later, Took," they spoke.

As we walked back to the truck, I took a look around. Right before I pulled the door opened, I spied a car chilling in the cut. I eyed it and I swear I thought I could see Brooke sitting inside. It was far away, so I really couldn't be for sure. The car wasn't one that I have seen her in before, and it was two people in the car. I pulled the back door opened, then jumped inside.

"Bro, go that way when we leave. I need to check something out."

"What's up?"

"Drive past that grey car over there, I'm trying to see who is inside."

"I got you."

I kept my face to the window, looking in that direction while Junior backed up. The tint on the back windows were dark, so they wouldn't be able to see me looking at them. Junior crept by slow, and I was able to get a good look. It was Brooke and she was with that nigga from the park. That same nigga that ran up on me when I was chilling with her, and asked me about drugs. I sat back in the seat after we passed them. My first thought was *how long had they been following me?* My second thought was *that bitch.*

CHAPTER EIGHTEEN: YANIYZAH

Langston and I walked around the store, checking everything out. The inspections were done, and the walls had been painted pink and purple. Half of the shelving was up, but it was still plenty of work that needed to be completed. Overall, I am happy with the progress that has been made. In a few short weeks, we will be able to open the doors to the public.

"It's looking good in here, right?" Langston asked.

"Yeah, it's coming along perfectly."

"What else do you need?"

"I don't think I need anything else for the store, just the clothes. Two orders came in yesterday, and I'm expecting two more this week. I also have a shoe order that's coming after that. I still have to order accessories though. Neka has a small lip stick and gloss line, so I'm contracting those into the store."

"What about employees? You need to get someone in here to help you out."

"Shannon is going to help. I probably can get Courtney's help too."

"I know you want your friends to help you, but that can be bad for business. Friends and family will take advantage of you the most."

"I know that much. But Shannon has always been there for me, so I have to look out for her."

"She's cool, I don't too much care for that other one though."

"Who, Courtney? Why?"

"It's just something about her that I don't like. I know you think she is your friend, but I see different."

"What did she do to make you say that?"

"I'm just a good judge of character."

I stood there looking at him for a second, looking for some type of reaction. He has only been around Courtney like twice, so I didn't get why he doesn't care for her. She is a little on the wild side, but he hasn't seen it. I don't think.

"Okay, I'll look for other workers."

"Good, now let's get out of here. Big Mama is expecting us for lunch."

"I hope she is not mad at me for not taking Imani by there yet."

"Let's see," he smiled.

When Langston pulled up to Big Mama's house, I sensed hesitation from him. I look up towards the porch and there was a lady seated with Big Mama. With everything going on around us, I had no clue of who she was. As far as I know she could be a FED.

I placed my hand on top of Langston's and stared at him. Finally, he looked over at me dead in my eyes.

"What's wrong, babe?" I inquired.

"That's my mama."

"Okay, so what's wrong?"

"I don't fuck with her like that."

"You haven't said too much about her, where has she been?"

"Locked up. I hate that she is out. I already know that she gon' start that drinkin' and drug shit back up."

"Just pray that she doesn't."

"If Big Mama's praying ain't help, I sure can't say a prayer to help her ass."

"Maybe she'll be different this time around."

"I highly doubt it."

"Don't be like that. And just so you know, since I've met almost all of your family, it is time for you to meet my father."

He rubbed his hand over his face. I know my father is the last person he wants to see, but I think he will change his mind once they talk. My father was trying to low key look out for us, and Langston doesn't want anything to do with him. I didn't bother telling Langston about the lawyer because he has one of his own already. But I did keep the card in case of an emergency.

Langston finally opened his car door, then came to open mine. After he grabbed Imani out of her seat, we headed up the sidewalk. By this time, Big Mama was standing on the edge of the porch, smiling at us. Langston was half stepping like I was when he first brought me here. It's funny how we've switched positions. I didn't know what to expect from his mama, and I didn't care. She couldn't be any worse than everybody else's mother I know. All I know is people with crazy mamas.

"Good afternoon, L," Big Mama beamed. She was standing there smiling harder than I had ever seen her smile before. For the first time, Langston wasn't smiling like a little kid back at her.

"Hey," he dryly responded.

"Niy, you finally coming by to see me? I told you that you didn't have to wait on L to come visit."

"I know, we're trying to get the store ready, so I've been handling that."

"I understand that much, but you got to bring this baby by here if you want her to know me."

Big Mama reached out for Imani, and she went to her with no problem. We climbed the two steps, then stood there looking at the woman looking at us.

"I guess you can't speak?" she finally asked in a tone that indicated that she was a heavy smoker.

"Wassup," he spoke nonchalantly.

"Well, aren't you gonna introduce me to yo' lil friend?"

"This my girl Niy. Niy, that's Pam."

"Pam?" she jerked her neck. "I guess this muthafucka done lost his damn manners? I'm his mama, Pamela."

"Nice to meet you Ms. Pamela," I smiled.

"You too. Is that your baby girl?"

"That's our baby girl," Langston answered.

"So I have a granddaughter? And ain't nobody told me shit?"

"'Cause you're always locked up," Langston smirked.

Before she was able to respond, Langston pushed the front door opened, and pulled me inside behind him.

"Why are you being so rude to her, babe?"

"Because I don't have any respect for her. The only thing that she has done for me is bring me into this world. It's bad enough that I have a fuck nigga for a father, but to have a bum bitch for a mother too? That shit ain't right in my eyes, so I treat them accordingly."

"Maybe she will do better this time around."

"I highly doubt that shit. And you better stop trying to be nice to her; next thing you know she will be beggin' for something."

Big Mama walked in the house with Imani, so we cut that conversation short. I had no idea of what type of mother Pam was to Quanda and Langston, but I wish that he would at least give her a chance before counting her out this time. I believe that your parents always deserve more than one chance to get things right. It's not like when you have a baby they send you home with a handbook to learn from.

"Alright, y'all," Big Mama spoke while handing Imani over to me. "Let me check on these rolls. We'll be ready to eat once they're done."

"Big Mama, I think we gon' just go out to eat."

"Why, L? I cooked this food for y'all."

"You know I can't be up in here with her. I wish you would have warned me that she would be here so that I could have prepared myself."

"If I told you that she was here, L, you wouldn't have shown up."

He chuckled, "You're right about that."

"Do this for me, son. I'm not asking you to be her best friend, just be civil today. "

"She bet not start actin' up or I'm out."

Big Mama shook her head and waved him off as she waddled towards the kitchen. Langston and I took a seat on the couch, then I stood Imani up to let her walk around. She was getting better at this walking thing. We hold her so much that she barely gets to practice, but from the looks of it, she has it down.

Ms. Pam walked through the front door, and I could see Langston's mood changing. I didn't understand why because Ms. Pam was smiling at Imani. She wasn't even paying Langston any attention. I rubbed his hand to give him comfort, but he was still tensed. Since Ms. Pam's attention was on Imani, I reached between Langston's legs that he had gapped open, and slid my hand across his crotch. He finally took his eyes off Ms. Pam to look at me. Slowly he rubbed his tongue between his lips, then winked at me. I knew that if nothing else, that would get his attention.

"How old is this baby that she is already walking?" Ms. Pam asked.

"She's 10 months," I answered.

"Ten months and already walking? Oh, she's getting out the way for another one?"

"Another what?" Langston asked before I could.

"Baby, what else?"

"We're not having any more babies anytime soon," I assured her.

"Mm hmm."

"Okay y'all," Big Mama called out. "Everything is ready."

Langston jumped up first to go wash his hands. Imani slowly waddled behind him, falling in the process. After falling a few times, she kept her hands and feet on the floor, and bear crawled the rest of the way to the bathroom. I laughed as I followed behind her.

As soon as we sat down to eat, my cell sounded off. I figured that it would be Shannon texting, but when I unlocked the phone, the text was from Montrez.

BD: I still love u.

Ever since I called him from my phone, he has been texting me every day. I've been ignoring his texts, but that didn't stop him from doing it daily. He is a certified asshole, so I know if I tell him to stop, he will just do it more. I am so scared of what Langston will say if he ever saw a text from him. Quickly, I hit delete to make sure that he didn't. When I threw the phone into my purse and looked up, Langston was looking directly at me. I tried to act normal so that he wouldn't think anything of it. He was so into his mother being here that he probably won't ask me about it.

Lunch turned out better than expected. It was more less because Langston didn't talk to his mother too much. He was picking and choosing which question of hers to answer. Ms. Pam didn't care one bit, she continued talking like he had answered every one of them. I can tell that she is the only person that didn't spoil Langston, and that may be an additional reason why he didn't care for her. He likes attention; from the looks of it, she does too. Big Mama spoiled Langston, so I am sure that she spoiled her only daughter as well. I can't wait to see how this situation between them pans out.

When we left Big Mama's, Langston and I hopped into separate cars. He gave me the keys to the car and had Junior to come scoop him up. Although I knew that he had to go to work, I had a slight attitude about it. He promised that we would still spend time together; so far that has only been once or twice. I know that he purchased the store to keep me occupied while he did his thing. But until the store is open, I still have plenty of free time to think about him. That wasn't a good thing because it left me feeling lonely. Even with me back in town with my friends, I feel lonely when Langston isn't around.

Going home wasn't an option for me, so I headed towards my father's house. Seeing Langston with Ms. Pam gave me the urge to see my dad again. I want to revitalize my relationship with him since he is the only family I have here. Seeing how carefree that Imani went to Big Mama made me want her to have the same reaction to my father. After all, he is her grandfather.

Pulling into my father's driveway brought back several memories. I thought about all of the times I used to fly up the driveway trying to make curfew. And about the times I used to sneak out, putting my car in neutral, and letting it roll out of the driveway. I would pick Shannon, Courtney and Aspen up, and we would go hang out with whatever guys we met the prior weekend. Those were fun times, but it also led to me having a baby at 17.

By the time I got myself and Imani out of the car, my father was opening the backdoor. As I walked towards him, he was smiling and waving at Imani. She was smiling back, but when he reached for her, she laid her head on my shoulder.

"At least you smiled at Pop Pop this time," he chuckled. "How you doing today, Yaniyzah?"

"I'm good, Daddy."

"I see, because you never come see me."

"I'm trying to change that," I answered as I stepped inside. "Is that okay, or am I overstepping?"

"No, no, I'm happy that you are coming around. And I love

seeing my granddaughter, she is so beautiful. She kind of favors your mother," he smiled. "Those eyes."

I had never paid much attention, but as I look at her closely, she does have my mother's eyes. The only thing I ever saw was Montrez in her. Her lips and nose, for sure are his.

"Yeah, I can see that."

"Come on inside, I was just about to make me something to eat. Do want anything?"

"No, I just ate lunch with Tookie, his mother and grandmother."

"Oh? How was it?"

"It was nice. His grandmother cooked for us."

"I'm guessing that they like you."

"I know his grandmother does. Today was my first time meeting his mother. I'm not sure what she thinks; it doesn't matter because he doesn't care for her too much. She wasn't there for him growing up, so her opinion doesn't really matter."

He opened his mouth like he was going to say something, then he pressed his lips together and formed a smile. Whatever he was going to say, I'm glad that he decided to keep it to himself. His opinion mattered to me, but only a little bit.

"So when am I gonna meet this guy since you have met all of his people?"

"I've mentioned it, but we haven't talked about it. I'll see about getting us together, maybe Sunday, but I'll let you know."

"Fair enough."

I took a seat at the kitchen table, and watched as my father prepared his food. Imani stood in front of me clapping her hands together, so I sung 'Patty Cake' to her. She always gets excited about that song because she knows tickling is involved. Her goofy butt loves to laugh out loud.

After helping my dad eat his food, Imani conked out. I took her upstairs to my old bedroom. Everything was still in the same places that I left them when I last walked out of here. I took a look around at my old track, cheerleading and softball trophies. Looking at it all made me think back on all the things I could have become. Instead, I decided to be disobedient to my father.

I thought about the only picture I had of my mother and I, so I pulled the nightstand drawer open. There it sat right on the top looking right back at me. As I removed the picture from the drawer, I couldn't help but smile. The first thing I noticed were my mother's eyes glowing, just like Imani's, looking back at me. The longer I spied the picture the more I saw Imani in her. A tear fell from my eye like it always does when I saw pictures of my mother.

I miss her so much, and I wish on a daily that she was here to help me.

I guess I was in the room longer than expected because my father pushed the door open. Once he saw that I was a little emotional, he came and took a seat next to me. He gazed down at the picture before securing his arm around me.

"I miss her too," he spoke. "It's not a day that goes by that I do not think about her."

"I wish she was here so bad."

"So do I. I've been so lost without her," he looked me in my eyes. "And you too. I haven't had a full night's sleep since you left."

"I understand that much because I've went months without sleeping. I've just gotten to the point where I am sleeping peacefully."

"I know that you are out doing your thing, Yaniyzah, but know, if you ever want to come back home you can."

Smiling, I placed my hand on top of his. "It's a nice gesture, but I'm fine where I am."

He shook his head yes. "I figured that much, but the door will always be open for you two."

"Thanks, Daddy."

We hugged it out, then began to reminisce on my mother. He started telling me old stories about them that I had never heard. Like how happy he was the day my mother told him that she was pregnant. They had been trying forever with no luck. When they decided to give up and look into adoption, I was conceived the following month. He even admitted to overreacting about my pregnancy, and apologizing for abandoning me. I forgave him easily because it was all my fault. If I hadn't been doing the things he told me not to, I wouldn't have ended up in that situation. He had always spoiled me, so it wasn't like he was a bad parent. He was more disappointed than anything. He had high hopes for me and I let him down. I may not have done things the way that he would have liked, but I will eventually make him proud of me.

Shannon called, reminding me that I was supposed to come get her. After lunch with Langston and his family, she had totally slipped my mind. She is going to help me sew the dresses together, and in return, I will sew in some hair for her. I said my goodbyes to my father, and assured him that I would be in touch with him about meeting Langston. When he comes home tonight, I will make sure to bring it up again.

After scooping Shannon, I pulled up at the beauty supply store. My plan was to stay in the car, but Imani was restless and wanted to get out of her seat. I snatched her out of her seat, then we strolled into the beauty supply store. When we stepped inside, there was a lady and a man behind the counter. I held on to Imani's hand while we followed behind Shannon.

"Girl, I hate going in stores where muthafuckas watching me like I'm gon' steal some shit," Shannon casually mentioned. I looked up and saw that the female worker was at the end of the aisle, straightening up. "Like a bitch gon' steal some damn rubber bands and glue. The fuck!?"

I laughed, "You stupid."

"For real, that shit be pissing me off."

"Girl, get the edge control so we can go."

We walked to the next row, and sure enough the lady came to that aisle.

"Damn, bitch! Are you gon' let us shop in peace or nah?"

"Do not curse at me," the lady finally responded.

"Well, bitch, quit following us like we gon' steal some shit."

"You bitch."

"No, you a bitch. Don't start with me before I get to slanging racial slurs around this muthafucka."

"Shannon, chill," I tried to calm her.

"Get out of my store before I call the police."

"Fuck you, this store, and the muthafuckin' police, bitch. Dog, cat, rat, and mouse eating ass muthafucka. Ole' lo mein ass hoe, teriyaki ass bitch. Don't get no shit in the hood if you're scared that black people gon' steal yo' shit.

"I'm calling the police."

"I said I don't give a fuck, call them hoes. I'll be gone before they get here anyway," Shannon took her arm and slid it over everything as she walked towards the door. "When the police get here, tell 'em I did that shit too."

"Get out!"

"I am, but not before I fuck this shit up."

"Come on, girl."

I pushed Shannon on out of the door, but not before she pushed the rack of stockings over. Shannon is always somewhere acting a fool, especially when she feels disrespected. I couldn't even say anything because I knew she had the potential to act up.

Langston walked through the door just as I was finishing up Shannon's hair. This time he had enough sense to walk in without yelling out sexual gestures. You could hear Imani's feet stomping towards him against the hardwood floors. I heard them laughing as they embraced each other. Langston turned the corner with Imani hanging around his neck.

"Niy," he called out then paused. "Oh, y'all in here doing hair and shit."

"Just finishing up."

"Who you in here getting cute for? Punchie?" Langston asked, directing his question to Shannon.

"For myself. He's just lucky enough to get to see me," she laughed.

"Excuse me then."

He placed Imani on the sofa, then walked over to give me a kiss. I wanted to kiss him harder than I did, but I didn't want to do too much. Once Langston gets started, he wants to go all the way. Imani is still up, plus I still have to take Shannon back home.

Shannon and I finished up the dress we were working on earlier. It was getting late, so I decided to go ahead and take her home. I wanted to spend some time talking with Langston before we went to bed tonight. Imani was fast asleep, so I laid her in her crib, then went to let Langston know that I was stepping out. When I walked into the bedroom, I heard the shower going. I pushed the bathroom door opened and eased inside.

"Babe," I called out.

"Yeah?"

"I'm 'bout to take Shannon home, I'll be back in a little bit. Imani is in the bed already, so you don't have to worry about her."

"Okay, be careful."

"I will."

As I eased back out of the door, I heard my text alert sound off. It wasn't until I tried to enter the passcode that I realized it wasn't my phone. I looked at the phone and it was a message from Joy. I know that she is his ex, but what I didn't know is how she got his new number. We both have new numbers, so he had to have given it to her. I could read the beginning of the message and it read: *When you came over yesterday.* My heart dropped at the sight of those words. He claims to be so busy, but he had time to see her. Tears began to develop in my eyes; I blinked a few times to make sure they didn't fall. I hated the fact that I saw that message because I trusted Langston completely. He didn't mention seeing her, so that made me wonder. Could they have something going on?

My text message alert went off in the other room and brought me back to reality. I stood in front of the mirror to get myself together before stepping out. I didn't want to look like anything was wrong, and have Shannon questioning me the entire ride. I smiled a few times, spread the lip balm on my lips, then marched out.

"Come on, girl," I said grabbing my phone and purse.

"'Bout time, I thought y'all was having a lil' quickie or

whatever."

I laughed, "Nah."

As we walked towards the door, I unlocked my cell phone. Unlike Langston, I didn't have preview messaging on my phone. When I clicked on the message, it was from Montrez.

BD: Hey sexy.

I rolled my eyes, then dropped the phone in my purse. I will have to talk to him, but if it gets out of hand, I will end up blocking him. I don't want Langston to accidently see one of those ignorant messages and think that something is going on. It's bad enough that he is talking to his ex. I don't want to push him closer to her, because he thinks that I am doing something.

CHAPTER NINETEEN: TOOKIE

Loud ass giggling woke me up from a good ass dream. After walking down that long hallway, I was just about to see the face of the muthafucka that's snitching on me. It almost pissed me off, but I realized that it was a dream. I was never going to be able to get a look at the person's face in a dream. I sat up on my elbow, and rubbed my eyes with the other hand. I recognized Shannon's voice, but the other one I couldn't make out.

"Niy!" I called out.

The chatter grew silent, then I heard her coming up the hallway. She knows that I don't like people in the loft, especially ones that I do not know.

"Yeah?" she asked, closing the door behind her.

"Who you got in there?"

"Shannon and Courtney, why?"

"Why Courtney in there? I thought I told you about hanging out with her."

"Babe, she's my friend, I can't just leave her out. On top of it all, she is Shannon's sister, and she is not gonna leave her out."

"I don't want her in my house."

"Alright. We're about to leave anyway to go shop for tonight."

"And don't go getting no skimpy shit, I don't want to have to beat nobody's ass for disrespecting me tonight."

"Whatever," she chuckled. "What you doing today?"

"Going to get my haircut first. I might turn a few corners, but that's it."

"A few corners? Where?"

"Why you asking me all these questions?"

For the past few days, all she has done is ask me questions. I'd finally agreed to meeting her father, but she was still hounding me. I don't know what is going on with her questioning me all of a sudden. I'm trying to play it cool, but she needs to know that I don't answer to anyone.

"I'm just asking, dang. Why you got to be so defensive?"

"I'm not being defensive, but you know I don't like talking about the moves I make."

"It's me that you're talking to, not some random chick."

"I know that much, but you got people all in the house, who knows if they're ear hustling. Talk to me later about this shit."

"Fine," she said, then pulled the door open to walk out.

I don't like this new lil' attitude that she is carrying around. I'll have to talk to her later to see what that is all about. She hadn't spoken up about whatever is bothering her and that wasn't going to work for me.

The barbershop was packed like it always is on a Saturday morning. I wasn't too much tripping because I wanted to hang out a bit. It's been a minute since I've been able to kick it at the shop. This is the place where you can get the most information about the hood, so I was hanging around to see if I was able to get the word on the street. Things were tranquil around here, but I'm still ruffling the trees.

"My nigga," Scoota dapped me up when I sat in his chair. "I see you getting fresh for tonight."

"You already know I got to step on the scene with a fresh fade."

"No doubt. I'm falling through tonight myself."

"What?" I sung. "You gon' step out?"

"Yeah, it's the opening of cuddle season, so I need something to keep me warm at night."

"I feel ya' on that shit. A nigga got to have something to rub on during these cold nights."

"Yo' girl ain't got no single home girls?"

"You don't want them chicken heads. Besides, Punch already got his claws in the only cool one."

"Ole big ass," he joked.

"Like you said, it's cuddling season, and who don't like a lot of warmth."

He laughed, "You ain't shit my nigga."

"Don't I know it."

It wasn't much hood chatter going on in the barbershop today. Most of the conversation was about the Cowboys' new quarterback, Dak Prescott. I left there and headed to Big Mama's. I wanted to see if my mother was still there, and if she had stolen or begged for anything yet. I don't like the idea of her staying with Big Mama, but I know that Big Mama wouldn't have it any other way.

My mother is Big Mama's only living child, so she will never give up on her. I think it has more to do with my uncle passing away at a young age. He died in a motorcycle accident when he was 19. I was one so I don't remember him, but Big Mama has plenty pictures of him around the house. My grandfather passed away from grief five years later. Big Mama said that he never forgave himself because a huge argument between them led to him leaving the house that night. Grandpa never told anyone what the argument was about, so no one know the real reason behind both of their deaths. Grandpa left a fat ass life insurance policy behind that Big Mama split between Quanda and myself. She put it in one of those CD accounts, then gave us access it on our 21st birthdays. I took out 150 thousand and left the other half in there to build for another 10 years. I had money all over the place, but most of it I didn't have access to. I have three months of stacked up cash that I couldn't do anything with either. Not to mention the money I already had that needed to be cleaned. I can't wait to get this store open to get this money cleaned up. I don't like having this amount of cash in my possession, even if it is in safe places.

When I pulled up to Big Mama's, she was sitting on the porch as usual. My mother was sitting out there with her, smoking a cigarette. I knew it wouldn't be long before she was puffing those stanky muthafuckas again. As I got out of the car, I noticed an undercover car parked down the street. I made sure to smile and wave like the president just in case they were taking my picture. Fuck it, I want them to know that I see them too.

"What's going on old ladies," I spoke as I approached the porch.

"You back already," Big Mama joked. "I thought for sure that I wouldn't see you for another two weeks."

"You got jokes today, but it's okay."

"I'm just messing with you, L. Where is Niy?"

"Out spending money."

"Must be nice," my mother huffed.

"It is."

"You hungry?" Big Mama asked.

"Nah, I'm good. But what do you have in there?"

"Some chicken and dumplings."

"I'll take some to go."

Big Mama got up to go inside of the house, and I took her seat next to my mama. I didn't want to sit there, but it was the only chair available on the porch. So badly I wanted to remove the blunt from my pocket and spark it up. I'd much rather be under the influence of something when I talk to my mother. Big Mama doesn't like to see me smoke weed, so out of respect, I don't smoke around her.

"How has everything been going for you?"

I looked over at my mother, "Everything is great."

"I'm happy to hear that Took, I really am. This time I'm gon' really try to stay clean. I know I say it every time, but I'm serious about it. Now that I am a grandmother it's time to get my life together."

"Oh, now that you are a grandparent you want to get your life together? What about when you had two of your own to take care of? It ain't like you got to take care of your grandkids."

"Tookie, I know I was a fucked up mama, I ain't denying that shit. But I can be a better grandmother than I was a mother. I don't want my grandkids to see me like y'all did."

"Yeah, whatever."

"You seem to be a great father."

"I am. I learned how to do it wrong from you and my pops."

"Anything would be better than we were, huh?" she chuckled. "I know you want to be a better parent than us, son, but are you sure that's your baby? I mean, I looked at her long and hard, and she don't look like nobody I know. She barely looks like her mama."

"She's mine."

"Any how do you know that? Did you get a blood test?"

"Nope, she's mine because I say she mine."

She stared at me for a second, "Oh, okay, I see." She put her cigarette out, then blew out a long train of smoke. "Well, be careful. That baby is moving fast, and that's the sign of another baby coming. And the way that baby was bent over in front of her, I would say that she is already pregnant."

"You have no clue as to what you are talking about."

"Alright," she said in a tone that suggested she was right.

I know that Niy isn't pregnant because she had a period. I'm the one that made her start the bitch. She's been taking her pills because I've seen the pack. The shenanigans are already starting with her, and I don't plan on sitting here listening to it. Big Mama pushed the screen door open, then stepped out with a big bowl.

"I put enough in here for all of you."

"Thanks, Big Mama."

I stood up from the chair to let her take a seat. My intentions weren't to ever stay long, and after speaking with my mother, it was definitely time for me to go. Before I was able to open my mouth to tell Big Mama bye, Quanda pulled up in front of the house. I'll stick around a little longer to see if she had any information for me, then bounce.

Quanda didn't have any new information for me so I went on home. Since I wasn't buying anything new for the party tonight, I had to go home and put something together. There was no need to go buy anything when I already have something at home. I have plenty of clothes with the tags still on them to put to use. If all else fails, I'll still have a little time to run to the mall.

When Niy and I pulled up in the Vette, all eyes were on us. This was normal for me, so I kept a smile on my face while helping Niy out. My name was being called from different directions. I couldn't tell who it was, but I waved at the entire crowd. Niy interlocked her fingers with mine, then we headed to the front of the line. For it to be late, the line was thick on the outside.

The inside of the club was lit as fuck. It was wall to wall people dancing and barely enough room to move. I couldn't tell who was who right now, so I pulled Niy towards the VIP area. I'm sure that is where all of my people are anyway. On our way, I dapped up every nigga that dapped me up. I felt like I was missed, and I was definitely feeling the love I was receiving. I didn't appreciate the taps on the ass from females, and I didn't acknowledge any of it. I am here to have a good time, and I'm not entertaining foolishness tonight.

"'Bout time yo' peel head ass made it," Punchie greeted me.

"You gotta talk to Niy about that. Her ass always taking two days to get dressed."

Niy rolled her eyes at me as she made her way towards Shannon and Courtney.

"'Sup, Took?" Ro spoke, handing me the bottle of Hennessey.

I dapped him with my free hand, "Chillin', man. Pass me a cup with a few ice cubes in it. 'Sup Onion?"

"You got it bro."

"Where Toot at?"

"That nigga say he on his way."

"A'ight."

After fixing my drink, I went to stand by the balcony railings. I looked over the crowd while I sipped my drink. It didn't take too long for me to run across a familiar face. Brooke, Marlana, or whatever the fuck her name is, was walking through the crowd. I exhaled deeply as I shook my head at her. I wonder why she is always the one following me when I know her face. It could be someone else watching that I don't know about. I took my eyes off of her to look around the crowd some more. I started looking for other familiar faces, or anyone that looked out of place. That was hard to do being that it was so many people moving around below me.

When YFN Lucci "Keys to the Streets" came blaring through the speakers, Yaniyzah came to dance in front of me. I was so focused on finding Waldo that I had forgotten about her. The fact that she had been acting snappy made my mind focus on business only lately. She wanted me home more, but I couldn't do that right now. I'm back picking up the money, plus I'm trying to get the store completed. I just need her to chill out a little while longer, then I'll be able to put my feet up a little.

"I guess you're done with acting silly and shit?"

She stopped swaying her hips to turn and face me. "What you talking about?"

"You gon' act retarded now?"

"I'm not."

"Yeah, okay."

"Anyways, I'm gonna go make me a drink, do you want one?"

"Yeah."

She walked off and I directed my eyes back towards the crowd. A female looked up at me then waved. I looked back to see where Niy was before waving back. It was friendly flirting, but I didn't want Niy to see me and trip.

I saw Sloan walking through the crowd, so I made my way down. It wasn't closing time, but I wanted to see what the money looked like. Before I could make it to him, I was stopped by Joy. I can't deny that she was looking better than bad. She was trying to converse with me but I was on a mission. I told her that I would get back with her before I leave tonight.

Finally, I was able to catch up to Sloan. He was busy smiling in some chick's face, so I continued to patrol the crowd while he did his thang. It wasn't an emergency, so there was no need to cock block. I had a few people that I could chop it up with until he was free. I tried my best not to stop and talk to females long because I know Niy's eyes were probably on me. There was no way that I was going to look up to find out either. She would definitely think something was up if I went looking for her.

Sloan walked up on me while I was speaking with Big Sorry and A. Lee. Our conversation was pretty much over, so I walked with him to his office.

"Bro, you brought the people out tonight," Sloan smiled.

"How I do that?"

"Once word got out about you being back, you know every wannabe baller came out to stunt. Man, I'm glad that you are back."

"I see. You all jolly and shit."

"I'm just happy that shit is getting back to normal around here. Especially with winter knocking on the door. So listen, I've been thinking about opening up a lil' hookah lounge, you wanna go in on it with me?"

"How much you talking?"

"'Bout 80, depending on what has to be done."

"Shid, I want to, but I got money tied up in this store shit. I don't want to spend up all my clean money. I don't need the FEDs fucking with you about our business."

"The FEDs fuckin' with you?"

"This one DEA bitch is riding my dick hard on some dumb shit, but I ain't fadin' it. At the same time, a nigga ain't tryin' to give them some extra shit to look into, you feel me?"

"You can be a silent partner. Can you do 40 clean and 40 dirty? It won't be a problem for me to clean 40."

"Yeah, I can do that."

"It'll take me a few weeks to a month to find a place. You don't have to bring the money until after the paperwork is done."

"Bet. You 'bout to have Niy mad as shit at me. She's already bitchin' about me not being home much, she's probably gon' bug out over another party scene."

"I'll take care of most of it to keep her off yo' ass. I just need your approval on my suggestions."

"Just let me know what's up."

"I will. Here you go," he said handing over the check. "You should have cleaned more cash than that."

"It's cool, like I said, I don't want to draw any unwanted attention to me or my money."

"Understandable."

"Same time next week I'll swing by."

SHAMEKA JONES

"A'ight."

I pulled the door open and walked out.

When I walked back out to the club, my eyes were met with Brooke's. She had her goofy grin on her face, so I smiled back. I wanted her to know that she wasn't ruining my night, and I wasn't going to let anything that she had to say change that.

"Same ole same ole, huh?" she asked.

"Of course, this is what I do."

"You're still claiming that?"

"It's what I do. I mean, you're here watching me, so you see what I do." I pulled the check from my blazer pocket. "This, sweetheart, is what you call working."

She laughed, "Cute."

"Jealous?"

"Of what?"

"You tell me. I can't have a good time without yo' ass poppin' up somewhere."

"I'm just waiting on you to slip so I can catch you."

"Where you got your net hid?" I laughed. "Good luck with that, a'ight." I walked away, leaving her standing there alone.

248

Maneuvering back through the crowd was even harder than before. Most of these muthafuckas were drunk and all over the place. This is exactly why I can't chill down here with the regular folks. Everyone is fucking up your gear and incoherent about the shit. Just as I made it to a clear spot, someone grabbed my hand. I turned around and it was Joy.

"Hey, wassup."

"You didn't answer my text."

"You know I don't be doing that texting shit."

"Why didn't you call?"

"Because I got a girl and I haven't had any free time to hit you back."

"Whatever. I just wanted to talk to you about the other day—"

"Um, excuse me?" I heard Yaniyzah ask from behind me.

"Hey, baby."

"Who is this?"

"This is Joy. Joy, this my girl—"

"You got me fucked up," Niy interrupted me. "Let's go."

Yaniyzah grabbed my hand and snatched it. I looked at Joy with the *I got to go* expression on my face.

Niy pulled me all the way to the VIP area before I broke loose from her. She looked at me with anger and drunkenness in her eyes. I didn't understand what her deal was. I was just about to introduce them, so there would be no misunderstanding. Niy always reacted first, then asked questions later. That shit gets on my nerves sometimes.

"Baby, chill, why you mad?"

"You think I'm gon' let you introduce me to some side chick?"

"Side chick? What the fuck are you talking 'bout side chick?"

"I'm not stupid."

"I know you're not. She's my ex, that's it."

"So you're back seeing her?"

"No, this is my first time seeing her in a while."

That statement seemed to make her even angrier. I didn't know what to say to her, so I stood there looking at her drunk ass sway.

"You got me fucked up *Tookie!*" she emphasized my name.

True, I had seen Joy, but Niy didn't know anything about it. Junior was the only one with me, and he didn't even come inside of the loft to talk to Niy about it. She didn't have the passcode to my phone, so I know she didn't see that bullshit ass apology that Joy sent. Or did she? Nah, there was no way that she could figure out my passcode; plus, I remembered deleting it.

"Come here," I said pulling her closer.

"Get off me. You think you're slick but you ain't that slick. I see through the bullshit."

"What bullshit?" I laughed. "Stop trippin'."

"Stop lyin'. And I'm ready to go. I know you got yo' money from Sloan already."

"Stop playin' me so close, ma."

"Stop talkin' to bitches!"

"Are we gon' do this all night?"

"We can."

"Fuck. Well, at least let a nigga take one more shot, shit."

"Me too."

"Don't look like you need no more."

She marched off towards the table. I was right behind her, shaking my head. Hopefully this drink will put her over the top, and knock her ass out. I didn't feel like hearing her mouth about Joy or no other bitch that I'm not fucking.

Yaniyzah stood with her arms crossed while we waited for the car. I couldn't do anything but shake my head at her because she was tripping for nothing. Maybe she needs some dick to get her back in line. When the car drove up, she swung the door open before I had a chance to. I laughed and held my hands up as I stepped back.

"Ain't shit funny."

"Yeah it is."

She sat down in the car, then slammed the door in my face. I trotted around to the other side, and threw the valet a bill before jumping inside.

"Yo', what's with all the attitude?"

"Why you lie?"

"What I lie about, Niy?" I asked as I drove off.

"About that Joy girl."

"I ain't lie about her."

"Yes you did. Today is not the first time you have seen her since we've been back Langston."

"Well, say what's on yo' mind then."

"I am!" she yelled. "I don't want you talking to, texting or seeing that bitch!"

"I don't, so I don't understand why you're trippin',"

Just then, the radio announced through the Bluetooth that I had a text message from Joy. I forgot that it automatically connected when the phone was in range. But at the same time, I wasn't expecting to get a text from Joy tonight. The way Yaniyzah's eyes dug into to me could have set my soul free.

"You haven't talked to her, huh?" she turned to face me. "So how did she get your new number?"

"Man, I don't—"

"Don't lie! HOW THE FUCK DID SHE GET THE NUMBER!?"

"I think I'm a lil' deaf in this ear," I said pointing to the one she was yelling into. "You mind speakin' up a little?"

"I'm happy that you seem to find this shit amusing!"

"Because you trippin' for no reason." I rubbed my hand over my face, then let out a deep breath. "A'ight, man. I saw Joy the other day for a brief moment. She was holding some money for me from a while ago, and I went to go get it. That's it."

"Why didn't you just say that at first? Why did you have to lie about it?"

"'Cause I don't need you knowing my every move. All you need to know about is what concerns you and let me handle the rest."

"You are my concern, and when it comes to other bitches, that is my concern also."

"Ain't no other bitches to be concerned with, I'm not a cheating ass nigga. I'm gon' tell you now, I don't like that jealous shit, so don't start it. I'm trying to build with you, and you all worried about an invisible bitch."

"She's not invisible. I saw her tall ass tonight."

"You need some dick, don't you? All that built-up energy got you talking out the side of yo' mouth. You do know that I am a man, right?"

She folded her arms back across her chest and sat back. Thank God because I was growing tired of her elevated tone. I don't tolerate being yelled at; I was letting her make it because she didn't know any better. Sooner or later, I will have to get her ass in line. I can't have her thinking that it's okay to be wilding out on me at any given time. She doesn't run shit that I don't let her run.

CHAPTER TWENTY: YANIYZAH

I've been sick as a dog ever since I got drunk at the club the other night. After a round of makeup sex with Langston, my stomach has been turning ever since. Even with me throwing up all of the liquor, my stomach still isn't right. For the first time since the day we got back, Langston spent the entire day at home with us yesterday. Although it was a no-work Sunday, I was happy about him spending the entire day with us. Now that it is Monday, I'm sure it will be business as usual.

Langston walked into the bedroom with breakfast on a TV tray. I sat up against the headboard as he came closer.

"How you feeling?"

"Okay I guess."

"I made you some oatmeal and toast. Hopefully it'll coat your stomach."

He set the tray on the bed, then picked Imani up and placed her next to me. It was a bottled water on the tray that I opened first. Langston sat on the edge of the bed going through his phone.

"I hope so. I'm tired of feeling nauseous."

He looked up at me. "You've been taking them pills, right?"

"Yeah," I frowned.

"I'm just asking 'cause we don't need no new babies around here. A'ight?"

"I concur."

I wondered what made him mention babies. Throwing up could have given him that idea, but I know the liquor caused that. But it made me begin to think twice about everything. I had a period, it was short, but I had one.

"I need you to do something for me. Ro 'bout to bring some money over here, I need you to count it for me."

"What you 'bout to do?"

"I'm gonna take a ride with him." I looked at him with my eyebrow raised. "It ain't on no drug shit."

"Alright, but what about meeting my daddy?"

"When you want to do it?"

"You want to do it tomorrow? Lunch or dinner?"

"I don't know yet. Let me think about what I have to do, I'll let you know later."

"Okay."

I couldn't help but smile. Finally, he has agreed to meet him without hesitation.

"You're smiling like the joker, so I guess that makes you happy."

"It does."

"Get some food in yo' belly, and throw something on before Ro gets here."

He stood up from the bed and walked out of the room. Imani used my arm to stand up, then reached over and grabbed a piece of my toast.

"Greedy."

"Ma-ma," she smiled.

"Mama," I mocked, then kissed her lips.

Before I was able to finish my breakfast, Ro was ringing the bell. I ate the rest of the food, then threw on some sweats and a t-shirt. After changing Imani's diaper, I emerged from the bedroom. I rinsed the bowl out, then placed it in the sink to wash later. Ro and Langston was sitting on the sofa talking, so I strolled over to take a seat.

I placed Imani on the sofa next to me then sat back. Langston slid the bag over to me without stopping his conversation with Ro. I unzipped the bag to take a look inside. It was filled with bills that had rubber bands around them. I had never seen so much cash at one time before. A chill came over my body that made me want to smile, but I maintained my cool.

"Take care of that for me," Langston spoke standing up from the sofa. "I'll be back in a lil' bit."

"How much is it?"

"That's what you need to tell me," he winked. "Let's roll, Ro."

"Alright, Niy, check ya later. Tell yo' girl Courtney I said wassup," Ro said before walking off.

I rolled my eyes and shook my head behind his back. The last thing I was going to do is tell Courtney that he spoke. Ro has a girlfriend, and I didn't want him to think that I condone shit like that. If he wants to speak to Courtney, he has to do it himself.

After I got Imani settled in her playpen and turned on *Paw Patrol*, I took a seat at the table with the bag. I poured the bundled up bills on the table to start my count. As I counted it out, I wondered if this was Langston's money. I had no idea of how much money he was really making, and honestly, I never thought about it. He has no problems with spending it, so it has to be a grip. If this is what he is bringing in weekly, or even monthly, I see why he spends like he does.

I wasn't even at the halfway point when my cell began to sound off. Once I wrote down the current count, I went into the bedroom to grab my phone. Montrez was texting, and it made me regret jumping up to grab it. He wants me to bring Imani over to his mother's house again, but I didn't feel like dealing with them today. My ears are still ringing from the last time I stopped by. I still hadn't mentioned a word of it to Langston, and I don't know if I should. I think I should keep this bit of information to myself a little while longer.

Since Montrez had already broken my concentration, I decided to call Shannon. I wanted to catch up with her and see what she knew about Courtney and Ro. I'm out of the loop on this one, but I want to be nosey.

"'Sup, cow?" Shannon answered.

"What you doing?"

"Getting dressed, Punchie 'bout to come pick me up."

"So you two are an item now?"

"I don't know yet. I'm still trying to feel him out."

"I hear you don't rush into nothing. Is Courtney talking to Ro now?"

"She got his number at the club, but I don't know what they got going. Didn't you say he had a girl or something anyway?"

"Yeah, that's why I'm asking. He just left here with Tookie, and he told me to tell Courtney what's up."

"Um, well that doesn't surprise me. You already know how my sister is so I don't even know why you are surprised."

"I just don't want me or Took to end up in no drama."

"They are grown so that is their mess. Anyways, what you doing, you getting out today?"

"My stomach still fucked up, I ain't trying to go nowhere."

"Aw shit, you not pregnant are you?"

"No. I don't think so."

"What do you mean you don't think so."

"Tookie said something earlier that had me thinking. I started my period last Saturday before the party, but it was for only like a day and a half. I've been taking my pills ever since."

"How long did you go without the pill before you started taking it again?"

"Like two weeks."

"Y'all didn't use condoms?"

"I mean, we did a few times, but Langston didn't like that shit. To be honest, neither did I."

"You might be, I can't say for sure though. Just go get a test."

"Fuck, Shannon, I can't have another baby. Not to mention,

Tookie is adamant about not having one."

"You talked to him about it?"

"No. He asked me about my pills earlier and said that we don't need no new babies around here."

"He won't have a choice if you're pregnant."

"Shan, aren't you listening? I can't have another baby right now."

"What you gon' do?"

"First off, I don't even know if I'm pregnant. Secondly, if I am, I'm getting rid of it."

"Don't say that, Niy. I don't think it will be so bad."

"It doesn't matter what you think. I didn't know Montrez well before having a baby with him and you see how that turned out. You think I want to have another one with another guy that I'm still getting to know?"

"You said yourself that he is great with Imani."

"He is, but niggas are always good stepdads, it's when they really have to step up to the plate that they flake."

"I don't think Tookie is like that. I told you off top that Trez wasn't shit."

"I'm not taking that chance right now."

"Tell you what, after I finish riding with Punch I'll have him to drop me off over there. I'll grab a test for you to take, and we'll have this conversation later."

"Okay, call me when you're on your way."

"Later."

Talking to Shannon had my mind really racing. I looked over at Imani who was holding on the side of the playpen bouncing to the music. My thoughts went back to Ms. Pam saying Imani was moving fast. I've always thought that, but I took it as me being a first time parent. She was growing fast on me I didn't think twice about her trying to walk. There's no way that I can be pregnant again my luck couldn't be that bad.

Langston pushed the door to the loft opened, and I damn near jumped out of my skin. My head had been all over the place, so I hadn't started back counting the money. Quickly I picked up a stack and slid the rubber band off. He walked over behind me, then wrapped his arms around my neck.

"You still counting that money slow poke?"

"Yeah, it's a lot. Plus, you know I had to deal with Imani first."

"Gon' put the blame on the baby."

"For real."

"Whatever. Give me a kiss."

I tilted my head back to give him full access to my lips. He walked around to the side of me, and picked me up out of the chair. He took the seat in the chair, then place me on his lap. I continued my count without missing a beat. After squeezing my breasts and kissing me on the nape of my neck, he picked up a stack to count.

"That paperwork for the store is complete," Langston spoke. "So whenever you want to open it, it's a go."

"Really? I thought we had to wait 30 days for the license?"

"It came in the mail today. Have you finished those dresses?"

"I have two done."

"Well, looks like you need to get to work."

"I have the stuff that I ordered already, plus the stuff that Kayla brought."

"What about workers? Did you get around to that?"

"Not yet."

"That's the shit that you need to be doing instead of worrying about me being at home all day. If you were busy doing the stuff you're supposed to be doing, you wouldn't have time to think about me not being home."

"Regardless of how busy I am, I still think about you when we aren't together."

"That's sweet and all, but we have to take care of business first. All that other shit can wait. It ain't like you don't see me every day, we wake up and go to sleep together. We eat breakfast and dinner together, and even lunch sometimes."

"I'm not saying that's not appreciated. I just like to be around you is all," I lowered my voice."

"Don't sound down about it. It does make a nigga feel good to know that he is being missed though." I giggled, then rocked my hips against his lap. "Don't do that unless you're ready to go all the way."

"I am."

"Well, you need to go put Mani to sleep, it ain't like you counting fast anyway."

"You're firing me?"

"Yep. Thank you, but your services are no longer needed."

"Oh, you gon' Shaunie O'neal me?" I laughed. "See how you do me?"

I stood up from Langston lap to go tend to Imani. Before I walked away, he made sure to grab a handful of my ass. That instantly turned my body on to preheat. We haven't had mid-day sex in a while, so I am looking forward to it.

Imani did everything but lay down when I took her out of the playpen. She clapped my hands together to make me play patty cake. After that, she wanted to get down, then she wanted something to drink in her sippy cup. Sleep was the last thing that she was trying to do right now. I wasn't going to wrestle with her, so I let her walk and crawl around doing her thing. Langston was still at the table counting the money anyway.

My cell alert when off, so I got up to go check it. It was Shannon texting me to tell me that she and Punchie were on their way. I guess that will eliminate the midday sex we were planning to have. That was messed up because Imani looked to be finally settling down.

"Babe, Shannon and Punchie are on their way over here."

"Word?"

"Yeah, Shannon is coming by to help me out."

"Good, now you can do some work," he laughed. "And later."

"I already know."

"Take her," he said, referring to Imani that was in his lap.

I picked her up, and walked towards the bedroom. Langston began to throw the banned-up money back into the bag.

While putting Imani down for her nap, I ended up dozing off with her. I woke up when I heard the doorbell ring. I rubbed my hair down to make sure it wasn't sticking up before emerging from the bedroom. Langston was dapping Punchie up when I stepped out.

"Hey girl," Shannon spoke.

"What's up, cow? Where y'all coming from?"

"Shopping and eating," she smiled. "Where my niece?"

"Taking a nap."

"She's always sleep."

"Shit, no she's not."

Langston and Punchie started towards the living room, but I pulled Shannon into the bedroom. I wanted to speak to her to see if she had told Punchie anything. Rather I'm pregnant or not, I don't want Langston to know about it.

"Did you get it?" I asked.

"Yeah."

"You didn't tell Punchie did you?"

"No, he kept asking why I had to stop by Walgreens though. I just told him that my throat was scratchy and I wanted to get some medicine. By the way, you owe me $20."

"Whatever. Give it to me so I can hide it."

"When are you gonna take it?"

"I don't know."

"Just take it now and get it over with."

I took a deep breath as I took the box from her. The last thing I wanted to be doing right now is taking this test. Now was the best time to do it since Punchie is keeping Langston company.

My leg shook uncontrollably while Shannon and I waited on the results to appear. This took me back to when we were waiting on the results for Imani. We were in the same positions with me sitting on top on the toilet, and her sitting on the side of the tub. She was looking down at her watch keeping track of the time.

"Niy!" Langston called out.

I jumped up off the toilet like I had springs in my ass. My heart was beating overtime as I darted out of the bathroom. I opened the bedroom door, and made my way down the hall. Langston and Punchie were seated in the living room looking back at me.

"What y'all doing?"

"Nothing, talking."

"Oh. You want to go to the movies?"

"Yeah. What about Imani though?"

"I'll see if Neka will watch her for us. If not, I can get Big

Mama."

"Okay. I'll tell Shannon and get Imani's bag together."

Quickly, I hurried back towards the bedroom to join Shannon. I'm sure the results from the test has been revealed by now.

When I pushed the door open, I startled Shannon as she came out of the bathroom. She jumped, clutched her chest, then sighed in relief when she saw it was me. I could see that she had the Walgreens bag tucked halfway into her purse.

"What they want?" Shannon asked.

"To go to the movies. Where is the test?

"I wrapped it up."

She dug into her purse and removed the test wrapped up in tissue paper. Shannon had a smile on her face, so I took that as a sign of good news. I took the test from her and tore the tissue off like it was Christmas morning. My eyes fell right on the test that read positive. Panic filled my body because I was expecting a negative test. I looked back up at Shannon who was still standing here smiling. That began to piss me off because this wasn't a celebratory moment.

"The fuck are you smiling at?" I couldn't help but ask.

"I know you're not happy, but I think it's a good thing, Niy."

"What makes you think that?"

"It's just a feeling I have."

"Well, I'm getting rid of it, and you're helping me."

"Niy, you need to talk to Tookie about this first."

"Shannon!"

"Okay, whatever."

I wrapped the tissue back around the test, "Now take and get rid of this for me."

She shook her head, then reluctantly took the test from me.

CHAPTER TWENTY-ONE: TOOKIE

Today was the day that I officially get to meet Yaniyzah's father. To say that I was looking forward to it was an overstatement. I was still straddling the fence, but it was too late to back out now. I've already agreed to meet this guy, and I know Yaniyzah will not want to postpone it any longer. She is looking forward to it, so I didn't want to let her down.

Yaniyzah was in a deep sleep, but I couldn't stop thinking about the meet. As far as I know this guy is one of the people hunting me. He could be using Yaniyzah to ultimately get to me. She didn't seem to think so, but I wouldn't put it past him. Cops are cops at the end of the day, and using people is how they make their cases.

My mind was also on the shit that Ro had put in my ear. He informed me that after I left the club the other night, he saw Toot and Joy cozied up together. That bothered me, but not as much when he told me he saw Brooke talking to them. Everything about that situation makes me uneasy. I don't want anyone that I know or even associate with speaking to Brooke. Sitting here thinking about the shit is fucking my head up. I needed a distraction, and the best distraction for me is sex. The only time that I don't think about other things is when I'm having sex.

I rolled over to snuggle up behind Niy. She didn't move, so I threw my arm over her, and cupped her breasts. That didn't make her wake up, so I gave them a squeeze. Finally, she moved a little. I sucked on the back of her neck, then she let out a soft moan.

"You want some booty?" she asked.

"Mm hmm."

"Good," she said turning around to face me. "'Cause I'm horny too."

"You said the magic words."

She laughed, then pulled me in for a kiss. I rolled over on top of her, and pushed her legs apart. She secured her arms around me while I grinded against her. My muscle was beginning to power up, so it was almost go time. I continued kissing, sucking and leaving passion marks on her body.

My head was between Yaniyzah's legs, tongue kissing her pearl. She moaned as she thrusted her hips towards me. The sounds that were coming from her mouth was turning me on. I was ready to dig in her guts, but I enjoy eating her pussy. It has a sweet taste to it that I am addicted to. I stuck my finger inside of her and she was waterpark wet.

"Damn, Niy, you got some sweet, wet ass pussy."

She giggled. "Do I?"

"Girl, you're sitting on a goldmine and you don't even know it."

"I do know."

"How you know?" I asked as I slid up her body.

"'Cause you always saying it."

"That's right, and that's why this pussy gon' always be mine."

I kissed her while rubbing my dick around her clit. Niy reached down between us, and pushed my dick down to her hole.

"Oh, you ready to fuck," I stated as I slid inside of her.

"I told you I was horny. I'm ready to cum."

"How many times you wanna cum?"

"How many times you think you can make me?"

"Let's see."

I already knew how to make her cum fast, so I dug deeper into her. Deep stroking her is the fastest way to make her body erupt. I want to go ahead and let her get that first nut out of the way. She pulled me closer to her, then wrapped her legs around me.

"Ooh babe, that feels so good."

"It sure does. Shit! Keep throwing that pussy back just like that."

"Fuck, you 'bout to make me cum."

"Spill that shit all over this dick."

"I am," she whined. "Oh God I am. Fuck, fuck."

She held me tight as her body shook. I stopped my stroke to wait for her pussy to stop pulsating. When she loosened her grip, I started back stroking her.

After a few strokes, Yaniyzah pushed me off of her, then straddled my legs. She leaned forward to give me some head. My eyes were planted on her watching her every move. I like to watch her give me brain because she did it with so much passion. She looked to enjoy tasting me as much as I do tasting her.

"Damn baby, you getting it." She reached up and traced my abs with her fingertips. "Come on and ride this dick."

"You ready for me?"

"Always. Get yo' sexy ass up here."

I pulled her up my body, then she mounted my dick. As she slid down, I gripped her waist.

"Mm," she mummed.

I popped her on her butt, then grabbed her cheeks to open them up. She held my chest as she bounced up and down on top of me. Her pussy was so good that I couldn't help but throw this dick back at her.

"Shit, girl, it seems like this shit gets better each time we fuck. What you doing to it?"

"Nothing."

"Got dammit it feels like it. Ride that shit to the tip."

She slowed her rhythm a little and rode my dick to the tip. I squeezed her ass cheeks hard to keep my toes from curling. Her pussy was snatching something serious, making me think twice about her being on top.

"Fuck, Langston, I'm cummin' again." I lifted my head up so I could see. "Shit!" she screamed, then collapsed forward on my chest.

I laughed, "That one took a lot out of you, huh?"

"Yeah," she smiled while rubbing my chest. "You are so fine, baby."

I chuckled as rolled over. I crawled out of the bed, then pulled her to the edge of the bed, and flipped her on her stomach. After sucking her pussy once more, I pushed myself back inside of her. She arched her back, and threw that ass on me.

"Work that dick ma," I slapped her ass. "You deserve something special for this shit. What you want, a car, a house, diamonds? Whatever you want it's yours."

"Whatever I want?"

"Whatever, baby, it's yours."

I probably shouldn't have said that shit, but right now I mean it. She never really wants anything, so she can have whatever.

"I want you."

"You got me."

She didn't respond this time. I wonder what she means by she wants me. She has me completely, so I'm not sure what she is asking for. If she is hinting at marriage, she will have to continue that. Although I probably will marry her, I wasn't going to do it anytime soon.

After we both came, I laid in the bed with Yaniyzah laying across my chest. While I rubbed my hands through her hair, she rubbed her hands all over my chest.

"Babe?"

Fuck. I knew her ass wanted to talk.

"Yeah?"

"I know you say that you're building for us, does that mean we will get married?"

"I mean, eventually."

"Do you want kids of your own?"

"I don't even know. I have Imani and that is enough for me."

"But what about your bloodline continuing on?"

"Who says that's good for the world?"

"I don't think it's such a bad idea."

"Why you so worried about that? We ain't having no babies no time soon, we can worry about that shit in 'bout three or four years."

"Why you getting an attitude?"

"'Cause you talkin' about a baby and shit. You want a baby or something?"

"No, I don't *want* a baby."

"Well, quit talkin' 'bout that shit then. We got a baby and we not having no more. Fuck you think this is, a daycare center?"

"You're so fuckin' rude," she groaned as she lifted herself off of me, and climbed out of the bed. "I'm trying to have a serious conversation with you."

"Me too, I'm serious about not having no damn babies. Take them fuckin' pills, and don't be tryin' to trap a nigga."

"Trap? Don't go speakin' no trap shit 'cause yo' pull-out game is weak!"

She marched into the bathroom and slammed the door behind her.

"My pull-out game ain't weak! You just make sure you take them damn pills!" I yelled.

I don't know what has gotten into her, but she had better get it out before she pisses me off. She knows damn well that we don't need another baby around here right now. Imani is a handful by herself, she doesn't need any assistance with fucking shit up.

When I woke up for the day, I didn't smell food cooking like normal. I take it that Yaniyzah is still mad at me about our conversation a few hours ago. It didn't too much matter anyway because I had a ride to take in a minute. I had overslept, so Junior was already on his way to get me. I had to make the money drop early, since I was meeting Yaniyzah's father later.

"You still mad at me?" I asked when I walked into the kitchen.

She looked me up and down, then rolled her eyes. "Where you 'bout to go?"

"Turn a few corners."

"Don't forget that we are meeting my father today."

"I haven't forgotten. If I'm not back in enough time, I will meet you there."

She smacked her lips together and huffed. I didn't pay it any attention. I kissed her on the cheek, then headed towards the door. On the way out, I grabbed the duffle bag of cash. Whatever is eating her I'll have to deal with later.

I met Junior in the parking garage of the loft. Before we rolled out, we had to get the money secured. I sealed the money as tight as I could, so all of it should be able to fit. As I got to the last few stacks, I knew it would.

"What's the deal for today, bro?" Junior inquired.

"We just have the money drop."

"Cool. You wanna stop by granny's?"

"I can't today. I have to go meet Niy's father later on."

"Word? Wait, ain't he a FED too?"

"Hell yeah, man. I'm trying to remove that aspect of him far away from my mind and only think of him as Niy's dad."

"That means that he will be all up in yo' business regardless."

"I'm prepared for the third degree, but I will be watching his ass."

"Straight up."

We jumped in the truck and headed out. Right now, I had to focus on what I was about to do. I'll think about Niy's father when it's time to.

As soon as we exited off the expressway, my cell rung. Joy was calling me for the fifth time. Even though I had a little time to talk to her, I wasn't going to answer. Whatever she has to say I do not want to hear. I was trying to steer clear of her out of respect for Yaniyzah. If Niy does happen to talk to Joy for whatever reason, I don't want her to be able to say that she's had further conversations with me. I want to be able to show Niy all of the unanswered calls, and unopened text messages if Joy tries to say different.

Junior pulled around to the back of the house and backed in. Jose and Israel were already back there waiting on us. That's why I fuck with them. They were always on time even when they didn't know the time.

"There's my brother," Israel beamed.

"Is, what's up, man?"

"You back?"

"Yeah, I'm back."

"For good this time?"

"Yup, I'm back for good this time."

"Perfecto. You got money?"

"You know it."

I ushered him to the back of the truck, while Junior did his magic to open the compartments. Once they popped opened, I stepped back to let him do his thing.

The plan was to stop by Toot's house when I left here, but we spent more time at Israel's place than I expected. I lost track of time catching up with them. The meet with Yaniyzah's father is in a little bit, so I had Junior to take me back home. From the looks of things, Niy and I aren't on the same page right now, and I need to get us back there. The last thing I want is for us to be upset at each other when we go to visit her dad.

When I entered the loft, I heard Yaniyzah getting off of the phone. She stepped out of the bedroom to look at me, then she walked back inside. The fact that she didn't say anything confirms my thoughts about her being upset. I'm not exactly sure what I did, but I have to fix it before we leave the house. Before I talked to her, I went into the kitchen to grab an apple and a water. I hadn't eaten anything today, and I need something in my system.

I made sure to take a deep breath before I entered the bedroom. I had no idea of what I could be walking into. No matter what it is, it has to be resolved today. Yaniyzah was standing on the side of the bed, combing Imani's hair when I eased inside. Once Imani saw me, she started trying to crawl away.

"Hey, babe," I spoke.

"Hey."

There was no enthusiasm in her voice when she spoke. I picked up Imani who had crawled to the edge of the bed.

"Hey, Mani," I kissed her on her cheek. "You getting yo' hair combed?"

"Trying to."

I sat Imani back in her spot in front of Yaniyah, then took a seat next to her. I know as long as I am up walking around, Imani will want me to pick her up.

"What's going on with you though?"

"Nothing."

"Don't say nothing when you've been acting salty all day."

"I haven't been salty; I just don't appreciate the way that you talked to me."

"I'm sorry for going off, Niy. I know I said some shit that was mean, that's because I was in the heat of the moment. You know that I don't want to do or say anything to make you upset. I want the shit that you want just not right at this moment. Marriage, kids, all that can wait until we are perfectly stable. You got the store, and Sloan wants me to open another club with him. We have too many other things to worry about right now to be concerned with that simple shit."

"Alright, I won't bring it up again."

"Can I have a kiss?"

She placed the last bow on Imani's head, then leaned over to kiss me. It was more of a peck than a kiss, so I know she's still upset. I can see now that it's going to take me more than a few hours to fix her attitude this time.

Pulling up to Yaniyzah's father house, I still had mixed feelings. I'm sure that he already has an opinion of me, just like I have one of him. I've never tried to impress anyone, and I will not start today. I will try not to be as cocky, but I will be me regardless. Either the nigga like me or he don't.

"We're here," Niy smiled. It was the first smile I had seen from her all day.

"Yeah, we are."

"Are you nervous?"

"Nope."

"Good, because my dad is cool."

I pulled the door handle and jumped out. Niy hadn't said more than three words to me all day, now she chooses to talk to me. I wasn't with that fake shit, so I wasn't going to converse with her right now. Whatever I need to know about her father I will find out on my own. I opened her door, then grabbed Imani from the back seat.

The door opened up as we approached the steps. Yaniyzah's father walked out, and stood there like Big Mama with his fist on his hips. He had a welcoming smile on his face, but I kept a straight face.

"I'm glad y'all made it."

"Thank you for having us, Daddy. This is my boyfriend Tookie."

"Langston," I shook his hand.

"Nice to finally meet you, Langston."

"Likewise."

"I'm Don, come on inside."

As we walked through the house, I took my time scanning the rooms. The house was decorated very nicely. Now I can see why my money didn't impress Yaniyzah. From the looks of it, she grew up comfortably.

When we made it to the kitchen, Don opened the oven and pulled a pan out. I knew that we were having dinner here but I thought it would be catered. Yaniyzah never mentioned that he could or was cooking for us. It made sense because Yaniyzah can cook her ass off. She had to be taught by her father since her mother passed away when she was younger.

"I hope you like ribs, Langston," Don mentioned. "Niy didn't tell me what you like."

"Ribs are fine by me."

"Niy, grab those plates out of the cabinet, while I put the food out. So Langston, are you from here?"

"Yup, born and raised in Dallas, Texas."

"What about your parents, are they both still living?"

"Yeah."

"Do you have any children?"

"One daughter."

"Okay, and how is your relationship with her mother?"

"We're together."

He laughed, "Oh, you are referring to Imani."

"Yes, she is my daughter."

"Okay."

My cell phone rung and interrupted the conversation. I looked down and saw that it was Quincy calling me. I didn't want to be rude, but it's been a minute since I've spoken with my brother.

"Excuse me, this is my brother and I have to take this.

Superstar, what's going on?"

"Chillin', man, what's up with you?"

"His brother plays professional basketball," I heard Yaniyzah say as I exited the room.

"You already know, same ole same ole."

"I hear ya. Big bro wanted me to let you know that he is sending you something. It should be there in a few days."

"Who?"

"Big *bro*."

"Oh, okay. Yeah, that's cool."

"Everything cool on yo' end?"

"Yeah, I'm meeting Niy's father right now."

"Well, nigga get back to that. I didn't want shit, I just wanted to drop that on you."

"Alright, man, I'll call you later."

"Bet that."

I walked back into the kitchen, and they were sitting at the table waiting for me.

"I'm sorry, but I had to take that."

"It's okay," Don smiled. "Niy told me that Quincy Williams is your brother. How cool is that?"

"It's alright I guess. I just see him as my annoying ass lil' brother."

"That's alright," he said still smiling. Somehow I think that knowing Quincy is my brother made Don happy. His questions were no longer being thrown at me. He was still being inquisitive, but it had more to do with Quincy. I didn't mind talking about him as long as it kept me off his radar.

It didn't take long for Don to direct his attention back to me. I wasn't tripping because this is what I expected. He sounds just like Niy asking me all of these questions, and wanting the answers to them now. That wasn't normally how I roll, so it made me uncomfortable just a little. Not because he was asking invasive questions, but because he was asking questions period.

"Do you see yourself marrying my daughter?"

"I mean, we haven't known each other that long, but I do like what I know about her. If things continue to go like they have been, I can see us being married one day."

"But you're already shacking up together so that's like being married. What's the point in waiting to make it official?"

"I have to make sure that I am ready. Marriage is not a

commitment that I want to rush into."

Yaniyzah looked up at me, then over at her father who was looking at her. I guess they had some kind of ESP type shit going on with each other. While they sat quietly looking at each other, I took a few bites of my salad. I haven't eaten all day, and Don was a good cook.

"Do you love her?"

"Of course I do, her and Imani."

"Okay."

He started back digging into his food, so I followed his lead. I guess the bottom line was knowing if I loved his daughter. He got the answer he was searching for and left me alone. Since things were silent, it was easy to hear Niy's text alert sound off. She looked at it then focused back on her food. Her text alert has been going off a lot lately, and she has been ignoring some of them. I trust her so I never bothered to look at the phone. Plus, I didn't want her in my shit. The next time that we are alone and it happens, I will ask her about it.

CHAPTER TWENTY-TWO:
YANIYZAH

I woke up early as hell this morning. After Langston had his bitch fit about not having kids, I set me an appointment to get an abortion. It was something that I wanted to do, and after speaking with Langston, it was a definite decision for me. I was going to tell him about the baby, but he didn't give me any comforting words to help me tell him. He started hollering about me trapping him, and I didn't want him to think that is what happened. I don't want a baby either, so I think this is the best thing to do. There is no way that I am having two babies in two years.

Montrez had been blowing my phone up all week about seeing Imani. I had been ignoring him, but I decided to text him back last night. Since I needed a sitter while I get the abortion, I agreed to let him keep her for a few hours. Hopefully, that will keep him off my phone for a while. I had a sitter, so now all I need is a ride home. After grabbing Imani and her bag, I slipped out the door quietly. I had to make sure not to wake Langston. Imani was still sleep so that was perfect.

As I walked down to the garage, I dialed up Shannon. She is the only person that knows about the baby, so she was the only person I thought to call. I know that it is last minute, but she usually comes through for me in clutch situations.

"Hello?" she answered with sleep all in her voice.

"Bitch get up."

"Why?"

"I need you to do me a favor."

"What?"

"I need you to come pick me up."

"From where, in what?"

"I'm going to go get the abortion and I need a ride home."

"You didn't tell Tookie, Niy?"

"No."

"You need to tell him."

"I'm not 'bout to go through that with you right now, can you do it or not?"

"Niy, I don't want Tookie mad at me."

"I thought I was yo' bitch."

"You are, but I'm at Punchie's house right now. I know you don't want me to get him to bring me up there, do you?"

"No. I'll come get you, and you can go with me."

She let out a deep breath, "Alright."

"Send me his address, and I'll text you after I drop Imani off."

"Ugh, you get on my nerves."

"Yeah, yeah."

I locked Imani into her seat, then jumped under the steering wheel. After checking my surroundings, I peeled out of the parking spot.

When I pulled into the apartments, Montrez was already standing in front of the building. I guess he was happy about being able to keep Imani. Sooner or later, I'm going to have to tell Langston about these visit, but right now is not the time. First, I need to see if Montrez is serious about being in Imani's life permanently. If that is not his plan, then there is no reason to tell Langston about it. I pulled right in front of him and stopped.

"Why you taking so long to let me see my damn seed?" he groaned.

"Good morning to you too."

"Man, fuck all that shit. Why don't you bring her to see me when I ask?"

"It's not like we stay up the street, and you can't run me. Imani doesn't have a car, so she moves when I move."

"Well, you need to set a schedule or some shit for me to keep her. I'm not dealing with this whenever you want to let me see her shit."

"You're throwing a lot of suggestions around for a person that don't even take care of her. We can talk about all of that when you start paying for her necessities."

"So now it's 'bout the money?"

I chuckled. "Trust me, it ain't about the money. But since you're demanding things, you need to do it all. Not just seeing her."

"I'll see what I can do."

"Whatever. Enjoy your time with her, and I will be back in a few hours."

"Where yo' ass going this early in the morning anyway?"

"That's your business right there," I said pointing at the back window. "Tend to that."

"What-the-fuck-ever, man."

Montrez snatched the back door open, and pulled Imani out. She was still sleeping, thank God. When she wakes up, she will probably have a major fit. She should sleep for about another hour or two if he doesn't bother her. Hopefully I'll be back soon so my baby won't be tortured too long. She didn't know him well, and

I'm sure she will cry. I kissed her on her forehead, then handed Montrez the bag. As I turned to get back in the truck, he slapped me on my ass.

"Don't disrespect me."

"Shut up. You wouldn't even have all that ass if it wasn't for me."

"That's what you think."

"That's my ass, and it's always gon' be my ass. I was the first one to tap it, and I'm gon' be the last one to tap that shit."

"In your dreams, nigga."

"In my wake, too."

I closed the door in his face and grabbed my phone. I was done listening to the garbage spilling out of his mouth. He will never hit this again. After I texted Shannon that I was on my way, I took off.

I sat in the car waiting forever for Shannon to come out. She knew that I was out here, so I don't know what's taking so long. I didn't want to keep texting her phone but shit. I impatiently waited with my feet still on the brake. When she hops in, I want to be able to burn off. I kept looking at the phone to see if she had called or texted but nothing.

Finally, Shannon came trotting out of the house. Punchie came out right behind her, but stayed on the porch. I looked at the clock and I had 20 minutes until my appointment. She jumped in the car looking like she had an attitude. I pulled away from the curb before I said anything to her.

"What's wrong with you?"

"You."

"What I do?"

"Got me and Punchie arguing. He wanted to know why I had to leave all of a sudden."

"What you tell him?"

"That we had to do some shit at the store."

"Did he believe you?"

"I doubt it."

"I'm sorry, Shan. I'll talk to him if you want me to."

"Don't worry about it, I'll fix it later. So, you're really about to go through with this shit?"

"Yes. And after Tookie got to barking about not wanting a baby again, I know it is the right decision."

"I don't think so, but whatever."

"He is adamant about not having kids, Shannon. What else do you expect me to do?"

"I expect you to tell him the truth and give him a choice."

"I don't want to do that and mess things up between us."

"You so dumb. Anyway, who's keeping Imani while you're out doing dumb shit?"

"Montrez," I smirked.

"I'm guessing Tookie doesn't know about that either." I bowed my head and looked at her. "Mm, mm, mm," she shook her head.

When I turned on the street that led to the clinic, it was lined with people on both sides. Some were even in the streets blocking traffic. They were standing around holding up those anti-abortion posters, chanting. I eased past them, then drove into the parking lot. They were all eyeing my car, waiting for me to get out. It frightened me a little because I don't know what they are going to say to me. I don't want them looking at me like I'm a monster either.

As soon as I shut the engine off, my cell began to ring. I dug it out of my purse, and saw that it was Langston calling. My heart started beating fast as I weighed my options on answering or not. If I answer, he will ask where I am, which might not be a good idea. My appointment is in five minutes, so I didn't have time to stand out here and chat with him. I silenced the ringer, then pushed my door open.

I couldn't help but to look around the room when I entered the clinic. All of the females that were here to get abortions had a dude by their side. It made me feel bad that Langston wasn't here with me. Shannon took a seat, while I walked up to the front desk.

"Fill out this form," the lady said, handing me a clipboard without even looking at me.

"Okay."

I turned to take a seat, and my cell started ringing again. Langston will probably keep calling until I answer. I grew nervous thinking about what he is going to say later. He is going to want to know why I wasn't answering my phone. Since Shannon told Punchie we were going to the store, I will stick to that lie. I will tell Langston that I accidently left my phone in the car. He probably won't go for it, but it was the best that I could think of right now. By the time I see him I will have perfected my lie.

While I filled out the forms, Shannon stayed on her phone texting. I'm sure that she is going back and forth with Punchie about what's going on. She said that she doesn't need me to talk to him for her, but I think that she will change her tune. If Punch doesn't believe her, then I will have to step in to confirm things for her, and vice versa. I just hope that I haven't messed things up for her. Shannon finally snatched her a baller like she's always wanted, I don't want to be the reason that she loses him.

When my phone rung for the third time, I turned the ringer off. It was obvious that Langston wasn't going to stop calling, so I had no other choice. He is going to be pissed at me, I know this for a fact. I never not have my phone on me, so he may not believe the story about me leaving it in the car. I filled out the last page on the clipboard, then walked it back to the desk.

My leg shook uncontrollably while I waited on my number to be called. For the first time, I was having second thoughts about this abortion shit. Not because I wanted the baby, but because I was feeling guilty about not telling Langston. Keeping secrets from him made me feel some type of way because he was so good to me. Yeah, he lied about seeing Joy, but I believe the story that he told me.

"Number 6824," the lady called out.

"Oh shit, that's me."

Shannon looked at me with sadness in her eyes. I placed my purse and phone in her lap, then walked towards the lady.

"How are you today?"

"Fine, I guess."

"Follow me."

Slowly, I followed her down the long hallway. There were dozens of pictures that lined the wall. Although it was an abortion clinic, they had posters of other options on the walls.

When she pushed the door opened to my room, my heart felt like it was going to jump out of my chest. I sped my breathing up to try to control the anxiety I was having.

"Change into this gown, and I will be back."

"Okay," I answered nervously.

I held my chest and took a seat. Different thoughts were going through my brain. I've come this far, so there was no turning back now. I stood back up, then slowly began to undress. Chill bumps developed on my body as soon as the cold air hit my skin. I hurried to take the rest of my clothes off, and slipped the gown on.

There were two knocks on the door, then the nurse entered the room. My heart began to beat again thinking about what was getting ready to happen.

"First, I'm going to get a sonogram to see how far along you are."

"Okay."

"Just lay back for me, then we can get started."

Slowly, I laid back against the bed. My hands and my legs were shaking at this point. I closed my eyes and took a deep breath. Before I could completely exhale, I heard the unthinkable.

"YANIYZAH!" It was Langston. "YANIYZAH, WHERE THE FUCK YOU AT, YO?"

CHAPTER TWENTY-THREE:
TOOKIE

Yaniyzah put that pussy on me so good last night that I fell into a deep sleep. My cell kept vibrating against the nightstand, interrupting my sleep. I rubbed my eyes, then looked over next to me. Niy wasn't in the bed, so I reached over to look at the phone. Punchie was calling, but by the time I picked the phone up, he had hung up. The phone showed that I had three missed calls from him. My first thought was that something had happened to one of them. Before I could complete that thought, the phone sounded off again.

"Yo, what the fuck is going on, bro?"

"Bro, do you know that Niy is pregnant?" he asked.

"The fuck you talkin' 'bout?"

"Yo' girl is pregnant, dog."

"She what?" I said sitting up straight. "Nah, bruh, you must've heard wrong."

"No bullshit. She came over here to pick Shannon up a minute ago. She's going to have an abortion right now."

I jumped up out of the bed, and threw some pants on. "Please tell me you lying right now, bruh."

"My nigga, I just told yo' stupid ass that I wasn't bullshittin'.

Get the fuckin' wax out ya ear and listen. Shannon finally told me the truth after I cursed her ass out about leaving."

"Where they at?" I asked after slipping a shirt over my head.

"Ruth's Women Clinic."

"Alright, man, good looking out."

"You want me to meet you there?"

"Nah, I need you on standby just in case I get locked up."

"Don't go crazy, bruh."

"Fuck crazy, I'm 'bout to go insane on her ass. Let me call you back."

As I hung up in his face, I stepped into my boots. I scrolled through my phone and dialed Niy's number. When her voicemail picked up, it immediately ran me hot.

"Niy, I just heard some foul ass shit, and I swear it bet not be true!"

I ended the call, grabbed my keys from the bar, and hurried out of the door. I swear if she kills my baby I'm killing her ass. I pulled up the direction to the clinic on my phone as I made my way to the Corvette. On a regular day, I don't drive this car, but today I need the speed.

I called Niy's phone over and over as I drove with no answer. I left message after message with no return call. All I could think about was her ass in there laid up on some table getting the life sucked out of her. That thought made me hit the gas, and run right through the red light. A ticket is the last thing that I was worried about getting right now. My focus was on getting to the clinic before it was too late.

As soon as I turned the corner, I was met with a bunch of marching muthafuckas. They were all in the streets with their signs marching back and forth. I laid on my horn as I revved my engine. I was trying to give them a warning instead of mowing them down like grass in the middle of the street.

"Get the fuck out the way!" I yelled as I drove through.

I didn't even bother to park in a spot. I pulled right up to the front door and stopped. I don't plan on acting civilized, so I need to have an easy escape.

I walked inside of the clinic and scanned the room. Shannon was looking right at me when I laid eyes on her. She didn't say a word to me, she just pointed towards the door. At first I was going to stop at the front desk, but that would waste valuable time. The door Shannon pointed to opened and a nurse stood there with it wide open. She was getting ready to call out a number when I walked right past her.

"Excuse me, sir."

"YANIYZAH, YANYZAH, WHERE THE FUCK YOU AT, YO!?"

"Excuse me, sir, you're not supposed to be back here."

"Bitch, shut the fuck up talkin' to me!"

As I walked down the hallway, I began to push doors open. A lady stepped out of one of the rooms at the end of the hall to see what was going on.

"Sir, you can't be back here."

"Fuck you, is Yaniyzah in there!?"

She stood there looking at me as I bolted towards her. When I got closer, she stepped back into the room and tried to close the door. I pushed the door so hard that it hit the wall behind it. Yaniyzah was sitting on the table looking scared shitless.

"Bring yo' stupid ass out of here, yo," I said, grabbing her off the table by the front of her gown.

"Babe, I'm sorry," she cried as she grabbed her clothes.

"I DON'T WANNA HEAR THAT SHIT, NIY!"

I grabbed her by the back of her neck, and escorted her out of the door.

"You're hurting me."

"I'mma do more than hurt yo' ass."

"Stop."

"I ain't stopping shit! What the fuck is you thinkin'?" I popped her upside her head.

"I—"

I jerked her hard by her neck. "Shut the fuck up 'cause you wasn't."

The door that led back to the lobby was still wide open, so I pushed her right through it. I didn't even think to look for Shannon as I walked her ass out the front door. She was squirming and trying to remove my hand from the back of her neck. That didn't do anything but make me grip it harder. I held onto her neck tightly until we were inches away from the car, then I slammed her right into the passenger side of the car.

"Ouch, Langston."

"Get in the fuckin' car!" I yelled as I pulled the door open.

The protestors must have caught wind of what was happening because they were cheering me on. With tears in her eyes, Yaniyzah sat down into the car. I marched around to the other side and jumped in.

"IS THE FUCKIN' BABY DEAD!?"

"No," she cried.

I threw the car in drive, then took off.

"I swear if you wasn't a female I would beat the shit out of you right now. What the fuck was you thinking?"

"You're the one that said you didn't want any kids."

"I don't give a fuck what I said!"

"I didn't want you to think I was trying to trap you. That's what you said the other day."

"I DON'T GIVE A FUCK! You don't go making decisions like this without telling me."

"ALRIGHT ALREADY!

"DON'T HOLLA AT ME!"

"YOU'RE HOLLERING AT ME!"

"'Cause I'm tryin' to keep from beatin' yo' ass," I gritted my teeth.

"You didn't want a baby, what did you expect me to do?"

"I expect you to make a smarter decision than the one you made today. This shit right here is stupid as fuck."

"I'm sorry, Langston, I was just doing what I thought was right."

"How in the world of fucks did you see this was a good idea?"

"You don't want a baby and neither do I."

I looked over at her, "Where is Imani?" She leaned over against the door and sat quietly. After stopping at the red light, I looked over at her quizzically. I know she heard my question. "YOU HEAR ME!?"

"She's...with her...father."

I stared at her for a second to let her answer sink in. Where the hell does she get off telling *me* that she is with her father.

"The fuck you say to me? HUNH?" I tried to reach over to grab her, but she pulled the door handle and jumped out of the car. "GET YO' ASS BACK IN THE CAR!"

"NO! I'm not gonna let you snatch on me."

"Get yo' stupid ass in the car, and quit making a scene!"

"You stupid!"

My cell started ringing through the Bluetooth. Quincy was calling me, but right now wasn't the best time to talk.

"Bro, I need to call you back," I answered.

"What's wrong?"

"Niy out here acting a damn fool, I swear I'm 'bout to beat the shit out of this bitch."

"Whoa, calm down. What happened?"

CRACK! Yaniyzah's fists came smashing through the window next to me.

"DON'T DISRESPECT ME AND CALL ME NO BITCH!"

Yaniyzah was standing there in her bra, with her shirt wrapped around her fist.

"Bro, I swear I'm 'bout to give her ass a fresh fade with no clippers. She don' broke my fucking window."

BRO!" Quincy yelled. "TOOK!"

With cars blowing behind me, I jumped out of the car to get Yaniyzah. As soon as she saw me getting out, she took off running down the street. I ran behind her full speed until I caught up. I scooped her up from behind, and carried her back to the car.

"Put me down, Langston!" she kicked. "I'm not getting in the car with you."

"You're really pushing my buttons, Niy. I'm begging you to stop before I knock yo' ass out."

"If you put yo' hands on me, I'm calling the police."

I threw her back into the car, and slammed the door behind her. By now, people were really cursing me out about holding up traffic. That made me even more upset because I didn't do shit like this. I don't have my business all in the streets. Niy was sitting as close to the door as she could when I jumped back inside. I didn't say anything to her this time, I just took off. The light was red, but I didn't give a damn. I need to get out of this enclosed space with her before I really end up putting my hands on her. I've never put my hands on a woman before, but I have never been pushed this far either.

Once we made it to the loft, I walked straight to the key rack. I grabbed the keys to the 745, then turned to face Niy.

"Go change yo' clothes and go get my daughter," I said holding the key up.

"I'm not gonna get her if you're gonna be yelling."

"Go get my fuckin' daughter."

"Langston, I'm serious, if you—"

I reached back and smacked her on her ass with all my might. She still had on that hospital gown shit, so I got nothing but ass.

"GO get my FUCKIN' daughter right now Niy! I ain't playin' games with you, go get her before I get upset."

I could see the tears developing in her eyes, but she didn't drop any. She snatched the keys from my hand, then stormed off towards the bedroom.

I sat on the sofa in silence while Niy went to get Imani. While I had some time to think, I thought over the past few days. Now the attitude that Niy has been having is starting to make sense. When she mentioned a baby a few days ago, I went left. I thought that maybe she was having baby fever, shit, I didn't know that her ass was already pregnant. I know I was mean about it, but if she would have told me she was pregnant, I would have handled shit differently. There is no way that I would have agreed to an abortion. My family don't believe in that shit. Even though I didn't want another kid, I didn't want to kill the shorty either. That is my first planted seed, so I definitely want it to be here. This couldn't come at a worst time, but it's something that I have to get ready to handle.

Although I am cool with the baby, I am still pissed off at Niy. First I find out that she was about to kill my seed, then she tells me that Imani is with her father. She must have her head screwed on all the way backward to be doing some dumb shit like this. How could she go off and leave Imani with him, and she don't even know him? Niy doesn't let anyone keep Imani, so it was a major shock for me to hear that she was with him. That's another thing that we will have to discuss, but I will save it for later. I just want to hold Imani when she gets here, and make sure that she is okay.

CHAPTER TWENTY-FOUR:
YANIYZAH

It's been two days since everything went down between Langston and I. After admitting to letting Montrez secretly see Imani, Langston decided that he would sleep in the guest bed in Imani's room. He was still walking around the house not talking to me. Not even as much as a good morning, and it was irritating. I really didn't think that he would be this upset about the abortion. He's the one that made it seem like a baby was not even an option right now. I knew he would be mad about Imani seeing Montrez, but I thought I would have more time to explain things to him. He didn't give a damn about my explanation; he didn't even give me a chance to finish explaining it to him.

Langston wasn't talking to me, and I wasn't talking to Shannon. Although I am a little happy that I didn't get a chance to have the abortion, I am mad at her for telling Punchie. She is my best friend, so her loyalty should have been to me. The least she could have done was tell me that she had told him. At least then I would have answered when Langston was calling. When I finally checked my voicemail, Langston was yelling all over it. He left me five messages about knocking me out, kicking my ass, and telling me that I better pray that he gets to me before the abortion is done.

When I stepped out of the bedroom, Langston and Imani were sitting at the table eating. For the past few days, he hasn't let Imani out of his sight. Every time he left the loft, he has taken her with him. It didn't bother me any because it gave me a chance to nap and work on clothes. I looked at Langston and smiled, but he didn't return the gesture. I'm trying my best to give him the space that he needs to get over what happened. You would think two days would be enough time to get his head right, but he was still treating me like it just happened. I know I went too far by punching the window out of his car, but when I heard him call me a bitch, it sent rage through my body. I don't give a damn how mad he gets, it will never be okay to disrespect me.

I've grown tired of the silent treatment, so I made sure to come out of the room in my booty shorts and bra. My voice couldn't get Langston's attention, but I know that my body can. That is the one thing that he can't resist for too long. I leaned over into the fridge, making sure to take my time removing the carton of eggs and the roll of thawed sausage. When I turned to face Langston, his eyes were planted on me.

"You gon' catch pneumonia in the ass with that lil' shit on," he groaned.

"I'm in the house. What's wrong with what I have on?"

"Nothing if you 'bout to shoot a workout video or some shit."

His sarcasm wasn't humorous to me, but at least I have him talking.

"I wouldn't mind shooting a workout video…with you, if you know what I mean."

He stared at me while he gulped down the last of his orange juice. I'm sure the wheels in his head were spinning, but he didn't react to my statement. That wasn't what I was expecting to get from him. To save face, I turned around to start on my breakfast.

While I chowed down on my sausage and eggs with syrup, Langston and Imani stretched out on the sofa. Watching cartoons were a part of their morning routine. I sat watching from afar, feeling left out of the loop. Even though this was their bonding time, I still wanted to be included. I scarfed down the rest of the food in my bowl, so that I would be able to join them.

Before I was able to wash my bowl, Langston was headed towards the bedroom. I already knew that he was getting ready to leave soon, but I wanted him to talk to me. It doesn't matter what he says to me, I just want to exchange words. This silent treatment is getting to me because I'm used to talking to him. I put the bowl in the dish rack, and quickly dried my hands. I trotted to the bedroom, then eased my way inside. Langston was standing at the foot of the bed, changing his shirt.

"You're leaving?" I asked.

"Yeah."

"When are you gonna talk to me?"

"I'm talking to you now."

"I mean seriously. You're sleeping in the other room, and you walk around here all day ignoring me."

"Because I don't feel like talking."

"You don't feel like talking, or talking to me?" Once again, he just stared at me. "Are we broken up, Langston? If you don't want to be with me anymore, just say something. I can leave you know."

"Leave this house if you want to and see what happens."

I folded my arms across my chest and tilted my head to the side. He stood there looking me up and down like he was waiting for me to say something. I wanted to, Lord knows I did, but I didn't want to keep arguing with him. I'm ready to make up and be happy again. Langston pushed past me without saying another word. I stood in place while he walked out of the room, then out of the front door.

Not knowing what else to do to make Langston talk to me, I thought about going to Big Mama. The problem with that idea is that I would have to tell her what happened. I didn't want to tell her that I was pregnant, and I damn sure didn't want to tell her that I went to have an abortion. The other problem was that I didn't want to leave the house. I didn't want to risk being gone when Langston gets back. I picked up my cell to call the only other person that knows how to deal with him.

"Hello?"

"Quanda, this Niy, you busy?"

"Not really, what's wrong?"

"I need to talk to you about Langston. I've pissed him off, and he hasn't talked to me in two days."

"Damn," she laughed. "What happened?"

"I-I'm pregnant."

"Oh. Wait, he's mad because you're pregnant?"

"It's more less because I tried to get an abortion behind his back."

"You what!? Why would you do a thing like that?"

"I know it was messed up. He said he didn't want a baby right now so I thought that was the best thing at the time. Not only that, but I've been taking Imani to see her father behind Langston's back."

"Girl, you got a lot going on. I don't even know what to say to help you out. Langston is stubborn, so all I can say is let him get over it."

"So, there is nothing that I can do?"

"Just keep talking to him, he'll eventually come around. Plan a romantic night or something, sex always work with men."

Since the booty shorts didn't work on him, I guess my next step is to walk around butt naked. Quanda isn't helpful, so it will be left up to me to make this right. After all, I am the one that caused this chaos.

"I'll figure something out."

"Well, I guess it's safe to say congratulations?"

I chuckled, "I guess so."

"Yay," she cheered. "I'm happy even if he isn't. I'll call and talk to him."

"Alright, Quanda, talk to you later."

Once I hung up with Quanda, I sat in silence, thinking. I'm wanting for Langston to talk to me, but I haven't made up with Shannon yet. It's not her fault that she told her man the truth to save her relationship. She was never down with the idea of an abortion anyway. I should have known where she stood because she was the same way when I got pregnant with Imani. She was the only person that thought I should have her. She has always been there for me, and I still need her to be.

"Oh bitch, you want to talk to me now?" Shannon answered.

"I'm sorry, boo."

"Don't be trying to sweet talk me, I ain't Tookie."

"He's not talking to me either. He won't even sleep in the same bed as me."

"Good, maybe you'll learn your lesson."

"I have. I miss both of y'all. Say you'll be my best friend again."

"If that's what you told him, I see why he hasn't forgiven you yet."

"What?"

"Bitch, you need to grovel."

"Pleeease Shan—"

"Not to me bitch, to him. When he walks through the door, drop to yo' knees and suck his dick."

"I thought you said grovel."

"Shit, you'll be on yo' knees, so it's the same thing."

I laughed, "See, that's why I love you. You are so clutch."

"Whatever. You owe me a purse for my services."

"I got you, whenever Tookie lets me off punishment."

"Well, you better get to work."

"I know I do. Let me get my thoughts together, I'll call you later."

"Bye, and I forgive yo' fertile ass."

I spent half of the day planning for tonight. After talking to Shannon, I came up with an idea. In order to get Langston talking to me, I will have to capture his full attention. I went to the convenience store on the first floor of our loft to purchase flowers and candles. They had some whipped cream, honey, and a few other edible items that I picked up. Tonight, I will have to put on my best performance.

While I prepared for the night, I made sure to keep Imani up. I wanted her to stay up so that she would go to sleep early. Every time she would attempt to fall asleep, I'd play with her, then give her something sweet to snack on. She was growing restless, so I knew that it wouldn't work for too much longer. Once I put the meat in the oven, I sat down on the floor with her to play. After the food gets done, I'll feed and put her to sleep.

The music was playing softly in the background, while the candle lights flickered. I sat in the living room where the rose petal trail ended. There I sat on a bed of rose petals naked, and patiently waiting. I had a bottle of Hennessey on ice just for him. That should take the edge off if he is still acting cold.

When the lock to the front door turned, and I grew nervous. I changed positions to sit on my knees. I could hear his footsteps slowly coming towards me, then he appeared. He paused where he was for a moment to look me over. I had his attention, but for how long? As he made his way towards me, he removed the sweater that he had on. I looked him in his eyes while I palmed and massaged my breasts.

Once he was in arms' reach, I grabbed his pants by the waist to pull him closer. I reached over on the table, and poured him a glass. Without saying a word, I handed the drink over, then proceeded to take his pants off. He sipped on his drink but didn't take his eyes off of what I was doing. Slowly, I slid my tongue all around his dick, then sucked the head. He separated his legs further apart for balance. Now that his dick was at full attention, I poured some honey on it, and took him all the way inside.

"Mm," he moaned. "Shiiit."

I didn't say a word to him like I usually do. I concentrated on what I was trying to do. As I sped up, his hands gripped the empty cup he was holding. I used my hands to massage his balls, while continuing to slob his knob.

"Fuck girl."

He leaned over to sit the cup down on the table. After that, he pulled his dick out of my mouth, and stepped all the way out of his pants. He got down on the floor next to me, then pulled me in for a kiss. I missed this from him. The soft and gentleness that he possesses. While we kissed, I straddled him. He massaged my butt cheeks, then slid his finger into my pussy. I moved his hand out of the way, and slid down his pipe.

"I'm sorry, Langston," I kissed him. "Will you forgive me?"

"You think this is all you have to do to fix this?"

"Tell me what to do, I'll do whatever it takes."

He grabbed my chin and kissed me hard. "This is a good start. I apologize for screaming and grabbing on you, for real. And yes, I do forgive you."

It felt like the weight of the world was lifted off of my shoulders.

"I love you, baby."

"Me too."

That shit still bothered me, but I'm not going to touch on that right now. I'm only 10 seconds in the door, and I wasn't about to mess that up. I know that he loves me, but just hearing him say it will make me feel better. For the time being, I will accept 'me too'.

Langston smacked my ass, "Ride this dick, girl. I know you didn't make it sexy in here just to talk."

I smiled then slowly began to bounce on top of him. He

secured his arms around my waist and held me tight. For the first time in days I felt at ease. Walking around here on eggshells wasn't comfortable for me, so I am ecstatic that he is finally coming around.

"I miss you," I said, then tongue kissed him hard.

He moved his hips around, "Mm, me too."

"Yes, baby," I whined. "Fuck meee!"

"I'm 'bout to murk this shit."

He removed his hands from around my waist, and slid them under my thighs. While he sat on the floor, he lifted me up and down on his dick. I held on to his arms, feeling his muscles as they contracted. That made him extra sexy to me. I had never even talked to a guy that was as sexy as Langston was, so he has me head over heels for him. However long it takes for Langston to marry me, I will wait, as long as he stays true.

CHAPTER TWENTY-FIVE: TOOKIE

After fucking with Yaniyzah all night, I was groggy as hell when I woke up. I looked over to my left and Niy was calling hogs. She swears that she doesn't snore, but I always hear differently. I'll let her make it this time because I'm the one that put her in a coma. Last night I dug into her guts as long as I could. I had to make up for the days that I'd been tripping. My plan was to come home to make up with her anyway last night. Her punishment had gone on long enough, and I knew she had learned her lesson.

Since Niy was still sleep, I rolled over behind her and snuggled up close. Just as I got comfortable and closed my eyes, my cell started ringing. I reached behind me to snatch the phone from the nightstand. It wasn't my main phone, so I had to reach again for the burner. I didn't recognize the number, but I answered anyway.

"Who this?"

"This Marcus, I got your number from Anson."

"Oh okay, you got something for me?"

"I do."

"When can I get it?"

"Hold tight, I will send you an address, meet me then."

"Bet."

I rolled back over behind Yaniyzah, who so just happened to not be snoring anymore. I know her nosey ass is awake.

"Niy." She didn't answer. She laid there like she was really sleep. "I already know yo' snorin' ass ain't sleep."

She laughed, then rolled over to face me. "Whatever, I don't snore."

"Shiid. How you think I know you was up?"

"I still don't believe you."

"I'mma record yo' ass one day." I placed my hand on her stomach. "So, there's really a baby in here?"

"Yup."

"Damn, how this happen?"

"You not wanting to wear them damn condoms."

"Yo' ass just fertile, man. I've been fuckin' for years, and ain't never got a girl pregnant."

"Well."

"Now I guess you want to get married and all that other bullshit?"

"I'll be ready whenever you get ready. I don't want to rush you."

"The hell you don't."

"I don't."

I slapped her on her ass. "So you don't wanna marry me?"

"Of course I do."

"Alright."

"Alright what?"

"Alright, we're getting married then."

"What you mean," she frowned, but had a little smile on her face.

"You said you wanna marry me?"

"Was that your proposal?"

"Yeah."

She laughed and shook her head. "Oh my God, you are so crazy."

"What?"

"Most men say kind words, get on one knee, have flowers, oh, and a ring. You know, stuff like that."

I laughed, "Baby, I'm not most men."

"You at least supposed to have a ring."

I couldn't help but laugh at her. All the things that she wanted was in the bathroom. After fucking her to sleep, I went to the truck, and got everything that I had purchased for her. I spent half of my day yesterday shopping for her. My plan was to make up with her anyway and pop the question, but she had other plans for us last night. She had about 20 gift bags waiting for her in the bathroom, because I knew that would be the first place she would go. Also, it was six dozen roses, and three rings sitting on the counter for her to choose from.

"Fuck a ring."

"What you mean," she whined. "I wanna ring. It doesn't matter what it looks like, I just want one on my finger."

"Why? To show off to your friends?"

"Yes," she laughed.

She rolled out of bed and headed right to the bathroom. I waited until she got close to the door before slipping out. She opened the door to walk in then stopped abruptly.

"Baby—" she said as she turned around, bumping into me.

"Which one you want?"

Her face was lit up with joy, then tears ran out of her eyes. I grabbed her hand and kneeled down.

"I don't know what I'm supposed to say in a proposal, but I

want to get married. Your father was right. We are already shacking up, and with this baby coming, there is no need to prolong it. I mean, I was already in it for the long haul anyway, so let's just make it official."

"Okay," she cried.

I stood up, wiped the tears from her face, then hugged her tight. She looked up at me, and I planted a kiss on her lips.

"Don't cry."

"Do you love me Langston?"

"What?" I released my grip a little. "Didn't I just ask you to marry me?"

"I know, but you never tell me you love me. I say it and you say 'me too'."

"I told you when I met you that actions speak louder than words. I don't have to walk around saying 'I love you' all the time when I'm showing it. I'm just not into that shit like that. Now pick which ring you want, and don't ride my last nerve."

"I'mma ride something else," she smiled.

"I'm down, but first, get all of this shit out this bathroom."

After I had breakfast with Yaniyzah and Imani, I headed out to Toot's house. I hadn't talked to him and I had a few questions. The first one was what the fuck he was doing with Joy. And the second question is what was he doing talking to Brooke? My used to be best friend, and my worst enemy are two people that I don't want him talking to.

As I pulled up to Toot's house, I saw an undercover watching his house. I almost missed them, but the muthafucka had a camera up to his face when I passed by. Toot was standing outside waiting on me, so I'm assuming that he was taking pictures of him. Fuck. I didn't want to get out of the car, but I was already here. I shook my head, then jumped out.

"Yo, what's good my nigga?" he dapped me up.

"You tell me. You know you got people watching you?"

"What you mean?"

"About four houses down, it's a blue car sitting in front of it taking pictures."

"What?" he frowned, then looked down the street. "Hold on right quick, let me stop this package from coming through." He pulled out his phone to handle his business. I made sure to keep my back to the car, so that he couldn't get my face. I didn't want him to mistake me for the drop off person. "Let's go inside."

"Nah, let's chill right here. Besides, I don't plan on staying long."

"What's on ya mind?"

"What's this I hear about you hugged up with Joy at the club?"

"Man, I was drunk, I didn't mean shit by it."

"You fuck?"

"Man."

"So you fucked right?"

"I mean."

"Alright then my nigga," I shook my head.

"You mad?"

"What else you been doing behind my back?"

"Nothing, what you mean?"

"You talking to FEDs now?"

"Hell nah I ain't talkin' to no FED. Fuck wrong with you?"

"You talked to one at the club."

"When?"

"When you was all up in Joy's face, you don't remember talking to another female?"

"I ain't talk to no FED. The only person I talked to was that bitch you used to fuck with."

"Brooke, that bitch is a muthafuckin' DEA agent."

He had that surprised look on his face like I had given him an expensive gift. Whatever he has been doing behind my back is going to come back to bite him in the ass. It took everything in me not to hit his ass in the mouth. If that muthafucka wasn't out here taking pictures, I would have beat the shit out of Toot. He knows that Joy was the first girl that I ever loved, and he goes and fucks her. I don't know if she did that to get back at me or what, but that shit wasn't cool at all on either part. Toot has been my boy for all these years, and now I can't fuck with him no more. He is a scavenger ass nigga in my book. I backed away from him, then turned to walk away.

"Took!" he called out. "Bro, I'm sorry. TOOK!"

I didn't bother turning around to face him. That nigga broke my heart with that shit, and I can't even stand to look at him.

As soon as I got back in the car, I called Ro. I told him to meet me at our first kick-it spot. When we were younger, we would hide out there after we would steal some shit. Anytime either of us would run away from home, we already knew where to look for them. It's been a while since we had been there, and that had Ro asking me questions. Even though I was on a burner, I wanted to talk to him in person.

"What's up, bro?" Ro asked as soon as he stepped out his ride.

"You got to stop fucking with that nigga Toot."

"What happened?"

"Somebody is watching his house, and you already know he was talking to that bitch Brooke. I don't know if he has said anything to her, but you got to steer clear of him. He is hot right now, and I don't want you to get caught up."

"You think he snitchin'?"

"I don't want to put a stamp on it, but he is the only one that got funny shit going on. I'll find out later tonight though."

"Good lookin' my nigga, real talk. I'll put the youngins up on game too. Did you talk to him about Joy?"

"Yeah, that hoe ass nigga fucked."

"That's some low down dirty shit, boy."

"I ain't even trippin' like I should. It's all good though, Niy is what I need. We're engaged now anyway."

"Nigga, stop lying," he turned his lips up.

"Real shit."

"She asked you to marry her?"

"Nah, nigga," I laughed.

"I'm just saying. I can't see you on one knee saying sweet nothings and shit," he laughed. "Did you wear a suit?"

"Naw, muthafucka, you know me better than that. You already know that shit was hard for a nigga like me. I don't even know if I said some sweet shit to her or not."

"What made you ask?"

"Fucked around and got her ass pregnant." He burst out laughing. "But I was gon' marry her anyway, eventually."

"Now you 'bout to have Shanie lookin' at me all crazy."

"What's up with you and Courtney though?"

"She let me fuck. I'mma fuck with her a lil' bit."

"Be careful with that one."

"I already know. I have a whole phone just for her ass. She's a feisty one, and I like that shit."

"You know Punchie fucks with her sister, right?"

"I got this, bro."

"A'ight then."

"What you 'bout to do?"

"Go by Big Mama's—" his phone started ringing and cut me off.

"Hold on, bruh. Yeah? For real? Okay, I'm on my way."

"What's up?" I asked as he hung up.

"Shanie's water broke, she's getting ready to have the baby," he smiled.

"Congratulations, nigga! Get gon' and go have that baby. I'll be up to the hospital later on."

"Bet. I'M 'BOUT TO BE A FUCKIN' FATHER!" he yelled before jumping into his car.

Big Mama wasn't sitting on the porch like normal when I pulled up. I looked down the street and I didn't see an undercover car either. That was a good thing in my book. I used my key to unlock the door and let myself in. Big Mama was sitting on the sofa, reading her bible. She gave me a fake smile when I looked at her, so I knew something was wrong. I looked around, and the first thing I noticed was that the television was missing.

"Where the TV," I huffed.

"L, not now."

"What do you mean not now? She took it, didn't she?"

"L, I said, not now."

"Big Mama, I don't want her back in here. Every time she comes home she says that she will change but she never does. Stop trying to help someone that doesn't want help."

"Shut up Langston Qynnard!"

"But Big Mama—"

"WHAT.THE.HELL.DID.I.SAY!? Pam is my damn child. Mine! So I will always be there for her. Have ya own damn kids, then you tell me if you give up on 'em."

I knew Big Mama was mad when she called me by my first and middle name. The fact that she started cursing lets me know that she is pissed.

"I have kids, Big Mama."

"That baby you playing daddy to ain't yo' blood. No matter how much you love her, your blood is different."

Something clicked in my head to make me talk sideways to Big Mama. I don't like for people to say that Imani is not mine, not even my Big Mama.

"She's my fuckin' daughter! Don't ever say that I am playing daddy to her!"

"Who the fuck do you think you are talking to like that?" she rose up from the sofa. "Huh? You must have forgotten who the hell I am? I will kick yo' nigga ass all up and down that fuckin' concrete out there. I will send yo' ass home lookin' like you don' been through a cheese grater."

"I'm saying, she's my baby, Mama, and I have another baby on the way."

"You what?"

"Niy's pregnant."

She stood there looking at me with her lips tight, then she relaxed them.

"You better be glad that you said some good shit, 'cause I was about to beat yo' ass like Cookie did Hakeem. Boy, you better go ask South Dallas about me. Ask anybody from Metropolitan, to Pine, to Malcom X, they'll tell you that I was the one that shut all the parties down."

"I know, Big Mama."

"You better act like it. Don't let this old age fool you, I still hit hard." I couldn't help but laugh at her, and her balled up fists in my face. "Great grandmother, what a way to end the day."

"Yeah, and I asked Niy to marry me too."

A big grin spread across Big Mama's face. "Look at you turning into a man right before my eyes."

"Every male has to do it at some point in their life, right? I guess God is telling me that it is my time."

"That sounds about right. He is an on-time God."

"But for real, Big Mama, what you gon' do about Pam?"

"Her drug ass gon' have to go somewhere else."

I just sat there and looked at Big Mama. She just cursed me out for saying the same shit. I guess it has to come from her since she is her child.

"I thought you said—"

"I am going to help her, but I can't have her stealing my stuff. It's too soon for that to be happening."

"She does it because you let her."

"I don't watch TV no way."

"That ain't the point."

I thought about what I was saying, and decided to keep my mouth closed. Big Mama just cursed me out about saying stuff, so I didn't want to get on her bad side again. I didn't have anything else to save my ass with this time.

"You worry about your new family, Langston, I'll handle Pam."

"Okay, but when you need me to step in, you know how to find me."

"I know. Where is Yaniyzah anyway?"

"Probably somewhere showing off her ring to her friends."

Big Mama chuckled. "I can only imagine. I remember when Papa proposed to me. Oh, I was so in love. He gave me the best ring money could buy back then. I couldn't wait to show all of my friends either."

"I guess that's a female thang."

"Of course, we're getting ready to be wives. You have to gloat in front of the single women," she laughed.

"Y'all women are a mess."

My cell alert went off on my burner phone, so I already knew what time it was. I didn't want to cut my conversation with Big Mama short, but I had business to tend to. Marcus must have gotten the information on the snitch for me. I slid my phone in my pocket and stood up.

"You got to go, L?"

"Yes ma'am."

"Alright, well, be careful."

"I will."

"Love you, L."

"Love you too, Big Mama."

I drove down a long driveway that led to the address that was sent. It was a house sitting back on a big piece of land. As I got closer, I saw a car parked next to a shed. I drove up next to it, and stepped out. A guy, who I am assuming is Marcus, walked from the opposite side.

"Tookie?"

"Yeah, you Marcus?"

"Yes."

"Nice to meet you, man."

"You too."

I stood there looking at this boy that couldn't be no older than 18 or 19 years old. He was young in the face, but he gave off an older persona.

"What you got for me?"

"We already snatched the muthafucka for you."

"Word? Who is it?"

"I'll let you see for yourself. Follow me."

As I followed behind Marcus, it was like déjà vu. I had seen this scene in my dreams, but it was walls surrounding us. My heart was beating fast in anticipation. I've been waiting a long time to find out who can't keep their mouth closed. Marcus pulled the door open, and a female was sitting on top of a table with her feet resting on the arm of a chair. I looked at her, then back at him.

"That's my girl, Keko," he smiled.

"What's up, Keko?"

"Damn you fine," she spoke. "And you snitchin' on him?"

She pushed her foot forward, causing the chair to spin. When it turned around, Joy was sitting in the chair tied up. I could have pissed myself when I saw that it was her. I would have never guessed that she was the person running their mouth.

"Yo, how y'all know fa sho' fa sho'?" I questioned.

"It's all right here in black and white," Marcus said, sliding some papers across the table. "She was caught with Ira Charles Brown with 5 keys and 50 thou in cash. She turned informant."

"When were you with Inky?"

Her lips were taped up, so she couldn't answer me. I snatched the papers from the table to take a look. The date showed that it was almost a year ago. A year ago, we were still together. I reached over and snatched the tape from her mouth.

"What the fuck is this shit, Joy?"

"They blackmailed me, I had to."

"What the fuck was you doing with Inky in the first place? You was fucking that nigga like you fucked Toot?" She sat there crying, not saying a word. "ANSWER ME, BITCH!" I grabbed her chin.

"I'm sorry."

"Why the fuck would you bring me in that?"

"Ink did. I just went along with it to stay out of jail."

"She gave them everything," Keko spoke. "She told them where you hang, that's how that DEA bitch knew where to meet you. She gave them addresses, friends, and signed off on a photo lineup."

"Why would you do that, Joy?"

"Because Inky was threatening to tell you about us. I knew that you wouldn't go to jail about it though."

"How you figure when you know I dibble and dabble?"

"Everything was cool until you pissed that DEA bitch off. Then she started coming at me every day trying to get me to trap you, but you had left and changed your number by then."

"You snitch on Toot, too?" Again, she didn't say anything. "You're the most trifling bitch I ever dated. And to think I loved yo' ass."

"I loved you too, Langston, I still do."

"Yo, let me kill this bitch already," Keko huffed.

"Shut up," Marcus shot at her. "Don't you see these muthafuckas having a sentimental moment and shit. Rude ass."

"Please don't kill me," Joy begged. "I swear I will go away, and not talk to them anymore. Please Langston."

"You don' already said too much," Keko continued. "You got this man's life in your hands, but yours is in mine," she laughed.

"Ke!" Marcus shot at her.

"Okay," she folded her arms.

"I don't even know what to say to you, man," I spoke. "I mean, you was my girl and you fucked everybody. My best friend, Joy?"

"I said I was sorry."

"Sorry won't get it."

Keko looked at me with questioning eyes, but I turned away from her. As soon as I did, I heard a smack. Joy screamed out in pain, and I kept walking towards the exit. Although I was mad about Joy snitching and smashing the homies, I didn't want to see her get hurt. Keko's little ass seemed eager to beat and kill her. I don't want to be able to say I know for a fact that she is dead, but I know that she will be. And to think, I wanted to spend the rest of my life with that bitch. I trust Niy, but I will keep a short leash on her ass from now on.

It was late when I got home because I rode around the city

smoking. My mind was all fucked up from everything that has happened today, and I needed to calm my nerves. Between Toot, my mama, and Joy doing stupid shit, I couldn't help but smoke. The house was dark, so I knew that Niy and Imani were already sleep. I hope she don't trip on me for being gone all day. She probably didn't even notice with all the excitement she had in her when I left this morning. Niy was lying in the bed, calling hogs again. I stood in the dark, undressing, then I climbed in next to her.

"Niy," I shook her. "Niy, you sleep?"

"I was," she mumbled.

"I love you."

"Yeah, me too."

Ain't that about a bitch?

Thank you all for ride another roller coaster with me. I hope you enjoyed part two of this saga. I won't leave a long Thank you message this time, but I will show my appreciation by giving you a sneak peek into my next few releases. I couldn't decide between part 3 of this book and part 2 of No Mercy. Since I have kept you waiting on both, I'll drop the unedited sneaks to both. Enjoy, and one again, thank you for supporting a Shameka Jones novel.

A HUSTLER'S FANTASY TWO (UNEDITED) SNEAK PEEK

Chapter One: Tookie

A lot has changed in the last seven months. For starters, Yaniyzah and I have moved into a bigger house. Neka didn't like staying in the house that Quincy purchased for their family alone, so I bought it from him. She moved into a smaller house, and Yaniyzah and I moved in shortly after. I sold the house I had, and let my brother Jr move into the loft. He had become a great apprentice, so I let him stay there for free. I started schooling him on the laundering business a few months ago and he was catching on quick. It must be some type of smart gene running through my father's bloodline that skipped him. All of us used our head for more than just a hat rack like he did.

On to loves Imani and Yaniyzah. Imani is the best baby ever, other than her running through the house destroying thing she's great. She's even beginning to talk. Her favorite word right now is no. It irritates the hell out of Yaniyzah, but it was funny to me. Yaniyzah's attitude these days are hot and cold. Most of the time she is mean, the only time she is nice is when she is full or horny. Her attitude is ugly, but her body is banging. She has booty and breast poking out everywhere. I love her new body, but she can't stand it. She hates the big booty comments that she always gets. I rub and squeeze on that muthafucka every chance I get, so I don't make it any better. I also spoil her rotten though. Everything she wants or need I make sure to give it to her quick. Big Mama told me to keep her happy while she is pregnant to keep us from arguing. She explained the hormone shit to me, so I am being very patient. It's challenging at time, but I've done a good job if I say so myself.

The store was now opened, so I spend most of my days watching Imani or helping out there. Jr was handling the pick-ups for me now. After he get the money he brings it straight to me to count. I still counted and sealed up the money for transport. I am still accountable for it, so I have to verify that it is correct. Things we are working out perfectly for me. I am able to make money, and steer clear of everything. This is what I wanted eventually, but I had to do it sooner than planned. Now that I have a son coming into this world I had to change some things. I can't be riding around all day working, and leaving Yaniyzah to raise my son. Even worse, I didn't want to end up locked up. All things happen for a reason, so I'm taking it with stride.

I only have a few more lose ends to clear up before I am Scott free. Jefe still had me responsible for the drugs that Ro and the guys are pushing. It's time for me to introduce Ro to Jefe so that I can wipe my hands with it. Punchie wanted the connect, but he had FED's watching him before. Just because he didn't get knocked on the first go 'round doesn't mean that he is in the clear. Since Ro wasn't in any of the pictures Yaniyzah's father had he wasn't a target. Punchie will just have to continue getting his coke from Ro. I don't want to get Ro caught up, but I damn sure didn't want to get Jefe caught up.

My plan sounds good but there is only one problem. I haven't mentioned the trip to Niy, and it was two days away. Jefe sprung it on me yesterday, now I have to spring it on her. I doubt if she is going to take the news lightly like I did. It will probably result in an argument that ends with me eating her pussy to shut her up. Shit, with us is pretty predictable so I already know how to handle it.

When I heard the garage door I knew that Yaniyzah was home. Imani knew it too because she started running towards the kitchen. I rose up from the sofa to meet her, and to make sure Imani didn't fuck up anything while she waited. She's good for pulling all of the pots and pans from under the sink.

"Mama!" Imani yelled as soon as the door opened.

"Hey mama's big girl."

Yaniyzah sat her keys and purse on the island, then bent down to pick Imani up. She began to place kisses all over Imani's face.

"Can daddy get some," I smiled.

"Dada," Imani pointed at me.

I wrapped my arm around Yaniyzah, then kissed her lips, "Hey baby, how was work?"

"It was cool. I sold more than a few pieces today."

"That's good."

She looked to be in a good mood today, so I didn't want to say anything to spoil it. I place my hand on her big ass belly and rubbed it. It had gotten so big over the last month that I could hardly believe it. I knew her belly would get bigger, but it seemed like this happened overnight. Every time I see her it looks like it had grown

"Man, I'm tired. Neka gon' lock up for me tonight, can you call and make sure that she doesn't forget anything. I mean, I reminded her several times of what to do, so I don't want to be the one that calls her."

"I'll take care of it. Come on in here and let me rub yo' feet."

"That sounds good, what we eating for dinner?"

"It don't matter whatever you want."

I removed Imani from her arms, then we walked towards the den area.

While I massaged Yaniyzah's feet, I scrolled through my phone to make dinner reservations. I had a taste for Surf & Turf Pasta from Perry's Steakhouse. Niy loves their Lamb chops, so looks like that is what we will be eating tonight. I'm trying to butter Niy up to tell her about the trip, hopefully this does the trick. If not, she will just have to be mad for a few days.

"Baby, I don't know why you insist on squeezing yo' fat ass feet in these heels," I complained, as I slid the shoe onto her feet.

"I'm not squeezing I just can't reach my feet right now."

"Why you just don't slide on a pair of them flat shoes?"

"'Cause I don't want to, now buckle the shoe up."

"You know, Big Mama and Pam said you shouldn't wear these heels while you're pregnant."

She looked at me as if to say she didn't give a fuck. Slowly, I have begun to speak to my mother again. Come to find out she didn't take Big Mama's TV. She invited one of her old buddies over to visit, and he took it when she went to the bathroom. Not willing to face Big Mama, she was gone for two weeks before she showed her face again. However, she did come back with the TV. She said that she wasn't going to go back to Big Mama's until she did. Big Mama had rules about having people in her house, so she knew that she would be in trouble regardless. And the fact that the TV was gone was worse. Of course Big Mama welcomed her back with open arms after talking all of that shit. I expected that much so I wasn't even mad about it. I was actually proud that she wasn't on drugs, and she brought the TV back in good shape.

"Whatever Langston, let's go."

I pulled her up off the bed, then walked into the bathroom. My phone was in there, plus I wanted to brush my hair one more time. Yaniyzah walked in behind me to snap a few pictures of us.

Yaniyzah didn't want to wrestle with Imani during dinner, so we dropped her off at Don's house. Over the last several months Imani had grown to like him. He made sure to come pick her up every weekend like he was her father. I didn't like spending time away from her, but it did give Niy and I some alone time. Don was pissed at Yaniyzah for a good minute for getting pregnant again. I took responsibility for that because I was the one that didn't want to use the condoms. He knew that he couldn't fuss about me about so he let it go.

After valeting the car, Yaniyzah and I walked into the restaurant hand in hand. Once I gave the hostess my name she walked us to our booth. I let her slide in, then I slid in next to her. The hostess sat our menu's down, and said that the waiter would be over shortly.

"You look beautiful tonight Niy," I said, moving her hair behind her ear.

"Aww thanks babe, so do you."

"Thank you, but you are radiant right now. I am such a lucky guy."

"You sure are spreading it on thick, what you got up your sleeve?"

"What you mean?"

"Hello," the waiter spoke, as he walked up to our table. "Thank you for choosing Perry's Steakhouse for your dining needs tonight. Can I start you off with some drinks and appetizers?"

Water and Lemonade for me," Yaniyzah answered.

"Same for me."

"What about appetizers?"

"I'll start with the Cherry Pepper Calamari."

"And you sir," he turned to me.

"That's it."

"Okay. I'll bring your drinks, then your appetizer will be out shortly after. Are you ready to order now, or do you need additional time?"

"We're ready," I looked to Niy for confirmation.

She went ahead ordering what I already knew she would. After she was done, I ordered my food, then sent the waiter on his way.

Once the drinks and appetizers came, Yaniyzah forgot all about her question to me. At some point I know I have to tell her about the trip, but I didn't want to interrupt anything right now. She was smiling and eating, so I know that she is happy. I guess she could sense me looking at her, so she paused then turned her head to look at me.

"What," she asked chewing.

"Nothing."

"Why you watching me eat?"

"I'm just looking at you."

"What you got up?"

"Why you keep asking me that," I chuckled. "Ain't nothing up."

"'Cause I know you. Now what you got to tell me," she asked, placing another piece of fried Calamari in her mouth.

"I got to take a quick trip."

"A trip? Where to?"

"To introduce Ro to the boss man."

"When?"

"The day after tomorrow."

"The day after tomorrow? Why are you just now saying something?"

"I just found out myself. The trip is only for one day, so I'll be right back."

"Is that why you brought me out?" she turned her lip up. "You could've just told me this at home."

"That's not why I brought you out, I brought you out because we gotta eat."

"Of course I don't want you to go, but since it's only for a day I will not complain about it."

What a relief. I thought for sure that I was up for a good fight. Then too, I should have known that she wouldn't be too mad since she was stuffing her face. The waiter walked up right after the conversation ended to bring our food.

"Ooh baby that looks good," Niy complemented, as she dug her fork into my plate.

I sat there watching her, until she went in for the second bite.

"Damn babe, what I'mma eat?"

"I'm sorry," she laughed. "It so good though."

"You should have order you some then."

"I want this."

"Well, eat that and get out of my plate."

"Stingy," she groaned.

This happens every time we go out to eat. She will order her food, then eat off of my plate. Normally I would share, but today I am hungry. I haven't eaten all day and I'm sure she has, several times.

And as promised....

NO MERCY (UNEDITED) SNEAK PEEK

Prologue

Shemarcus

"Fuck Ke!" I screamed as I fell to the floor, and grabbed my leg. Keko stood there looking at me with evil in her eyes. As I scanned her eyes looking for remorse, but I didn't see any, her crazy ass shot me on purpose.

"Marcus, are you okay?" Tiffany asked knocking on the door. "I heard a pop."

Keko pointed the gun towards the door, "Bitch if you don't get the fuck away from my door I'mma pop yo' ass!"

By the way Keko was scowling I knew that she was serious. It's bad enough that she had shot me, I didn't want her to go to jail for shooting Tiffany. If she did there would be no way that I could save her.

"Tiffany, please get the fuck away from the door and leave me the fuck alone!" I shouted. "Please!"

"See what the fuck you made me do?" Keko spat. "Now get up so I can take yo' stupid ass to the hospital."

"How the fuck am I gon' get up and you shot me in the fuckin' leg? What's wrong with you?"

"Don't you ever try to protect no bitch that I am gunnin' for. And don't you ever think it's okay to play with my heart Marcus. I will kill you before I let that happen."

Keko is unstable when she is upset, so I know that she means what she is saying. I wasn't trying to play with her heart and I never will. I love this girl, but she is making that a hard thing to do.

"That is not what I am doing Ke. You know I love you, I was trying to get her out of here."

"She should have never made it on the inside as far as I am concerned. I will say this for the last time, keep that bitch away from you. I don't give a fuck if you have to kill her yo' damn self. Stay away from her Marcus!"

"Alright!"

I was in no position to talk shit to her right now. Whatever she says is law at this moment. But believe, as soon as I bounce back I will get her ass in line. She finally reached down to help me up from the floor. I cringed as I tried to stand up on the leg that I was shot in.

"Ahh! You're fuckin' crazy, you know that?" I questioned.

"I know."

"Call Anson. If we go to the hospital they will ask questions about me being shot."

"Okay."

"I should turn yo' silly ass in to the police."

She helped me to the couch then walked away. I pulled my t-shirt over my head and tied it around my leg. I was in so much pain, but most of it came from the reality of Keko shooting my ass. She already had me shook from the shit at the warehouse, now she done shot my ass for real. Again I was thinking, *maybe pursuing her was a bad idea.*

20 minutes later there was a knock at the door. Keko jumped up quickly to go answer it. Anson walked in with Shay and Drew behind him. Drew is Shay's best friend whom is also a nurse. After being in pain for so long I am happy to see their faces. Anson strolled over, looked at my leg then back at Keko. She stood there looking scared shitless because she knows that Anson is going to blow a fuse. Drew walked over and began examining my leg.

"How the hell did this happen?" Anson asked, Keko while pointing at my leg.

"He had that bitch in here," she folded her arm. "I've been drinking, and he knows how I feel about her."

"So you shoot him?"

"He was trying to protect that bitch he shouldn't have jumped in the way."

"I don't even know what to say to you lil' muhfucka's right now."

"I'm sorry Anson."

"I don't wanna hear that shit right now Ke." Keko rolled her eyes, then stormed off towards the back. "Go say something nice to her Shay 'cause right now I can't."

Shay stood there for a few seconds before turning to making her way. Anson took a seat next to me and watched while Drew fixed me up.

"What the fuck was you thinking? Why would you have another broad in here?" Anson asked.

Drew looked straight at me waiting for my reply.

"I was trying to get her out. Nothing happened."

"That shit is irrelevant she shouldn't have been here in the first place. You already know how Ke feels about her, hell I even know that shit."

"You're right. I was just trying to be cool with the girl. Hell, we've known her for years."

"But you know that she has a thang for you, so you can't be

making fucked up decisions. How the fuck you gon' work like this?"

I didn't even bother responding this time. Just when Anson decided to give us some jobs this shit happened. I swear I can't win for losing around this bitch.

"He will be alright," Drew announced. "The bullet went through. After I patch him up, he'll be good in a few weeks."

I cringed as she stuck the needle in my leg, "Ahh, thanks Drew."

"You're welcome. I bet you won't have that girl in here again."

I managed to let out a slight laugh, "I bet I won't either."

After Drew fixed me up, she gave me a few pain killers. For the next few days I have to rest and stay off of my leg. Being in the house wasn't my thing so I don't know how I am going to make it. And since Keko is the one that shot me I don't want to be stuck in the house with her. I really want to beat her ass but I'm not a women beater. Plus, I love her ass too much to hurt her.

"Drew," Anson spoke. "Go check on Ke and Shay, let me and Marcus talk real quick."

"Okay, and Marcus I'll send some more pain killers over if you need them."

She loaded all of her materials back into her bag, then started towards the back.

"You need to get this shit under control," Anson spat. "This right here is not okay by any means. I've been telling you for weeks to man up and you haven't done it. Now I'm wondering how you're gonna take control of a job when you can't even control Ke's lil' bitty ass."

"I can handle the work. Ke just gets away with shit because of the way I feel about her. I promised that I wouldn't do anything to hurt her and I'm not."

"Well, you better figure out something. She doesn't mind hurting you, so you need to reevaluate your promise to her. By no means am I tellin' you to hurt her, but somethings got to give. It's always good to have a rider on your team, at the same time, your rider needs to respect you. I love Shay with all my heart, but if she shoots me I ain't bullshitting my ass will be a widower."

I leaned my head back and looked at the ceiling. What the fuck can I do to make Keko respect me more? It's not in me to harm or hurt her in any type of way. I think my soft spot for women came from my mother being killed by a man. All I want to do is love all women no matter how crazy they were. That's is the main reason that I keep talking to Tiffany's thotiebop ass knowing that I shouldn't. Women are my weakness.

Keko

I sat on the side of my bed listening to Shay talk. She was going on and on, blah blah about me shooting Marcus. I know it was wrong to shoot him, but she's acting like I killed his ass. All I did was shoot him in his leg, and the wound wasn't even bad. I didn't want to shoot him, but he had to understand that I am not accepting any bullshit. I've heard of too many stories where females put up with all types of shit from dudes and never do anything about it. I'm not one of those females. Marcus will respect me as his woman or I will make him do it.

"...And I'm not taking you to drink anymore because you don't know how to act."

"Shay, please kill all that noise. You know damn well if it was Anson you would have done the same thing."

"Correction, if it was Anson I wouldn't have killed both of their asses."

"Exactly."

"But he is my husband Ke, he made vows to me. You and Marcus are just beginning to date. What if he would have shot back and killed you by accident?"

"Then my ass would just be dead right now."

"Girl!" she shook her head. "You need to stop that shit. With

361

that attitude, you gon' mess around and run him off. I'm telling you these things for your own good, I don't want Marcus to snap on you one day and really kill yo' ass. You already know he can do it and get away with it."

Drew walked into my bedroom, so we killed that conversation. She had no idea of what either of us did, and we have to keep it that way. I am curious to what she thinks about me shooting Marcus, but I wouldn't dare ask. I didn't want her asking me questions that I can't answer. The first thing that she would probably ask is where I got the gun from.

"Damn girl," Drew started on her own. "I wish I had the balls to shoot Karrigan when we were young and he was acting a damn fool."

"I was just pissed when I saw him with that girl in here. I saw her on top of him when I opened the door."

"I don't blame you girl, I would have shot his ass too," Shay teased.

"So what happened to the bitch?" Drew inquired.

"Marcus pushed her out the door, I'm assuming she is in her apartment."

"That don't make no sense how thirsty females can be. I bet she won't be up here no more," Drew laughed.

I smirked, "I bet she won't either."

Anson helped Marcus to his bedroom, then I walked them out. The only reason I went outside to see if I could spot Tiffany's yellow ass. I started to go knock on her door, but I didn't want to start the drama back up. Marcus wouldn't be around to save her ass, and it will end up being a sloppy kill for me. I didn't want to end up in jail being emotional behind a rat face ass bitch. One thing is for sure, if she tries me again, I will teach that ass a lesson she won't live to remember.

I eased my way back into the apartment. It was a few blood splatters on the entry way floor, so I cleaned it up before retreating to my room. I paced back and forth in my room trying to think of something to say to Marcus. I know I owe him an apology, but I didn't know what else to say besides that I am sorry. I still had on my club clothes, so I began to peel them off.

Standing in nothing but my birthday suit, I pushed the door to Marcus room open. He was in his normal position, laying on his back with his hands interlocked across his forehead. He lifted his head up to look at me, then laid back down. Damn, did that shot make him lose his eyesight? I strolled over next to the bed and took a seat.

"I'm sorry for shooting you Marcus. I'm not saying it's right but you know how I feel about that bitch. You knew that I didn't want her in here, especially when I'm not home."

"What type of apology is that? How you gon' apologize and blame me at the same time? Fuck outta here!"

"I'm sorry. I shouldn't have shot you. I fucked up and I own up to it."

"Admitting you are wrong does not fix my leg."

"But do you accept my apology though?"

"I don't know yet I need to think about it."

"Let me help you."

I stuck my hand inside of his basketball short and pulled his dick out. He didn't flinch or even bother to look at up me as I began to lick the tip. I could usually count on some eye to eye contact from him while I did it. His dick began to grow, and slowly he started to move his hips.

"Mm," he moaned silently. At least he is participating a little bit.

I continued to bob up and down his pipe, then his hand rested on top of my head. Normally, I didn't like for him to touch my head while I went down on him, but today I felt the need to be lenient. I owe him the best head of him life, so that is what I am going to give him.

Once I had the condom on his muscle, he stood up to take his shorts all the way off. I was laying on my back with my legs gapped wide open. Marcus snatched me up then flipped me over on my stomach. He danced his dick around my clit leaving me waiting in anticipation. He placed his dick at my vaginal opening, then rammed it inside of me.

"Ahh!" I cried out.

Marcus grabbed my waist to pull me back towards him, "Bring yo' ass here!" He slapped me on my ass so hard that I had flash back of my mama whopping me.

"Shit baby!" He grabbed me by the root of my hair and pulled my head back. He used his other hand to grab me around my neck. "Uhh!"

"You ever do that bullshit again I will kill yo' muthafuckin' ass! You hear me?" he asked as he squeezed harder. "I'LL KILL YO' ASS KE!" While he made his threats he continued to ram his dick into me.

"O—" I was trying to say okay, but he was squeezing me too tight. The way his hands are squeezing me he might kill me before I get a chance to try it again. I was trying to pry his hands from around my throat, but that just made him squeeze harder.

He let go of my throat, then slapped me hard on my ass twice. I tried to gasp for air as he started pounding my pussy again.

"Fuck Marcus! OKAY!"

"Ain't no okay," he barked, slapping my ass harder in between each syllable. "You're too fuckin' hard headed, but we're gonna fix that shit. Ain't we?"

"Baby," I whined.

"Ain't we!?" he slapped my cheeks again.

He was fucking the shit out of me and there was nothing I could do but take it. He had a grip on my hair so tight that I swear I heard it breaking from the roots. I guess since he wasn't going to shoot me back, he is going to inflict pain on me in other ways. He was deep in my stomach making me feel like I had to throw up.

Don't forget to friend me on social media

Facebook: Shameka Jones

Author page: Author Shameka Jones

FB Group: Shameka's Symposium

IG: yes.im.that.shameka

Twitter: missgemini83

 Shameka Jones was born in West Dallas, TX, June 7, 1983. She is the youngest of three children and the only girl. During her early teenage-years she took a liking to writing poetry to express her thoughts that she was too shy to speak on. After years of reading fiction novels and being surrounded by writers she was inspired to write her first ever novel. After several life changing events and a vivid imagination, she wanted to express herself with writing novels. Her biggest inspiration came from when she learned her mother was diagnosed with Parkinson's disease, she need an outlet to express her bundled up feeling and began to write to take her mind off of things.

Shameka signed to Royalty Publishing House January of 2015. She writes Urban Fiction Erotica novels and is the author of the **Secret Lovers:** What he don't know won't hurt him, series, Turned out by a Thug, **Sprung:** Turned out by love, Saint's Heaven, A Hustler's Fantasy and **No Mercy:** Me and my hitta. She is currently working on several different novels, and a project that she hopes to bring to the big screen one day. Shameka now resides in Oak Cliff where she spends most of her time writing and enjoying life with her huge loving family who means the world to her.

To get exclusive and advance looks at some of our top releases:

Click the link: (App Store) http://bit.ly/2hteaH7

Click the link: (google play) http://bit.ly/2h4Jw9X

TEXT ROYALTY TO 42828

FOR ALL UPDATES, NEW RELEASES, CONTESTS, SNEAK PEEKS AND SO MUCH MORE!

Looking for a publishing home?

Royalty Publishing House, Where the Royals reside, is accepting submissions for writers in the urban fiction genre. If you're interested, submit the first 3-4 chapters with your synopsis to submissions@royaltypublishinghouse.com. Check out our website for more information: www.royaltypublishinghouse.com.

Do You Like CELEBRITY GOSSIP? Check Out QUEEN DYNASTY!

Like Our Page HERE! Visit Our Site:

www.thequeendynasty.com

CPSIA information can be obtained
at www.ICGtesting.com
Printed in the USA
LVOW13s1832180518
577693LV00010B/519/P

9 781546 969310